TO CATCH A HUSBAND

By Sophia Holloway

Kingscastle
The Season
Isabelle
The Chaperone
Celia
To Catch a Husband

a&b

TO CATCH A HUSBAND

SOPHIA HOLLOWAY

Allison & Busby Limited
11 Wardour Mews
London W1F 8AN
allisonandbusby.com

First published in Great Britain by Allison & Busby in 2024.

All characters and events in this publication, other than those clearly in the public domain, are fictitious and any resemblance to actual persons, living or dead, is purely coincidental.

A CIP catalogue record for this book is available from the British Library.

First Edition

ISBN 978-0-7490-3187-9

Typeset in 11/16 pt Adobe Garamond Pro by Allison & Busby Ltd.

By choosing this product, you help take care of the world's forests. Learn more: www.fsc.org.

Printed and bound by
CPI Group (UK) Ltd, Croydon, CR0 4YY

For K M L B

CHAPTER ONE

Miss Mary Lound looked up from her embroidery, which she was working upon with more vehemence than skill, stabbing the fabric in an accusatory manner, and stared out of the window. She was not the sort of young woman who enjoyed needlecraft of any sort, and had it not been for the rain which had come down heavily all day, she would have been out, either upon horseback or her own two feet, for she was a brisk walker. She sighed heavily. It was terrible weather for July.

'I think that even though the sky is somewhat lighter, my dear, you ought to wait until tomorrow before taking the potted cheese to old Mrs Nacton,' Lady Damerham suggested, a little nervously. Mary had been very snappish all week, not that her parent blamed her for it. For her own part, Lady Damerham regarded what had happened as all just another misfortune laid upon them.

'You are quite right, Mama, but . . .' She shook her head, and was silent for several minutes, before blurting out, 'I wish I were a man.'

'Mary! Really, you say the strangest things.'

'Yes, but if I were a man, I could do something. As it is we are stuck, with no means of earning an income, and on the verge of penury. If I were a man I could join the army, or the navy, or . . .'

'You could write a book? Ladies do write novels and—'

'Me? Goodness, no. I would be pretty appalling at it, and I hardly think lady authors earn more than pin money. Besides, I can think of nothing worse than trying to write one of those fanciful romances with kidnappings and haunted houses and all that foolishness. Having said which, our situation has all the makings of something as silly. "Titled gentleman wastes much of his inheritance gambling, is succeeded by heir who is as thoughtless and has to sell the family estate to meet his debts, and departs for the wilds of North America, leaving his mother and sister nearly destitute." Yes, that is ridiculous enough to make a novel!'

'Not destitute, dearest. I have this house for my lifetime, remember,' corrected her ladyship, gently, ignoring the fact that upon her decease, her daughter would be homeless.

'You have the house, Mama, but how are we to manage? It might have seemed a good idea for you to have a jointure when you married, but it was pathetically small, and how Edmund and his fancy lawyer managed to persuade you to accept a miserable lump sum from the sale of the estate in return for nullifying it I do not know.' Mary was still fuming over this, for her brother had invited the lawyer to the house when Mary was out for the day visiting a friend, and had not used the family solicitor.

'But I had to, Mary. The poor boy would otherwise have been severely curtailed in what he could sell, and he said a debtor's prison threatened. I could not leave him liable to such a fate. He did have it in the estate sale that it was dependent upon me being able to remain in the dower house, do not forget.'

'I am not sure if he could have tried to sell otherwise, Mama. It is all very murky to me, and that letter from Lord Cradley, upon purchase, was unpleasant in the extreme.'

'It was not couched in the most genteel of terms, I grant you,' Lady Damerham admitted.

'It made it very clear you were to remain only because of the legal requirement, and woe betide you if you as much as stepped upon one yard of "his" land. "His"! The effrontery of it.'

'Mary, if you maintain this level of ill temper, you will drive yourself to an apoplexy. I am sure of it. There is nothing to be done, except to economise, and though we may have to turn off some of the servants, you know dear Atlow would not leave us, even if we paid him not a penny, as long as we gave him bed and board.'

'Atlow is indeed a dear, but we cannot exist with an ageing butler and a cook-housekeeper, and ultimately only one maid to keep a house this size clean and the fires laid.'

'It will be . . . difficult. We must be brave and . . . Are you absolutely certain you could not write a book, not even a small volume of poems, dearest?'

Mary shook her head and laughed, though it was not a laugh of joyous merriment, and promptly stabbed her finger with her needle.

It was thankfully not long afterwards when the butler announced that Sir Harry Penwood wished to know if the ladies were 'at home'. Atlow had moved with them from Tapley End to the smaller dower house out of loyalty, but also with relief at the reduced number of stairs, passages and galleries that had to be traversed. He gave the 'Sir' an emphasis.

'Oh, do please show him in, Atlow. How wonderful!' Lady Damerham pressed her hands together in delight, and when the young man entered the room, came forward instantly and hugged him.

'Dear Harry. Awful circumstances . . . so glad you are safe and home . . . your poor mother, I so feel for her . . .'

Sir Harry, looking over Lady Damerham's shoulder

as she addressed these disjointed remarks to him, gave Mary Lound a wry grin, and then responded, in a serious tone.

'Thank you, ma'am. I cannot say I had thought to be back in England for some considerable time but . . . Mama is quite well, and coping, as one does.'

'She was always so very stoic. I saw her but last week and she made no mention of your return,' sighed her ladyship.

'I did not give warning in case I was delayed on the journey and she fretted. You know her one great fear is the sea, and every time I have left England's shores, she has been convinced I will end up shipwrecked. Anyway, I am back, and to stay, of course.'

'Of course.'

'And I must, very belatedly, offer you my own condolences, ma'am, even though you must be nearly out of your blacks by now.'

'Indeed, another month and . . . besides, I – we – had time to accept . . . it was not sudden.' Her smile returned. 'We must offer you refreshment. I hope you have not got too wet coming over to see us. Oh, and while I think of it, your mama asked me for the receipt I have for damsons in a batter pudding when we met outside church the other week. A very weak sermon we both thought, which is most unusual for the rector. I had it ready the other day, but where . . . ah yes! Mary, dear, send for tea, or would you prefer something stronger, Harry?' Lady Damerham was already halfway to the door.

'Tea would be perfect, thank you, ma'am.' Sir Harry had almost forgotten how 'butterfly' Lady Damerham could be in conversation. He looked again at Mary. She had not changed, he thought, although he had not seen her in nearly three years.

'Do take a seat "Sir Henry",' offered Mary, with a grin and a gesture of her hand, as her parent shut the door behind her, 'as soon as you have pulled the bell.'

'If you call me "Sir Henry", even in jest, Mary, I am not sitting down but walking right out of that door.'

'I am sorry, Harry. I should not tease you, especially now. It must be both strange and sad for you, coming back when the locality has perhaps come to terms with Sir John's death, and yet here it is, made new again to you.' She patted the sofa beside her, and he came to sit down. 'It was a terrible shock, but at least the suddenness of it meant there was no suffering.' Her voice softened. 'He was very well thought of, and nobody doubts the estate is in good hands with you. You are selling out, yes?'

'Put my papers in as soon as I got back to England.' He sounded regretful. The army life had suited young Harry Penwood, and he had only had his company for six months. He felt it as work unfinished, especially with Wellington looking set to drive the French out of Spain entirely and back over the Pyrenees, after winning a victory only a few weeks past, and one which had given Captain Penwood his last taste of action.

'At least you have your ancestral acres, and in a good

state, too. No fear of poor husbandry there. I . . .' She paused as Atlow entered, and requested him to bring tea. When they were once again alone, she pulled a face. 'You find us suffering from the result of the opposite. However much Papa had to retrench, he never contemplated selling the entire estate, and yet Edmund did not even retain his patrimony for a single whole year, and we are left impoverished, and almost destitute.'

'But Lady Damerham has the dower house for life, surely?' Harry frowned.

'She does, but whether we can afford to live in it is another matter, and my portion is, would you credit it, only to be paid when I marry. So Papa failed to provide for me should I remain single, and thus most in need of financial support.' Mary did not attempt to conceal her disgust at her sire's lack of forethought. 'At this rate I am facing my declining years in some gloomy cottage, with a single servant and mutton once a week, if fortunate.'

'Put like that, you are in a difficult position, but you will marry, of course you will, and—'

'I am five and twenty, Harry. I never had a Season to be trotted up and down in London, and I have no regrets about that, but I know everyone hereabouts, and if any gentleman had found me to his taste, or he to mine, I think we would have discovered it by now.'

'Er . . .' Harry looked a little uncomfortable. 'You do not blame me for not . . . I mean . . . we are dashed good friends but . . .'

'Oh Harry,' Mary laughed, and reached out her hand to his. 'No. We are, as you say, the best of friends, and I daresay there are married couples out there who rub along far worse than we would do, but you and James were brothers to me, whilst Edmund . . . Do you know, I wondered, when I was a girl, if Edmund was a changeling. I did, really. I had read in some history book that King James the Second was meant to have had a baby boy smuggled into the chamber of his Catholic wife, in a warming pan of all ridiculous things, and a baby girl smuggled out. Well, I suppose that fired my imagination, and I wondered if Papa had smuggled in a changeling that was Edmund. He has always been so unlike James and myself. James would not have . . .'

Her smile twisted. She missed her brother James, would always miss him. The memorial in the village church was all there was, for he lay in a grave in Portugal, a grave perhaps already overgrown and forgotten. James would not have squandered the little inheritance that remained, would not have sold Tapley End, and never, ever, to the family with whom the Lounds had been at odds since the Civil War.

'No, he would not.' Harry understood, and it was one of the things that made him so much like a brother, when Edmund seemed unrelated. Edmund would have looked questioningly at her, frowned in incomprehension. 'But it is done, Mary. There is nothing you can do about it. Old Cradley has bought the estate fair and square. If I could have afforded it . . . well, however wrong it would have felt to own the place, I would have bought it rather than see it go to him. I could have made over Hassocks Farm to you, or sold it to you for a pittance, and the rent would have kept you in the dower house, at the very least.'

'It would still be charity, Harry, though meant, and probably accepted, in friendship. It just feels . . .' She shook her head. 'I know Edmund is not solely to blame. We all know Papa was a gamester, and if he had not been so plagued with the gout of late years, we might have been in the suds even before Edmund inherited.' She sighed. 'But you would have thought that he, Edmund, would have made a push to come about, not simply carry on where Papa left off and then shrug and say it was not his fault.'

'He did not say so?' Harry looked suitably surprised.

'Oh yes. He even had the impudence to say it was my fault, because if I had married well, then he could have sponged off my husband.'

Harry's jaw dropped, and it was some moments before he could respond.

'Well, if that don't beat all! In all this sorry mess, Mary, at least he is going off to the other side of the Atlantic Ocean to trap beavers or whatever. He cannot do any more harm from there.'

'True.' She paused for a moment. 'I do not suppose I should tell you, since you will no doubt sit as a magistrate as your father did, but I am a thief.'

'You?'

'Yes. When I heard who was buying the house and its contents, please note, I had the writing table from the green saloon brought over here, and the portrait of Grandmama that hung in the morning room. And I also brought Sir Robert and the Lady Elizabeth. I thought if they had to see a Risley living in the house they might haunt it, and I was none too sure Lord Cradley would not have had them burnt, as final proof of victory. I replaced Sir Robert with a still life that had been in the attic for years.'

'Well, then that is not theft but rescue.'

'You may shortly be on the bench, Harry, but your grasp of law is . . .'

'Tenuous? Not really. But look at it this way. Cradley is not going to use a lady's writing table, loathed your grandmama, and might indeed have committed your ancestral portraits to the flames. He has not been deprived of anything he would miss, and they are your ancestors.' He smiled.

'Bless you,' Mary smiled at him, but it wavered. 'I keep thinking this is all just a nightmare, but it is not. I cannot forgive Edmund. He did not even bother to see if anyone else would offer for the estate, and took Lord Cradley's frankly insulting offer as if it were manna from heaven. I would have been so ashamed if I had brought us to such a pass, that I would rather have drowned myself in the lake.'

'Has Cradley strutted about the place yet?'

'I believe he came over once it was all legal and final,

and sneered at everything before having it shut up. He even turned off most of the servants. That was about ten days ago. I cannot think what he would wish to do with the house, though it is far nicer than his own. For all that I complain of bad husbandry, his land is good, though no doubt he will increase the rents and take what he can from ours. He did send a very formal letter to Mama, expressly forbidding "trespass etc.", by which he very clearly meant me walking the grounds, let alone fishing. It is not as though he fishes himself, either.'

'You will miss that. Though it goes without saying that you can come over and try your luck on our beat of the river any time you wish.'

'I warn you, Harry, if I do, I will be striving to catch our dinner. Just think of the economy if I could avoid us having to buy fish.'

Lady Damerham was quite surprised to re-enter the room to find them laughing, and looked from one to the other. Since she did not like seeing people unhappy she did not complain.

'Here you are, Harry. It was just where I thought it was . . . at least the place where I thought it was after it was not where I first thought it was.' She held out a piece of paper, upon which the recipe was written in her neat, rounded hand.

'Thank you, ma'am. I will make sure that I hand it over as soon as I get home.' Harry, who had risen, smiled at her and took it, then looked to Mary again.

'Is it true, what my mama says, that Madeleine Banham is no longer a snub-nosed schoolroom chit who pouts when she is thwarted?'

'Well, I have not seen her thwarted for some time, so I cannot vouch if she has changed in that respect, but she has undoubtedly unfurled her petals into something of the local beauty. I think her mama is hoping to bring her out informally in Bath early next spring, and then they are taking a house in London, but I am not sure it is confirmed as yet. She would take, though, not a doubt of it. You had best join the queue, Harry, if you want to sigh over her.'

'Me? Not the sighing type, as you well know. Good to be warned, though, because I would look a perfect blockhead if I asked "Who is that?" and it was Maddy Banham. I take it her mama is just as French as ever?'

'*Absolument.*' Mary grinned and wafted her hands about in a theatrical manner.

'Lady Roxton is a very charming woman,' said Lady Damerham, trying not to smile.

'She is, Mama, but after nearly a quarter of a century in England she still sounds as though she landed in Bristol last month. Do you remember, Harry, how we used to try and drive the conversation so she would say "Wales", and it came out as "Wayoools"?'

'I do.'

'Very naughty the pair of you were, I have to say. Poor woman, it was not her fault she came straight from the murderous situation in France . . . how can people be so bloodthirsty? . . . and with a very weak grasp of our language. She was so beautiful, though, that Lord Roxton, not that he was Lord Roxton then, snapped her up very swiftly, despite his father's reservations about "Gallic volatility", and she has been a good wife and mother, whatever anyone says.' Lady Damerham always liked to be fair, though it left Mary and Harry both wondering who the 'anyone' might be.

'Indeed, Mama, but her accent is such one might use it as a caricature of a Frenchwoman speaking English, even now.' Mary offered Harry more tea, but he declined.

'Thank you, but no. I ought to get back before the heavy rain commences again. The clouds were gathering in the west as I arrived. I just wanted to see you both and . . . well, if battle lines are drawn around here, you always know that I stand in line with you, sword drawn, so to speak, and you can trust me to stand firm in the face of the enemy.'

'We know, Harry, and it helps. Of course, there has never been a Risley we liked much, but the current holder of the barony happens to be a particularly unpleasant and contrary specimen. It does mean that not only you but most of this part of the shire range against him. If only that helped pay the bills.'

'We must not be mercenary, my love,' admonished Lady Damerham.

'Not mercenary, Mama, practical. I am no

needlewoman, and if my gowns have to be taken in, I could look a positive fright.'

'I promise to warn you of that.' Harry gave her hand a squeeze, bowed more formally over Lady Damerham's to avoid another hug, and departed.

CHAPTER TWO

Miss Madeleine Banham was torn. Part of her, a very large part, lapped up the adoration of the local bachelors with pleasure, though a rather smaller part resented that most of them would not have cared if she had lacked every one of the accomplishments which she had worked so hard to perfect at the select Queen's Square seminary where she had spent her later schoolroom years. A pretty face and a good figure were all that they sought, and saw, but Madeleine was proud of her watercolours and her performance upon the pianoforte, to which she still devoted a half hour of practice every morning. When she did receive compliments about her art and music, she knew she would have received exactly the same had her ability been mediocre, because the gentlemen wanted to please her. It was slightly lowering. Her mama told her that it did not matter, but that very small voice inside her told her that her beauty and figure would undoubtedly decline, but she might be an even better painter and pianist at the advanced aged of thirty-five or forty.

She was a patently feminine creature, who floated rather than trod, had a laugh that was naturally bright and musical, and a voice that one besotted youth described as 'an angel with a mouthful of honey'. Since he had been so unwise as to say this before Miss Lound, this had led to her describing the problems an angel would have with diction, and the deleterious effect of sticky fingers upon celestial harps. Whilst Madeleine could see that it was a very silly thing to say, the thought had been sweet, like the honey, and Mary Lound was far too prosaic and practical. There were nearly eight years between the young ladies, and they had thus never been close. For her part, Madeleine thought the other rather an Amazon, and even 'mannish', for she had no fear of muddy skirts from traipsing around the countryside on foot, killed fish with her bare hands, and would rather spend an hour loosing arrows into a butt than dancing quadrilles and flirting. In fact, Madeleine was pretty sure that Miss Lound was incapable of flirting. It was no surprise, as her mama said, that she had never had a suitor and looked almost certain to remain a spinster for the rest of her days. Madeleine could ride, of course, but did not hunt, and preferred to hack gently about the locality, being social, and wearing a habit that showed her figure to perfection.

This particular morning, her papa had suggested she ride with him 'to get the roses back in your cheeks'. He awaited her in the hall, unperturbed by the fact that she was keeping him waiting, since she was always a little late for everything. Lord Roxton, a still handsome man in his late forties, enjoyed being congratulated on his daughter's good looks, even though he always ascribed it to her mother's beauty. Lady Roxton, having provided her husband with three sons and a daughter, had lost the trimness of figure as well as the bloom of her youth, but was accounted a very fine-looking woman 'for her age', which was, of course, damning. Madeleine descended the stairs, a vision in dark green, alleviated by her lace-edged, snow-white cravat and a curling feather in her hat which accentuated the red gold in her artless curls. Father smiled at daughter and nodded approvingly.

'Very nice, my dear. We must be careful if upon the more frequented roads, or we will have gentlemen driving into the ditches when they gaze upon you and cease to pay attention to their leaders.'

'Papa, you should not.' Madeleine blushed.

'I speak the truth, no more and no less. No wonder young Sopwell dripped his soup down his waistcoat when you smiled at him at dinner the other evening.'

'Mr Sopwell lacks polish,' said the girl who had yet to make a formal come out.

'He is a trifle green, but a good lad, and—'

'Are you going to ride upon the 'orses, or stand talking all morning, milor'?' Lady Roxton emerged from a small saloon and shook her head at her husband.

'We shall be off directly, my love.' His lordship was, like many husbands, firm in great matters, but under the uxorial thumb in minor ones.

She came forward with a soft rustle of skirts and brushed a probably non-existent piece of lint from his coat, looking up at him with an affection that Madeleine found slightly embarrassing and that made him feel a decade younger in an instant.

'*Bien*. Off with you, and be sure to return before the hour of one.'

He leant and kissed her cheek in a very mild salutation, but Madeleine looked away. Parents really did put one to the blush.

It had been over a week since Madeleine had been out riding, and her mount was a little fresh. She was a competent horsewoman, but her sire nevertheless did not engage her in conversation until she had stopped the animal sidling and brought it down off its toes, and he watched her, fully prepared to grab the bridle above the bit if required. When Copper was at last docile, they left the park and trotted along the Gotherington lane, stopping briefly to exchange civilities with the local doctor, who was looking somewhat weary after attending a difficult birth, and waiting for a flock of sheep to be transferred to pasture upon the other side of the lane.

'I fear we shall not go as far as I would have wished, my dear, if we are to be home in time for luncheon.' Lord Roxton did not sound too put out. 'But now the fields are stubbled, we could cut back cross-country, if you are happy to do so.'

Madeleine agreed to this, as long as they used the gates rather than put their horses at them and jumped. They were on the point of turning about when a horseman came around the corner towards them, and pulled up when he recognised Lord Roxton, though his eyes did not linger upon the peer, but rather upon Miss Banham.

Sir Harry Penwood did not sigh; he stared.

'Good Lord,' he breathed, reverently. Lord Roxton's lips twitched.

'That, Sir Harry, is not exactly complimentary.' Miss Banham looked coyly at him from under her lashes, and if he had been stunned, for her part she was a little impressed. When she had last seen him, three years past, she had only been on the cusp of finding gentlemen interesting, and Harry Penwood had the disadvantage of being known well since he had been at the playing pranks stage. He had looked nice in his regimentals, she remembered, but was rather dismissive of a young lady still in the schoolroom, and as yet to bloom into womanhood. There was nothing of the youth in the broad-shouldered man before her, except his ill-concealed amazement.

She had certainly bloomed, he thought, as his brain

regained the ability to function.

'My . . . my apologies, Madeleine, or rather, Miss Banham.' He touched the brim of his hat and nodded also at Lord Roxton. 'Good to see you again, sir.' He gulped.

His lordship was quite used to seeing men's Adam's apples bob up and down when they first beheld his daughter, and smiled, though it faded with his words.

'Glad to have you back among us, though I regret the circumstances, of course. Very unexpected. Shock to us all.' Lord Roxton was not a man of crafted phrases.

'Yes, sir. I hope Lady Roxton is well. I can see that M . . . iss Banham is in perfect health.' Harry glanced at her. He dare not do more because his eyes felt as if they would be on stalks.

'My wife is very well, thank you. I realise that Lady Penwood will not be socialising, of course, but we would be more than pleased if you come over to the Hall to see us some afternoon, would we not, Madeleine?'

'Oh yes. But you will not tell us about gory battles, will you? Mr Bromley did so, and Mama and I disliked it excessively.'

'You can be sure that I will not do so.' Harry could think of nothing less suitable for a lady's ears, and was himself more than content to leave the least happy aspects of soldiering in a box of memories to be opened rarely, and in private. There were, of course, the lighter moments, the funny stories, which, in expurgated form, might be brought out in mixed company, but they were not about war and death but living in the field, and among friends.

'It is good to have another younger fellow in the vicinity. Brightens things up. Far prefer having balls to evenings of whist with the aged and decrepit, and you cannot have dancing without gentlemen fit to caper about.' Lord Roxton liked dancing.

'I confess, sir, I have not had much occasion for "capering about" these last few years, but I am sure I remember the steps.' Sir Harry was thinking how good it would be to dance with Miss Banham.

'I thought Lord Wellington encouraged dancing, when the army is out of the fighting season.'

'Oh, he does, but that is mostly among the staff, and those quartered close enough. Never found myself in the right place at the right time.'

Miss Banham's horse began to fidget. Papa had a tendency to take over a conversation and lead into subjects she found very boring, like politics, and the war. Whilst he did not notice her becoming bored, he did notice the horse.

'Well, we must be on our way. Have to be back by luncheon or her ladyship will give me a rare dressing down, and we have already been held back by a flock of sheep.' Lord Roxton winked, to remove any idea he was in fact under his wife's thumb. 'Do ride over and see us soon, Penwood.'

'You can be sure that I will, sir.' Sir Harry touched his hat with his whip, and rode on, in somewhat of a daze. When he encountered Mary two days later in Cheltenham, where she had gone with Lady Damerham to purchase gloves, he laughingly chastised her for not giving him a true warning of Madeleine Banham's transformation.

'I nearly fell off my horse,' he admitted. 'She is so much changed.'

'Not changed, just grown. Be fair, Harry, she was still stitching samplers when you last saw her.'

'Very true, but . . .' He gave a deep sigh of appreciation.

'Oh Harry, you said you were not one to sigh over females.' Mary shook her head at him.

'Never have until now, but then I have never seen a girl as beautiful as Madeleine Banham.'

Mary laughed, but was conscious of a feeling that was not, could not be, jealousy, for she did not think of Harry Penwood other than as a dear friend, but was yet a form of annoyance at the way Madeleine Banham could put men under her spell with little or no effort, and not just silly young men either.

'I had thought better of you. Before you swoon at the sight of her, try and discover if you like what lies beneath the beauty.'

'You sound like my mama.' Harry grinned.

'Thank you so much. I now feel positively aged, not just on the shelf.' There was the slightest hint that the remark had touched her on the raw, and Harry Penwood had known her long enough to note it.

'You, madam, are only "on the shelf" if you choose to be so. You could have had half the shire at your door if you wanted, but you have not wanted. Be honest, Mary, you found "youthful admiration" foolish, and kept saying you had no desire to wed and become a man's possession, like his gun dog or his collection of porcelain. Now, I quite see how that would be so, but if you treat fellows with disdain, or even contempt, you will not find them on one knee, begging you to accept their suit.'

'I do not treat you with contempt, or disdain.' She sounded defensive.

'No, by Jove you do not, because we have grown up together and you pushed me into the horse pond and I sat you in a cow pat when you were six. I love you dearly, as I would a sister, and it is me being fraternal who tells you truths you would rather not hear.'

'He is right, my dear.' Lady Damerham, who had said nothing during the interchange, and was a little daunted by her daughter upon occasion, patted Mary's arm. 'I am sure you could find a husband if you tried, even now, though it would be a little difficult with the gentlemen who live closest. If we went to Bath in the spring, perhaps, in modest lodgings, you might . . .' She halted as Mary glowered at her. 'It is that or writing a book.'

'Writing a book?' Harry blinked and looked at one and then the other.

Mary's frown disappeared, and she laughed, which relieved Lady Damerham a great deal.

'Mama is convinced that if I want to earn some money to keep us afloat, I have to write a book, one of those awful romances.'

'Good grief! You are the last person I could imagine doing that. Mind you, I daresay you could write a nice little book on fishing.'

'I cannot better Mr Best, alas, nor Mr Ustonson.'

'But neither are lady anglers.'

'And I do not want to differentiate between the genders when it comes to fly fishing. It is one thing where a man's "superior" height and strength are of no importance, and remember what happened when Edmund sneered at my catch and said "Quite good . . . for a girl"?'

'You hit him across the face with a two-pound trout. James and I nearly fell in the lake laughing.' Harry's grin returned.

'There should never be the qualification "for a woman" in fishing.' Mary gave him a tight smile.

'And well I know it. However, if it sold copies . . .'

'I could not do it.'

'A fish romance, then – two trouts with but one single thought, besotted bream, courting carp, dallying dace?'

'Now you are being too silly for words,' Mary giggled, which was not something she did very often.

'How about "dashing former army officer falls for local beauty"?' he suggested, not entirely joking.

'No.' She looked more serious again. 'I cannot claim to be close friends with Madeleine Banham, but she is not yet officially out, and may not know the "rules". Just be careful, Harry, that you do not see encouragement in what she thinks is mere friendliness. We females can be heartless pieces, you know.'

'Thank you for the warning. We shall see what happens, but I am definitely going to make a reconnaissance and visit Lord Roxton in the next few days. I may have been bowled over by her looks, Mary, but I am not such a sapskull as you think.'

'You could not be,' she retorted, swiftly.

'Wretch.' He shook his head but was smiling.

'Come over and see us also, dear boy,' requested Lady Damerham.

'Yes, do that, Harry, despite my insults.'

'I will.' He bowed and went upon his way.

'There is always Harry, I suppose,' suggested Lady Damerham, thoughtfully, 'but I am not at all sure he could see you in the light of a wife.'

'I am absolutely certain that he could not, Mama. Now, you wanted lilac gloves.'

It was a whole week before Harry Penwood fulfilled his promise and came to take tea with them, and he brought his mother, since he felt she ought not to remain entirely without social contact, even in only the second month of her mourning. She sat with Lady Damerham, who was both sympathetic and disjointedly pragmatic.

'I think sitting at home, with everything about her reminding her of my father, is inclined to keep her in low spirits, though she pretends to being "much improved". Since we have all known each other for decades it is perfectly acceptable,' said Harry, quietly, to Mary, his eyes on his mother.

'And Mama understands her situation, even if she and Papa were not close, as Sir John and your mama were. I think widowhood can be very isolating.'

'Yes.'

'So, tell me, are you still under Madeleine Banham's spell?' Mary tilted her head to one side and gave him a questioning look. He coloured, which gave her the answer before he said a word.

He had paid his call upon Lord and Lady Roxton and been greeted with open friendliness by both of them. Madeleine had been, if anything, a little more reserved, which he liked, though he might not have been as pleased if he had known why. She was not a girl prone to shyness and was quite well aware of her own powers of attraction, but upon hearing from her husband that Sir Harry Penwood would undoubtedly be calling upon them in the near future, Lady Roxton had drawn Madeleine aside and given her warning.

''Arry Penwood is not some green boy who will make the eyes of the sheep at you, and let you treat 'im like a lapdog. 'E has not so very many years, but 'e has been a soldier, and that makes *toute la différence*. You cannot play the tricks with such a man, so look, and think, before you smile just so and add 'im to your list of *conquêtes*.'

'You make him sound quite dangerous, Mama.' Madeleine laughed, but frowned also.

'Not *dangereux*, but not a man with whom you can trifle.' Lady Roxton paused for a moment. 'You are very young, *ma petite ingénue*, but of great *beauté,* so men will adore you, men of many sorts.'

'You do not think Sir Harry a bad sort, Mama?'

'Not at all, but the adorings of boys are not the same as those of men grown.'

This slightly cryptic 'warning' left Madeleine unsure how she ought to react to Harry Penwood, and thus it was a rather more serious Miss Banham who handed him his teacup and listened to his description of dolphins swimming beside the ship that brought him home, which he considered suitable for ladies and tea. He found it the more captivating.

'She is not a featherhead, which is good to know,' declared Harry, 'and so many beauties are. I suppose they think all they have to do is smile, and that learning is irrelevant. She asked sensible questions about the dolphins.'

'The dolphins?' Lady Damerham was distracted from her conversation with Lady Penwood, and looked very puzzled, having only a rather hazy idea that they were either very big fish or very small whales, and perhaps whales were fish, or ate fish, though she was almost certain fish did not eat whales.

'Yes, ma'am. I was describing them swimming alongside us as we came up the Channel.' He did not say that Miss Banham had assumed they were fish, since this would be met with derision by Mary, but then Mary knew about fish and sea creatures. A 'normal' young lady would have no reason to have learnt about them.

'So, she has an interest in natural history. I grant that is better than asking "what is a dolphin?"' Mary sniffed, and her mama studied the contents of her teacup and did not look at her daughter.

'And she did not flutter her eyelashes at me and look all coy,' added Harry, ignoring the fact that she had seemed quite flirtatious at their first encounter.

'I should hope not. Coyness is immodesty dressed up to be the opposite,' Mary said, forthrightly, 'and is not the same as being shy, really shy. Amelia Weston is shy, the poor girl. She looks as if she wants the ground to open up and swallow her if one does as much as exchange the time of day with her, and answers in a whisper.'

'Her mama has made far too much of her freckles, you know,' commented Lady Penwood, wisely. 'The poor girl is now exceptionally self-conscious, and everyone knows that those with red hair are likely to show freckles. One cannot help the colour of one's hair, though I believe some ladies do "help" it keep from grey.

'Walnuts.' Lady Damerham nodded wisely.

'Walnuts, Mama?' Mary blinked.

'Yes, you can use them, crushed of course, to dye hair brown. I am not sure whether it is the nuts or the shells, but it is definitely walnuts.'

Harry Penwood smiled, glad that Lady Damerham had successfully drawn the topic of conversation away from Miss Banham, and encouraged her to 'butterfly' her way even further from the original topic. Mary threw him a look which intimated that she understood what he was doing but would not stand in his way. After all, she thought afterwards, she did not want to make Harry, her dear friend, reluctant to talk to her. She must, it seemed, curb her tongue when it came to Madeleine Banham.

The following morning, Mary was seated in the small parlour, sighing heavily over irrefutable figures. It was she rather than her mother who cast her eyes over the weekly expenditure. Lady Damerham had always preferred just to hear the rough figures upon quarter days, but Mary had been used to studying the books monthly. Now, however, with economy as their watchword and a dwindling income that could not be augmented, unless Mary should take to the literary life, she was watching the pennies by the week. It did not make pleasant viewing, although she knew they were most certainly not being extravagant. There was a sufficiency at present, but each week saw the gradual diminution of capital. She heard the bell at the front door, and Atlow crossing the hall, followed by an agitated voice. Setting pencil and figures aside, she got up, and went out to see who had been admitted.

'What is it, Wilmslow?' Mary looked at the man

who had been steward of the estate for a quarter of a century, and whose family had served the Lounds for generations.

'He's dead, Miss Mary.'

'"He"?'

'Lord Cradley, miss. Just had a note come over from Brook House. Dead as a doornail, he is. Opened a letter that was delivered this morning, stood up from his chair in the library, blustering as was his wont, and keeled over dead.'

'Good grief!'

'Fair stunned everyone, it has. I thought as you should know right away, miss, and I was wondering if you could advise me.'

'Upon what, Wilmslow?'

'Well, his lordship – his late lordship I ought to say – was wanting me to set up an increase in all the rents that come up for the year at Michaelmas, and it has not been a good year, as you know. Should I—'

'We are well over a month from Michaelmas, Wilmslow, and with luck the heir will not have come, or not have studied the books, before the quarter day. Say nothing, and do nothing, and that is right and fair by those who deserve fairness.'

'Glad I am to hear you say that, Miss Mary. I was inclined to it, o'course, but since he was the master, and it was his wish . . .'

'He is not the master now, and for that the tenants of the Tapley End estate must be thankful, howsoever they may be good Christians and pray for his soul in church.'

'Aye, miss. All we has to do now is wonder about the new lord, and what manner of man he will be.'

'He is a Risley. That tells us enough, Wilmslow, more than enough.'

CHAPTER THREE

The obsequies for Lord Cradley were suitably well attended by the gentlemen of the local gentry and aristocracy, though, as Harry Penwood revealed, wickedly, to Mary afterwards, most were there just to be absolutely sure the old misery really was dead and buried. There was a notable absence of relatives, with the exception of a thin lady of mature years who was at the house and presided over the meagre provision of cold meats, sniffing loudly throughout. This was peculiarly distracting, and was put down not to excessive grief but a summer cold. Lady Damerham discovered, via the vicar's wife, that she was a second cousin who had 'religiously knitted socks' for him every birthday. This made Mary laugh when she heard it.

'Now that is genuinely funny, Mama. I have this image of her in my head, needles clicking away, and muttering psalms as the sock grew. "He breaketh the bow and knit two together, twice".'

'It is not an occasion for levity, my dear, though I perfectly see that once such an idea was in one's mind it would be hard to shoo away. I wonder if she thought it might remind him of her existence and mean he left her something in his will?' Lady Damerham frowned.

'He might have left the socks themselves to her, but I doubt he gave her a charitable thought otherwise.' Mary sighed. 'And now we will have the new Lord Cradley, who is a Risley of the cadet line.'

'Do not forget that he and the deceased were not upon speaking terms. It may mean that he is in fact a . . . a charming man.'

'As likely to find a whale in the Upper Pool, Mama,' retorted Mary, shaking her head. 'No, all we await is discovering what unpleasant type he may turn out to be, assuming of course that he comes to take up residence. The Risleys have always been grasping sorts, so it would seem probable that he will. What he does with Tapley End is another matter. Loth as I am to say it, he would be better moving into it from Brook House, for at least it has been maintained properly and is not the rambling mess that the Risleys constructed, adding bits every generation as they came into even more money.'

'Well, I am not sure the Lounds ever came into

"more money" after the Lady Elizabeth sold all her jewels to pay for the repairs after the Civil War, and Sir James was elevated to a barony by Queen Anne for that diplomatic affair. Your father never did say what it was all about, other than to say his grandfather knew when to keep silent and when to speak. I think the family has been losing money for the last century.'

'Yes, and too often by foolishness, not misfortune, which could be forgiven, but it does mean that the house makes sense as a building.'

This was true enough. There was a great hall, of moderate proportions and with later Tudor panelling, that formed half the centre of the house and gave onto the early east wing that terminated in a chapel. The first baron had extended to the west in the Queen Anne manner and created both public reception rooms next to the hall and airy, private chambers in the west wing. The house had grown over centuries, but always in the warm, mellow Cotswold stone, and with symmetry and scale. Brook House, by contrast, had been an empty field until the up-and-coming Tudor merchant Risleys had bought the land, and shown off their wealth with an array of decorative brick chimneys and bay windows that was followed over time by a grand dining room resplendent with plaster caryatids and spurious armorials, a grandiose Palladian portico and, in the last forty years, a 'mediaeval tower'. As Mary's father had said, most men built follies they could see from the house, not as part of it. In addition, the early demise of the late Lord Cradley's mother had left the house without a châtelaine and someone to oversee its care. It was thus rather tired-looking and unloved.

'He might feel he ought to remain in Brook House,' suggested Lady Damerham, thinking again of the new Lord Cradley.

'Then he is welcome to it as long as he stays there and does no harm to the estate.' Mary very obviously meant the former Lound estate. 'Oh . . . I lose all patience with the whole thing.'

A week passed, and with it July slipped into August, though the weather had been so inclement of late that it felt as if Michaelmas should almost be upon them already. It did nothing for Mary's gloomy humour. She foresaw an early autumn and long winter, and the winter months were her least favourite. Whilst she would be prepared to brave the elements in all but the worst weather, her mama became very agitated and worried over her contracting some inflammation of the lungs and limited her activities. Added to which she no longer had her two hunters. Last winter she had been in mourning, and now she was without a mount, so there was no hunting to which she could look forward and that made the winter gloom seem even gloomier, and the knowledge that this year they might attend the parties that proliferated about Christmastide did not fill her with eager anticipation. Meeting friends was all very well, and she enjoyed the talk and the food, but there was an air of, yes, competition, among the young women, and she was now aware that she was looked upon as 'poor Miss Lound, who could not find a husband'. Well, Miss Lound was now undoubtedly 'poor', in the pecuniary sense, but until now the lack of a husband had concerned her not at all. Miss Lound of Tapley End had not needed a husband, at least not from among the men she knew.

It was mid-morning, and Mary was coming down the main staircase, lost in her less than happy thoughts, when the bell at the front door echoed through the hall, and Atlow, with a measured pace that owed as much to his age as a butler's calm, went to answer its insistent tinkle. He opened it to reveal Sir Harry Penwood.

'Hello, Mary.' Harry Penwood drew off his gloves and handed them and his hat to Atlow with what was very nearly a grin. 'I bring news.'

'Good news, I should hope, from your expression.' Mary smiled back at him, casting her depressing thoughts to the back of her mind.

'Well, interesting news, even if not "good". I thought I would come over and tell you and Lady Damerham of it as soon as I knew.'

'Then best we find Mama and permit you to surprise us. Where is her ladyship, Atlow?'

'In the small parlour, Miss Mary. Shall I bring coffee there?'

'Yes, please.' Mary tucked her arm through Sir Harry's and looked at him with narrowed eyes. 'Very interesting news if your twinkle is anything to go by, Harry.'

'Wait and see.'

A few minutes later he was sat in a large wing chair by a good fire, for it was indeed so damp and chilly an August day that it felt autumnal, and with a cup of coffee at his elbow.

'So?' Mary folded her hands in her lap, feigning merely genteel interest.

'Old Cradley did not leave Tapley End to the Risley heir, who is that distant second cousin, or some such with whom he had a major falling out years ago,' he announced with aplomb. 'Brook House is entailed, and must go to that chap, like the title, but since he, Cradley, had just bought Tapley End he could do with it as he wished, and he has left it to the grandson of his aunt, his mother's sister. Not sure what relationship that is called, and it does not actually matter, but at least it does mean that there will not be a Risley striding about the place to mock the ancestors. That must please you, yes?' He beamed at both ladies.

'I suppose it must. Yes, actually it does.' Mary sighed. 'What a pity he had not died before he bought it.'

'Really, Mary, that is not very charitable.' Lady Damerham shook her head.

'Yes, but he only bought it barely a month before he died, so I am not wishing him a shorter life, not by much.'

Sir Harry laughed and told her she was a hard-hearted piece.

'We must be charitable,' said Lady Damerham, with more determination than belief.

'You can be for the both of us, Mama.' Mary was unrepentant. 'Do we know anything about this heir, to Tapley End I mean, not the title? Might he not just sell it on, since he has no connection with it? Or is he local enough to want to enjoy the landholding?'

'I do not know much at all, other than his name is Kempsey, Sir Rowland Kempsey, and he comes from Cumberland.'

'Good grief!' Lady Damerham exclaimed and spilt a drop of coffee into her saucer. 'Does anyone come from Cumberland?' Both her daughter and Sir Harry looked at her with puzzled expressions. 'What I mean is, people "go to" Cumberland, poets and those odd people who want to see more of nature, but does anyone actually live there, other than sheep and farmers?'

'We may not even find out, if he looks at the deeds, decides it is worth a tidy sum, and promptly sells it,' cautioned Mary.

'Now, there you are wrong,' corrected Harry. 'You see, the reason I know all this is that my bailiff was passing the time of day over a pint of ale in The Stag's Head yesterday evening, and your stewa—sorry . . . Wilmslow, let slip that the new owner is coming to view the property in the next week.'

'I must ask Wilmslow if he would be so kind as

to send Joshua Pilton's lad over to scythe the lawn next week,' remarked Lady Damerham, diverting the conversation for a moment. There was a short pause, during which Lady Damerham contemplated the length of the grass, Mary tried to sort her thoughts, and Harry Penwood sipped his coffee, whilst watching the emotions that crossed her face. He could read her like a book.

'We will have to leave cards, of course, to both gentlemen,' sighed Lady Damerham, returning to the main topic.

'Remind me when that shall be and I will have the headache,' murmured Mary, who very rarely suffered from any such indisposition.

'We must be civil, dearest.'

'As a household, I suppose that is true, but I do not think I could bear them here. The one is a Risley and the other owns the roof over your head. The only difference between us and Joshua Pilton is that he pays rent for his tenancy. It is demeaning. The new landowner will look down his nose at us as "a bankrupt's poor relations" and that will be far too close to the truth for comfort.'

'Which one, my love?'

'Oh, probably the both of them, Mama.' Mary shook her head. 'If only we had an income.'

'We will not reveal our circumstances.' Lady Damerham looked shocked.

'We do not need to, Mama. The entire county knows Edmund sold up and de facto fled the country.

The new owner is bound to hear it within twenty-four hours of his arrival.'

'Oh dear.' The widow clasped her hands together. 'Perhaps Harry could tell him that was all exaggerated?' She turned to Harry Penwood, who looked cornered.

'That, Mama, would be unfair. You cannot expect Harry to lie for us, and especially not a lie that would soon be shown up.'

'As opposed to one that would work a treat, Mary?' Harry cocked his head on one side and gave her a questioning look.

'Morally, it makes no difference, of course, but in practice it does. One has to be practical.'

'One does.' He gave himself up to laughter, and Lady Damerham wondered at the pair of them.

Three days later, having ascertained that there were no errands for her mama that might serve as a reason to go out, Mary went for one of her walks. Lady Damerham sighed over it, for she approved of gentle walking, when about the shrubberies, or shopping, or even to church in clement weather, but her daughter walked at a meaningful pace and with no more reason than she liked the freedom. There was something about the open air that Mary Lound always found invigorating, even on a day when the wind was tugging at the leaves upon the trees, trees whose leaves were just starting to lose their verdancy and rustled as if warning each other of the perils to come. The recent rain made walking across the fields a recipe for wet feet and disgustingly muddy hems, so Mary kept to the lanes, which were marginally better. On her way back, she took the more travelled road that led past the lodge gates to Tapley End and followed the perimeter wall to the less ornate ironwork that opened upon the short drive to the dower house. She had encountered a few of the locals whom she still felt were 'Lound tenants' even if the land was no longer in the family holding, and had discussed the autumn sowing with Joshua Pilton, and her husband's bad knee with old Mrs Gedling. They were not at all surprised to see Miss Mary out and about, and it was agreed by everyone that she had more care and interest in the land than her sire or her brother, and pity it was for the estate that it had not come to her.

The hedgerows were full of twittering sparrows, and a stoat darted across the narrow verge in front of her and disappeared into the ditch on the far side of the road, which made her smile. She heard hoofbeats, and out of the corner of her eye saw an equipage coming down the Tapley End drive to the lodge. She resolutely refused to turn and stare. Her smile became a sneer. So he was come, the man from Cumberland, to view his unexpected windfall. It was so unfair. Here he was, with an estate he had never even heard of until the solicitor's letter, an estate that could mean nothing beyond revenue, and yet it was in her blood, part of her. She lengthened her stride, and her gloved hands clenched.

She heard the gates creaking open behind her. Those

gates always creaked, no matter how much they were oiled. She did not alter her pace but strode on. The hoofbeats, at a brisk trot, grew loud behind her, and then suddenly she was sprayed with muddy water as the vehicle passed her. She let out an involuntary cry of annoyance and surprise as she was soaked.

The curricle, for she could see it now, came to a halt a few yards up the road, and a youthful tiger jumped down from behind and ran to the horses' heads. The driver turned in his seat as she approached and saw her expression. He had ignored her presence right up until her cry, when a sideways glance had revealed she was not some village wench with red cheeks and a bucolic gaze, but a young woman with a very pleasing profile and the demeanour of one used to giving instructions, not receiving them. To such a face an apology would be given.

He was wearing a low-crowned beaver set at a very particular angle to look nonchalant but suave. His pale, aquamarine blue eyes gave nothing away but gathered much; he possessed a deep, broad brow, and eyes set very wide apart. His cheekbones gave his face a sculpted look that would have been considered *de rigueur* on an ancient statue of a Greek god, and beneath a straight nose was a wide cleft that gave him a pronounced bow to his mouth that was both bizarrely feminine and yet powerful. In repose it hinted at petulance, but when he smiled, as now, it had a reptilian charm to it. Mary hated him on sight.

'My sincere apologies, ma'am. The least I can offer is to take you up and convey you to wherever you are going on this blustery afternoon.' His voice did not drawl, quite, but had a slow self-assurance. Mary had no doubt that her elderly pelisse and close, practical bonnet, added to the fact that she was on foot, had given him an erroneous impression of her. He probably imagined she was some local maid, vaguely genteel, who would be overwhelmed at the thought of being conveyed by a gentleman sporting six capes to his driving coat, and in a curricle with red wheels, however improper it would be to agree. Well, if he thought she was going to say yes, then he was in for disappointment.

'Thank you, sir, for your so *very* kind consideration, having already passed me without lessening your pace one jot. However, I am perfectly content to continue upon foot, and it would not do to sully such a fine turn-out with my now muddy garments.' Her voice was icy, but her eyes flashed fire. The gentleman tried again.

'Having been so inconsiderate, I feel that a little mud upon the seat would be the least penalty I could pay, ma'am.' The smile lengthened. He was a man used to getting his own way.

'Entirely insufficient, sir. I suggest that you continue upon your way and please, please, do not give me another thought.' She ended with heavy sarcasm, and he was taken aback. However, the wind was chill and his horses stamping, and in the face of intransigence he would be a fool to abase himself further.

'Then I can but repeat my apology, ma'am, and hope

that we will meet again in better circumstances.' He touched his hand to his hat brim, waited the moments while his tiger got back up behind him, and set his pair back in motion.

'It is not a hope I share,' muttered Miss Lound, her shudder one of mixed revulsion and cold as the wet reached through the arm of her pelisse, and the sleeve beneath. She glared after the receding curricle with uncharitable thoughts of wheels and ditches.

She was still fuming when she entered the dower house and drew off her gloves, tugging at them rather violently. Atlow pursed his lips and shook his head.

'There are some young gentlemen, Miss Mary, as think it a lark to spatter innocent pedestrians.'

'Well, this "gentleman" had not even the excuse of being a callow youth. I am only thankful that it is such an old pelisse and fit only for my long walks.'

'Let me take it and give it to Jane, miss, and get it dry before the range. She will have the worst of the marks brushed off, and can then set about rubbing out any stains that remain.' He set the gloves upon a walnut side table, and tenderly assisted her from the soiled pelisse. 'I will send up some hot water to your room. Ahem, there are some splashes of mud upon your cheek.'

'Oh dear.' Mary's fingers went to her cheek. 'I must look a mess.'

'A trifle disordered, if I might be so bold, miss.' As

one who had known her from the cradle, he knew that he might indeed be that bold, and received a rueful grin in response.

'I will change and then tea would be nice.'

'Her ladyship has Mrs Lissett with her, Miss Mary. Shall I inform her that you will join them shortly?'

'Yes please, Atlow.' Mary set her foot upon the stair. 'Oh, and you will be sure not to say anything about . . . no, of course you will not.' She could trust good old Atlow. Mrs Lissett was one of her mama's closest friends, but was a notorious local gossip who loved a little light embellishment. If she had the truth of the incident, it would soon become 'she was nearly run down'.

It was therefore a Miss Lound with her temper under strict control who entered the morning room some ten minutes later, with a polite smile for Mrs Lissett and an airy comment that it was 'very fresh outside'.

'Oh yes. Why my bonnet was very near blown from my head as I came,' declared Mrs Lissett. 'You really would not think it was still but the first week of August. I think the leaves will be coming off the trees by the middle of next month, and I always say the winter feels it is here when there is not a leaf left, excepting the holly and other evergreens, of course. It is not the best time of year to see the area, and what with the new Lord Cradley and the owner of your . . . of Tapley End,' Mrs Lissett had the grace to blush, 'due any day, one wonders what they will make of our little corner of Gloucestershire. They say that Lord Cradley is not a bit like his predecessor, but young and rather fashionable. I have no doubt he will set hearts aflutter.'

Mary vouchsafed a rather unladylike 'hmm' and frowned.

'We must hope he is more civil, at any rate,' said Lady Damerham, not wishing her daughter to give a long list of reasons why no sane woman should have her heart touched by a Risley.

'Oh, I am sure he will be. Fashionable gentlemen know just what to say.' Mrs Lissett was eager, after the irascible and unfriendly person of the late Lord Cradley, to encounter someone who exuded good manners.

'You mean, ma'am, that they are masters of insincerity.' Mary currently had a low opinion of fashionable men, especially those who drove curricles with red wheels. Two such in the vicinity might be too much for her temper. Lady Damerham gave her a swift look that was both mild reproof and supplication that she would withhold her frank views.

Mrs Lissett, unsure as to whether Miss Lound was serious or not, tittered hesitantly, which made Mary very nearly grind her teeth.

'I think Mary means that having a silvered tongue is not, in every case, indicative of a pleasing nature.'

'You mean he might be a,' Mrs Lissett dropped her voice, theatrically, 'rake. Have you heard anything that—?'

‘I have heard nothing, Mrs Lissett, I assure you,’ Lady Damerham interjected. ‘However, London beaux are noted for their cozening ways, and if he is as fashionable as you say . . .’

‘If he is that fashionable, our little corner of Gloucestershire can have no interest for him, and he will make his visit swift and brief, and we shall not miss him in the least,’ asserted Mary, adding, as her mother’s eyes pleaded once more, ‘for of course we will not have had time to become acquainted with him.’

Lady Damerham gave an audible sigh of relief. When Mrs Lissett departed she gave Mary a long look.

‘Something upset you on your walk, dear?’

‘Someone, Mama, very nearly upset me into the ditch. Sir Rowland Kempsey, I can report, has arrived in the vicinity, and drives a spanking pair of high-stepping chestnuts and a red-wheeled curricle that I am sure is all the crack. He came out of the lodge gates of the house and went past me at such speed, regardless of the large puddle in the road, that I was splashed right up to getting mud upon my cheek and was very nearly thrust into the ditch. When I remonstrated with him, his apology, if you can call it such, was to offer to take me up beside him and drive me home! Had you seen the look upon his face, Mama, you would have agreed with me that nothing should induce any decent woman to do any such thing. He leered like a libertine.’

Lady Damerham did not point out that, to her almost certain knowledge, Mary had never encountered a libertine, leering or otherwise.

'Well, there is nothing you can do now but calm yourself, dearest.'

'Yes, there is, Mama.'

'What?'

'I am going to fish in "his" lake as soon as the weather permits. That is what I am going to do.'

CHAPTER FOUR

Three days of very blustery weather delayed Mary putting this plan into action, but to her mama's relief, the fourth day was marked by hazy sunshine and a light breeze, which meant that Mary ceased to wander round the house like a caged tiger. It was late in the afternoon when she put on her fishing garb, an old round gown and a pelisse that fitted very loosely at the back, and which she had laboriously adjusted so that the arm seam would not restrict her casting. She topped this drab costume with a battered straw hat with a wide brim, tied beneath her chin with ribands that were fraying at the end. Taking up her fishing basket and her rod bag, she took the rear way through the dower house garden to the little wicket gate that gave onto the main park of Tapley End. The gate had a piece of wood nailed haphazardly across it, as proof of Lord Cradley's determination that she should not trespass. She curled her lip at this, and moved a few yards to the side, where the hedge was very thin, and had, it seemed, recently been made even thinner. Mary grinned. Wilmslow may have been commanded to bar the gate, and had obeyed, but he was no happier with a Risley running the place than she was herself, and it was obvious that a 'hint' had been left. She eased her way through the twigs, muttered over a snagged hem, and then, with a feeling of mixed defiance and exhilaration, headed towards the lake.

It was not an immense stretch of water, but large enough not to be called a mere pool, and had been formed by damming a spring-fed stream that passed through the park on its course to the river. Her grandfather had been a keen fisherman even into his late years, and had kept the lake well stocked, although only she had fished it regularly since his demise. She did not fish the smaller upper pool, which lay at the base of the hill. A little jetty by the old boathouse was Mary's favoured spot, and she knew the contours of the lake bottom there as well as the undulations above ground. On an August afternoon, this was where the trout would be.

Her well-loved rod was of red ash with a hazel top and standard whalebone tip, though only the ash was original after many breaks and hazel replacements, such as anglers were all prone to suffer, and came in three parts. It was not quite as long as many fishermen used, being no more than twelve feet in total, but it suited her well. She put it together and attached her brass multiplying winch, which had been the last birthday gift her grandfather had given her, when she was fourteen. She always thought of Grandpapa when she fished, and although it was a solitary activity, she never felt lonely. James and Harry Penwood had fished also, in the school holidays, and there had been some pretty intense rivalry, and occasional cheating. Generally, however, it was man against fish, or in her case, woman against fish. She relished that it was something where she could be as good as, if not better than, a man, for it was not a matter of brute strength. Her father, no angler, once said that he could not see what there was to be proud about defeating fishes, which were creatures of small brain, but like all anglers, Mary knew that a fish could be remarkably clever in avoiding one's hook, and landing a good fish was at least as skilled as returning successful from an afternoon's rough shooting.

She assessed the weather and the water, and selected her fly, dithering between a fern fly and a white palmer, which was her eventual choice. Once everything was in place, she took her landing net to lay beside her on the jetty and made her first cast where she had glimpsed a fish rise. It must have moved on, because nothing took the bait as she drew the fly back towards her with a delicacy that mimicked an insect upon the water. Fishing demanded patience, and Mary Lound, who was impatient with people, could be very patient with rod and line. She cast again, and her sigh was of quiet satisfaction. She could even look upon another fisherman, further along the bank, with a smile. There were enough fish for both her and the heron, grey garbed and hunched, and as intent as she upon the water.

There were two gentlemen in the yellow saloon of Tapley End, the older of the two sat reading a newspaper, one long leg crossed over the other at the ankle, and the younger, a youth of eighteen or nineteen, playing patience upon a small table. The cards conspired against him, and he laughed, and shook his head.

'I would make no gamester, for I cannot even win at patience.'

'I am glad to hear it . . . at least, that gaming holds no attraction for you.' The newspaper reader looked over the top of the pages and smiled.

'Fool's game, if you ask me,' the youth continued. 'Not but that I think a game of piquet in the evening is a very pleasant end to the day.'

'Is that a hint for after dinner, Tom?'

'No, no. Though not a bad idea. I might even beat you, if I am very fortunate.'

'There is that possibility, however small.'

Tom laughed again, stood, and walked over to the window, where the afternoon light gave a golden glow to the landscape, which was of carefully 'natural' pasture dotted with trees, about whose exact position great thought had been given some eighty years previously. There was a gentle slope to the right, down to where a lake added interest to the view, with a little stone bridge across the lower end hiding the sluice beyond from the house.

'By Jove, there's someone in the lake."

What? Drowning?' The older gentleman rose swiftly, dropping the newspaper, and came across the room.

'Er, no, but . . . there must be a little jetty I cannot quite see. It is a . . . good grief, it is a woman, fishing.'

'So it is. How unusual. This, Tom, is worthy of investigation. Come along.'

Mary was in a world of her own, and with a very nice speckled trout already laid upon a bed of dried grass in her basket. With a small twirl of her rod about her head in the advocated manner, she cast her line to a new hunting ground.

'Bravo.'

She turned her head at the exclamation, not pleased with the acclaim, and rather annoyed at the level of noise.

'Shhhh, you will disturb the fishes,' she declared in a low, insistent voice.

'My apologies, ma'am.' The speaker was a young man of slender form, whom Mary would have described as still 'coltish'. He doffed his hat, revealing a head of deep brown hair trimmed in the latest fashion. 'We came to see what you were doing.'

'Knitting.' The response was swift and accompanied by a glare.

'My brother ought to have said that we came to see who was fishing in the lake.' The older gentleman, a man of about thirty, had a measured voice in which Mary thought she detected an urge to laugh. He did not seem in any way surprised, however, and not at all put out. 'One wonders how it is that you are fishing here, ma'am?'

'I have fished here since I was twelve years old,' replied Miss Lound, brazenly.

'You have had permission?'

'It was actively encouraged.' She had no intention of apologising for her presence to strangers. She wondered why the new owner had brought friends with him upon his first visit. From her brief glimpse of him, the last thing she would have said was that he was a man of needy or nervous disposition who felt the need for support when arriving new to Gloucestershire. The gentleman was not easily put off.

'You have the permission of the new owner of this park?' The question was put as a matter of mild interest.

'Not exactly. But he has not forbidden it.' Miss Lound coloured a little. It was strictly true, since the new owner had not repeated his predecessor's prohibition. 'You may say I have "ancient rights".'

'May I indeed? I see. Do many local persons share

these rights? I ask merely so that I may know whether we are likely to see a steady stream of anglers about the banks over the next few days.'

'There is no need for concern, sir, and I doubt very much if Sir Rowland Kempsey would notice any depletion in his number of trouts.'

'You think not, ma'am?'

'The little I saw of him I would not have said he was a fisherman, for he showed no sign of patience.' Her colour was now less of embarrassment than annoyance.

'But—' The youth stopped, as his companion surreptitiously touched his arm.

'He did not?' The gentleman's brows rose.

'If he is a friend of yours, I should of course not make any comment upon his perceived character.'

'Oh, I do not know. Perhaps we shall hear of a side of him of which we were ignorant.'

'If you must know, he came out of the park and along the road in his fancy, red-wheeled curricle with no thought to a pedestrian, nor to the puddles, a few days past. Having deluged said pedestrian he then had the audacity to suggest I . . . they be taken up in his vehicle.'

'Oh dear. Were you very wet, ma'am?' The gentleman's lips twitched very slightly, and his eyes danced.

'Yes.' Miss Lound did not approve of the dancing, hazel eyes.

'Perhaps he felt it was in some way making amends?' he suggested, placatingly. 'After all, if you had been drenched . . .'

'No woman of decency, or sense, would have accepted the offer from a man with that particular smile on his face,' snorted Miss Lound.

'Ah,' said the gentleman. 'Is—' He stopped, for the lady was no longer paying him any attention. Her line had gone taut and she struck her rod as it bent, the line sliding between her fingers as the fish went running for cover. He said nothing more as he watched her play the fish, never letting the line lose tension, winching in little by little, letting the trout run each time a little less until it seemed to give up, whereupon she brought it in and bent to pick up her landing net. The gentlemen could see that the lady, and despite the worn garb this was definitely a lady, was quite expert. At that moment the fish appeared to revive, and she needed her free hand upon the line. The youth darted forward and picked up the net, which was slightly behind her, and, with no thought to his breeches, knelt upon the wooden boards and leant to scoop the trout up in the net with the eagerness of a small boy catching minnows. This was no minnow, but a fine two-and-a-half-pound trout, which Miss Lound despatched without any signs of squeamishness. The young man gazed at her in mixed admiration and surprise.

'What are you going to do with it, ma'am? Have it stuffed and mounted?'

'A fish this size? Mounted? No. Stuffed? Possibly. That depends upon Cook. This, and its companion, will be on the dinner table tonight.'

'You are going to eat them?' The young man felt it was somehow indelicate for a lady to actually eat something she had killed herself.

'Of course. It would be wasteful to catch a fish and not eat it, sir.'

'But you have just killed it.'

'Cooking it alive would be cruel.' She was, thought the older gentleman, playing his brother rather as she had the trout.

'But you are a lady.' The youth got to his feet, brushing his knees as he did so. He could not keep the shock from his voice. The thought of a woman as a hunter offended his soul.

'I am a lady who likes trout upon the dinner table.'

'Has it occurred to you, ma'am, that you have been caught poaching? The penalties are, I believe, quite severe.' The older gentleman interrupted, mildly.

'You are going to report me to Sir Rowland, sir?' Her eyes challenged him. 'Do you think he would have me arraigned before the magistrates?'

'I think you must be under some misapprehension, ma'am. My name is Rowland Kempsey, and I am the owner of this lake.' He let this sink in for a moment, and then added, 'I do hope you enjoy your dinner.' With which he touched his hat, gave a polite bow, and turned upon his heel, with the younger man thrusting the landing net into Miss Lound's hand and then mimicking his actions. She was left staring after them, making a fair imitation of a landed trout.

Sir Rowland walked pensively back towards the house. In truth, he was rather confused by his lady poacher. She was defiant, even belligerent, and had clearly taken another man to be himself. He wondered who it might be, but decided that the answer to that puzzle, at least, ought to be easy to discover. He halted in the great hall, and asked Mrs Peplow, the housekeeper, if there had been a gentleman call a couple of days prior to his arrival. In the absence of a butler, this redoubtable dame was the head of the meagre staff Sir Rowland had found in place, and whilst she was in the process of bringing back many of those who had been put off by Lord Cradley, the absence of a butler was a problem yet to be addressed.

'Why yes, sir. Lord Cradley, the new one, left his card, but I daresay Emma put it somewheres safe afore you arrived and has not recalled where. A good girl she is, to be sure, but a mite forgetful.'

'No matter, since we now know who the gentleman was. Thank you. Er, we found a lady fishing in the lake. I wonder . . .'

'Oh, Miss Mary, that would be. Well now, Mr Wilmslow said as he thought she would not keep away long.'

'You make her sound a little like a household ghost.'

Sir Rowland smiled. 'I take it we have not seen an apparition?'

'No, sir, course not. Mind you, if anyone was to haunt us it would be her, poor soul. So sad it was.'

Sir Rowland waited, patiently, for more information. He was, by nature, a patient man. Eventually, since the mournful tutting helped him not at all, he spoke again.

'In what way, Mrs Peplow?'

'Why, sir, she was born here, and lived every day of her life here, loved it more 'n Master Edmund – Lord Damerham, I should say. When he had to sell, she and her ladyship went to the dower house, which her ladyship retains for life, howsoever the land and bricks are yours now. Fair broke her heart it did.'

'That gives me the explanation I need. Thank you. I really ought to leave my card at the dower house and, er, also return the visit to Lord Cradley, who, it seems, drives a curricle with red wheels.'

Mrs Peplow vouchsafed a snort, which showed that she, like 'Miss Mary' did not think much of such an ostentation. Sir Rowland and his brother returned to the yellow saloon where cards and periodical had been abandoned.

'At least it is now entirely reasonable for "Miss Mary" – and I ought to have thought to ask the family name – to have no good word to say about "Sir Rowland", what with "his" treatment of her upon the road, and being the usurper of her family acres.' Sir Rowland shook his head. 'No wonder also that she felt the right to fish here. I fear extending her the offer to do so at any time she wishes might be seen as condescending, and even offensive, but, at the same time, not to do so would be churlish in the extreme. I can see, Tom, that we are going to have to tread very carefully hereabouts.'

'You may have to do so, Roly, but I will be gone by the end of September, remember. I want to have a few days in Hall before term starts. I shall look the innocent brother and observe your discomfiture as you tread upon eggshells.' Tom grinned.

'You show remarkably little respect for the head of the family.' The reprimand was given in a severe tone, but Sir Rowland's expression gave the game away.

'I do, don't I,' agreed Tom, his grin widening. There was silence for perhaps a minute and then he posed a serious question. 'Will this place suit you? I mean, it is sound enough, but a bit outdated, and some parts are real knights-in-armour stuff.'

'It is infinitely more convenient than Skillerslaw, and I have little doubt that Wilmslow will report the land as good and making a profit when I see him tomorrow. By the by, I would have you present at that meeting.'

'Why?'

'Because you are my heir, remember?'

'Yes, but only until you set up your nursery. You look healthy enough.'

'But we never know what may be around the corner. Our own father never thought to inherit, and yet he did so. Besides, I might be run down by Cradley in his red-wheeled curricle.'

'No, really.' Tom burst out laughing.

'And to go back to whether I will settle here, I think it very probable. I like what I see, and once this place is properly staffed again it will be very comfortable.' Sir Rowland looked about the room. It was not 'his', for there was nothing of his own in it, and from what he had gathered from his lawyer, the late Lord Cradley had only purchased the property a month before he died and had bought it, contents and all. The room still had the subtle mark of a woman about it, no doubt Lady Damerham. A thought, like a wisp of smoke, also entered his head that there might be the mark of 'Miss Mary' in it too.

His brother brought him from any further contemplation of the ambience.

'Not sure it will be comfortable living with your lady angler as a neighbour. If she were a fish she would be a pike, a great brute of a beast gobbling up everything in her path.'

'What an infelicitous comparison. I do not see anything piscine in her looks whatsoever, of whatever species.'

'True, but you wait. She might hit you on the head like that trout.'

'Ah, now that, I admit, is a possibility. I shall have to try and placate her.'

'Which is something that I would like to stay and

watch. You will not have an easy time of it.'

'No, I do not think that I will,' agreed Sir Rowland, thoughtfully. It did not seem to worry him, for he smiled to himself.

Mary Lound was not smiling, despite her catch. She did not like being wrong, and she liked being shown to be in the wrong even less. She told herself that since the man she had disparaged was not in fact Sir Rowland Kempsey, and that it had been a very natural error to assume that the gentleman in the red-wheeled curricle was him, she had no need to feel embarrassed. It did not help a jot. She returned to the dower house with cheeks that felt as if they burnt, and since it was not her fault that they did so it must be the real Sir Rowland's. He could have introduced himself at the outset, she told herself, rather than permit her to say what she did. Yet he had chosen to let her blunder on, and she was almost certain he had found it funny. Funny! Ha!

She entered the house by the back door, and went down to the kitchen, where Cook was overseeing the preparation of vegetables.

'Miss Mary. Now what brings you down here, miss?'

'Two fine trouts bring me, or rather, I bring them. I am sure that you can do something delicious with them for dinner, unless you are so advanced with your preparations. If so, they will be fresh enough tomorrow if left in the larder.' Mary took her basket and opened it to reveal the fish, and lifted them tenderly from their bed of grass.

'There now, your hands will be all fishy,' admonished Cook. 'Molly, bring Miss Mary a slice of lemon to rub on her hands.'

A youthful maid brought the lemon, and bobbed a curtsey as she handed it over.

'Thank you. Now, are they not fine fishes?' Mary was very pleased with the fish, if not their erstwhile owner.

'They are indeed, miss. From the lake?'

'Of course.'

'I hope as the new gentleman there does not take offence at you a-fishing, though the fishes ought to be yours, indeed.'

'Well, he has given his blessing to this meal at the least, so I do not think he will take umbrage.'

'That is nice, miss. I will bake these with a gratin of celery hearts and a cheese tart and cherry compote.'

'I look forward to it. Now I must go and change.'

Cook beamed at her in a motherly way as she gave a crooked smile and went up the back stairs to the hall, where Atlow, who had been winding the clocks, shook his head at her.

'I was taking the results of my successful fishing to Cook, Atlow. You know I like to see her to find out what she wishes to do with my catches.'

'Yes, Miss Mary. Her ladyship asked after you a while back, and I said as you had gone fishing, for I observed you with your equipment crossing the lawn.'

'I will go to her and assure her I have returned, triumphant, and not at all damp at the edges.'

'She is in the drawing room, miss.'

'Thank you, Atlow.' Mary went directly to the drawing room. Lady Damerham looked at her garb and gave a barely perceptible wince. Fishing attire was practical but not such that it showed off her daughter's face and figure to advantage.

'Atlow said you had gone fishing. You did not tell me, though.'

'Well, Mama, it was an impulse of the moment. The sunshine was not too bright, and I knew there would be shade where I wanted to cast. I caught two very nice trout, and Cook is preparing them for dinner.'

'Oh good.' Secretly, Lady Damerham did not find the taste of any fish thrilled her, but she was not going to admit it to her daughter.

'What is more, Mama, I met Sir Rowland Kempsey, who has a young brother with him.'

'Sir Rowland? The man who got you all wet? You met him before.' Lady Damerham sat very straight in her chair, wondering at such an encounter.

'Well, yes and no. It was definitely Sir Rowland, for he gave his name, but it seems the man who thoughtlessly splashed me with his curricle was not Sir Rowland, despite me seeing him leave the grounds of Tapley End.'

'How curious.'

'And how infuriating. Sir Rowland let me speak very

freely about my dislike of "Sir Rowland Kempsey", all the time knowing that I was talking about somebody completely different, and clearly enjoyed my ensuing discomfiture.'

'But what is he like?'

'As I said, infuriating.'

'No, really, dearest, I mean what does he look like?'

'Better than the curricle driver. He is tall, quite pleasant features, good voice. Annoying.'

'Is that all you have to say about him?'

'Not quite, Mama, because unless he is already taken, I am going to get him to marry me.' With which Miss Mary Lound left the room, head in the air, as her parent stared after her in horrified amazement.

CHAPTER FIVE

It had been said upon the spur of the moment, a thought that had sprung out of nowhere. She had voiced it from defiance, and a desire to shock, but as she climbed the stairs Mary halted. It was not, if one were rational, a bad idea. What was it that Harry Penwood had said? She could attract a man if she wanted to, but she had not wanted to do so. He was right. There had been no deep need in her to be married, to have a house of her own to run, since she had, effectively, run Tapley End, with a father often absent and then in poor health, and a mother who was not assertive. Of course, she ought to have considered that the day would come when her brother inherited and installed his wife as châtelaine, but it had seemed far off when she was eighteen and nineteen, and thereafter she had simply ignored the idea of matrimony. If Sir Rowland had been fifty and loose-jowled she would not have considered it now, but Sir Rowland was . . . She continued up the stairs to her room, thinking upon the man who really was Sir Rowland Kempsey. He had not, unlike the presumed Sir Rowland, repelled her, even if he had annoyed her by making her feel at fault.

'I must be practical,' she apostrophised herself. 'He is tall. I am a little over five and a half feet and he was much taller than I am, and taller than Harry, whom nobody calls short. That is not displeasing. He has eyes that smile, which shows he has a sense of humour, but then he was laughing at me, which is not pleasing. His features are regular, and he looks to be a gentleman who takes a reasonable degree of exercise, for he is not fat. His voice is quite deep, and pleasant.' There, that was very sensible. It did not take into account the smile on her lips when she thought of his smile, nor the slight increase in her pulse when she remembered his voice and manner, but she ignored those, very determinedly. This was a rational decision. If she was Lady Kempsey, assuming he decided to live in Tapley End, and she would take no irreversible step until that was known, she would once again have the running of her ancestral home. She would, it was true, belong to him, but if what he wanted her to do was what she wanted anyway, did that matter so much? 'What is the point of being free to be impoverished and count every penny, when being a man's property gives one comfort, security and dear

Tapley End? There is no point at all. Therefore, I must set about catching myself Sir Rowland Kempsey,' she said to her image in the looking glass.

She was not entirely sure how this was to be achieved, but upon consideration thought that she ought to cultivate the company of Miss Banham, and learn from her, however galling that might be.

In pursuance of her plan, she resolved to ride over to visit Lady Roxton, upon the slightly flimsy excuse that her mama wished a note delivered to her ladyship. Lady Damerham wondered why Mary was so keen that she send an invitation for the family to come over and dine, and even more so why she wished to deliver the note in person, but accepted that her daughter liked to be outdoors upon every possible occasion, and so complied. Riding over, rather than paying a call in the carriage, enabled Mary to feel more at ease, and made it an informal call. The butler, smiling benignly upon Miss Lound, assured her that the ladies of the house were at home and showed her into the morning room, announcing her as he did so.

Lady Roxton and her daughter were not alone, for Lord Roxton rose from a chair to greet her, and another gentleman also stood. Miss Lound stared at him.

'You!' She forgot the polite phrases of greeting.

'Oh, you will surely not have met.' Lord Roxton was not quite sure what her exclamation meant. 'Miss Lound, may I present Lord Cradley. Lord Cradley, Miss Lound.'

Lady Roxton gave a cautious smile. Mary Lound was, she felt, rather *farouche*, so socially awkward, and certainly far too inclined to speak her mind.

Lord Cradley made an excellent bow, with a smile upon his lips. Miss Lound made the smallest curtsey that was possible and glared at him.

'I am honoured, Miss Lound. Obviously.' The last word was added in a drawl, and his eyes dared her to retort. With a supreme effort she resisted, though her anger was clear, which he noted with a degree of pleasure.

'Obviously, my lord.'

'I regret, my lord,' Lord Cradley kept his eyes upon Miss Lound but addressed his host, 'that I have to confess Miss Lound and I, whilst not introduced, met upon the road some days ago, when I was so very careless as to splash her with muddy water from head to toe.' His expression was wry, and Mary seethed, for in revealing his 'crime' he had created an image of her in a ridiculous situation, and open to either mirth or pity, neither of which she wanted. 'I fear she may never forgive me.' He did not sound very fearful. In fact, he sounded rather amused. He also left her in a predicament, forcing her either to forgive him upon the spot, which she would not do, or sounding churlish if she agreed with his conjecture. Thinking quickly, she instead gave him a bright smile whilst her eyes were lit, not with mirth, but loathing, which he clearly found even more entertaining.

Madeleine, watching Lord Cradley rather than Miss Lound, found the twinkle in his eyes both a trifle wicked, and yet charming. Mary Lound would have told her the charm was that of a snake. His voice had a purr to it more than a drawl, a purr that was quite captivating. He was very clearly a man of the world, a little dangerous, perhaps the sort of man her mama would truly warn her against, but there was a frisson to the danger of him, and he was so very smart and fashionable.

'Such reprehensible behaviour, my lord, should certainly be atoned for,' she murmured, her eyes not quite meeting his.

'I did attempt to do so, Miss Banham, I assure you. I offered to take her up in my curricle and drive her home.' He sounded very reasonable.

'But having nearly ended up in the ditch once, my lord, I would have been foolish in the extreme to have risked it a second time.' This time Miss Lound's smile was broader, and her voice, if not as honeyed as Miss Banham's, was low and calm. She looked him full in the face.

'You doubt my driving ability, Miss Lound?' His eyes narrowed for a moment. That barb had found its mark.

'Upon what I have seen so far, sir, very definitely, but I admit that I could be in error. After all, you may have driven through that puddle through carelessness, poor handling of the ribbons, or a desire to be a little naughty.' She sounded almost patronising, and her choice of adjective implied he had behaved like a child. That stung.

'I think you should know, ma'am, that I am rarely

careless, accounted a very good whip, and if, though I deny it in this case, I chose to be "naughty", I would be very naughty not just "a little".' The purr was silkier, and very slightly menacing. He wanted her to know that showing him disdain was unwise. She did not flinch. He decided she was either very brave or very foolish, and he was not sure which. For his own part, he was not foolish, and he knew when to withdraw. Miss Banham, who was an enchantingly pretty innocent, might well be put off if he showed too much steel, and he did not want her put off at all. He therefore looked to Lady Roxton and gave her a smile of charm and apology.

'I think, ma'am, that my visit of courtesy is at risk of becoming very slightly less courteous. I shall withdraw, if you permit, delighted to have made your acquaintance and with an open invitation for you, and you too, my lord, to come to Brook House, though I warn you it will take another few weeks before I consider the place worthy of being visited. It has not had a woman's touch, or indeed that of a duster, for far too long.'

He swept her a bow, and glanced also at Miss Banham as he did so, silently indicating that his obeisance was at least equally to her, shook Lord Roxton's hand firmly, and departed, with a final flourishing bow to Miss Lound, who was standing as still as a statue.

As the door shut behind him, Miss Lound let out her breath, looked at her hostess and grimaced.

'My apologies, ma'am. I ought to have been more

emollient, but the gentleman wished to cross swords with me, and I cannot step back from a challenge. It is one of my many faults.'

''E is a man who finds 'imself *fort amusant*.' Lady Roxton gave a small Gallic shrug.

'But he is very smart, Mama. I do not suppose he will find our local society entertaining.' Madeleine Banham sighed.

'We are not complete rustics, Miss Banham, and if he does not like honest, unassuming society, then best he returns to wherever he came from without lingering,' said Miss Lound, trying to be positive about the locality.

Lady Roxton might deplore Miss Lound's forthrightness, but she silently agreed with her sentiment.

'But is it not exciting to have someone new and so fashionable in the district?' It was clear that Miss Banham was a little overwhelmed by the gentleman.

'Oh, for interest, perhaps yes, but I can offer you more than Lord Cradley. Sir Rowland Kempsey, and also his younger brother, have taken up residence at Tapley End, though I cannot tell for how long. Sir Rowland, from what little I could tell, looks to be a gentleman with enough "town bronze" to be guaranteed worthy of discussion.'

'You have met him?'

'Briefly, and informally.' Mary Lound did not want to bring up the subject of fishing. Miss Banham would wrinkle up her nose at the thought of any fish not upon a plate and well-seasoned.

'Ooh. How old is he? What does he look like?' Miss Banham could not help but let her youth show, and Miss Lound kept her amusement concealed within.

'I cannot give his age exactly, but I would think him perhaps thirty or thereabouts. His brother is considerably younger, probably a youngest sibling, and still in his teens. He has that gangly quality about him, but a nice enough boy. Sir Rowland . . .' Miss Lound paused, ostensibly conjuring his image from the depths of memory, but uneasily aware that he was remarkably near the surface, which annoyed her and intrigued her at the same time. 'Sir Rowland is a tall man, about six feet I would imagine. His figure was concealed by his coat, but even accounting for layers of clothing I would say he is broad enough of shoulder and trim enough of waist to be classed as the Corinthian more than the dandy. Having said which, I have not personally encountered either sort beyond my brother Edmund's rather desperate attempts to look fashionable. His eyes are brownish,' she tried to sound vague, 'and he possesses a sense of humour.'

'You were able to study 'im for some time, Miss Lound,' commented Lady Roxton.

'Only a few minutes, ma'am,' replied Miss Lound, and her ladyship drew her own conclusions from that.

'I do hope they both remain here,' sighed Miss Banham. 'Not that our friends are boring, but it is such fun to have new acquaintances.'

'You will have the opportunity for very many new acquaintances when you go make your come out in the spring.' Miss Lound gave her what she hoped was a friendly and encouraging smile. 'It will be very exciting.'

'Did you make a come out in Bath or London, Miss Lound?' Miss Banham's question made it sound as though, if she had, then it must have been decades ago.

'Neither, though I did spend several weeks in Bath a couple of years ago. The dressmakers there are of the highest quality, and it is a very lively place.' Mary ignored the unintentional insult.

Lord Roxton, who made a habit of spending a week in London before the Derby meeting each year, visiting old haunts, friends, and his tailor, smiled to himself. Bath was considered very much a backwater these days, so if Miss Lound felt it vibrant it said a lot about her ideas of social excitement.

'I am looking forward to it all very much.' Miss Banham's enthusiasm was genuine.

'And I am sure both will have lots of gentlemen as smart as Lord Cradley.'

'And Sir Rowland, as you describe him, does sound interesting.'

Just for a moment, Mary Lound's heart thumped. What had she just done? She had paraded Sir Rowland, in imagination at least, before the most likely young woman in the district to attract a man. Whilst she could not have pretended he was some ogre, she had been all too open and forthcoming. Even if Madeleine Banham did not flutter her indecently long and curving eyelashes at him, she was youthful, beautiful and charming, and she herself, Mary Lound, was five and twenty, without any feminine wiles, and no experience of being courted. If she was planning to catch Sir Rowland Kempsey, then she had just put a large hole in her own landing net. Then she thought of Harry.

'Sir Harry Penwood is returned also, do not forget, and after three years without sight of England must be as interesting as someone new.' It was grasping at straws.

'That is true, and he is much . . .' Miss Banham waved her arms about, in a gesture she had obviously copied from her mother, 'more interesting than when he left, but he does not cut such a dash as a London gentleman.'

Poor Harry. His chances did not look good. It occurred to Miss Lound that rather than 'cutting a dash' as an idle young man, he had been cutting at Frenchmen, but saying so in front of Lady Roxton would be the height of poor taste. However much the lady deplored Napoleon Bonaparte, she was French by blood and birth. She changed the subject.

'My mama would be so pleased if you said yes to coming to dine, Lady Roxton. It seems an age since we last entertained.'

'And you could invite Lord Cradley to make the numbers even,' suggested Miss Banham.

Since 'over my dead body' was not an appropriate comment, Miss Lound merely gave a small smile.

Lord Roxton, both a little more tactful, and more aware of the centuries-old feud between the houses of Lound and Risley, pooh-poohed the idea upon the grounds that his presence would constrict conversation.

'For I am sure by then everyone will have met him upon at least one occasion and be keen to exchange views. Lady Damerham is out of full mourning this month, is she not?'

'Yes, sir.'

'Well, then. Perhaps we ourselves might have not just a dinner but a supper party with dancing afterwards, and all the newcomers to the area can be invited, and we will be able to see how well they dance as well as please the young ladies.'

His spouse looked surprised at this idea, but not horrified. Miss Lound's smile became fixed. Being seen at a dance with Madeleine Banham was even more certain to cast her in the light of hopeless old maid. Comparisons were odious, but also frequently made. Of course she could dance, had mastered conversing whilst dancing and not looking at one's feet, but she lacked the fluid grace of one who danced naturally, and with pleasure. What a pity, she thought, that courtship took place so much indoors and at functions, rather than on long walks, or sat upon riverbanks, though a chaperone in either situation would be sure to want to walk more slowly, or frighten the fishes.

She returned home with Lady Roxton's assurance that they would be delighted to come to dinner the following Monday evening, and with the realisation also that observing how Madeleine Banham charmed men without having a man present was going to be impossible, since asking for advice was out of the question. It was as she dismounted at the stables that she had the idea of inviting Harry Penwood, and his mama, who might well decline. She did not want to see him making a cake of himself in front of her, but better him than Sir Rowland, and Lord Cradley was out of the question. She therefore returned to her mama with an assent and a request that she send another note, this time to Lady Penwood, making sure to say that the Roxtons were also to be present.

'If Harry is in two minds about coming, that will sway him,' said Mary, confidently, 'and, by the by, the man whom I mistook for Sir Rowland Kempsey was in fact Lord Cradley. No wonder I loathed him upon sight. I can now report he is even more insufferable than I first thought, and if you invite him to dinner, tea or a light luncheon, Mama, I shall go into strong hysterics.'

'Oh dear,' said Lady Damerham, already wondering how she was going to give a dinner that did not prove they were as poor as church mice and make Cook die of shame, and still maintain Mary's concept of strict household economy.

Her culinary concerns having robbed her of a good two hours of sleep during the night, Lady Damerham partook of thin slices of bread and butter and a cup of hot chocolate in her bed next morning, leaving Mary to breakfast alone. In contrast to recent days, the morning was one of blazing sunshine, and even if she had been perfectly sure that she might fish the lake, she knew there was little chance of a bite. However, she went out to the stables and had Silas, the groom, pull out a large butt of coiled plaited straw into the garden, and pin a target to it. She then went to get her bow and quiver and spent a happy half hour sending arrows into the target with good grouping. She was focused upon her breathing and her aim, and only as she was loosing an arrow did she catch movement as a man appeared from the path beneath the yew arch. The movement distracted her aim, and even as she started, the arrow left the bow and shot past the gentleman within three inches of his chest, burying itself in the outermost part of the target.

'What the devil . . .' exclaimed Sir Rowland Kempsey, halting abruptly. 'You nearly killed me! What on earth do you think you are doing?'

'Archery. You ought to have been more careful,' she snapped, rather more shocked than she wished to admit.

'Me? It is you, madam, who should have the care, placing your target where anyone might step into danger.'

'But nobody uses that path.'

'I just did.' He spoke with heat. Both parties had racing pulses.

'Well, the gate is barred. How could I guess it would be used?'

'I came through the gap, the one you use if the strand of brown wool I saw comes from your fishing attire.'

'Then it is a . . . a private gap.' She knew that sounded ridiculous, but she was horrified, imagining what would have happened if indeed her arrow had struck him, and her perturbation emerged as anger. She glared at him, and he glared back.

'Females ought not to be allowed to brandish anything more dangerous than a knitting needle,' he fumed.

'I could do a lot of damage with a knitting needle,' she retorted, and then took a deep breath and closed her eyes. After a long moment she opened them and spoke again, more calmly. 'I intended no hurt, sir. It was just . . . unfortunate.'

'Perhaps a red kerchief tied to the gate might alert me in the future when you take up your bow, Miss Lound.'

'Yes. Yes, that is a sensible thought.'

'It ought to have been yours.'

'Well, it was not, but thank you so very much,' she said, sarcastically, 'for providing it for me, a mere woman and thus incapable of "sensible thought".'

'That was not my insinuation.' His voice, like his heart rate, was reverting to something approaching normal. He became aware of her pallor, and the very slight tremor of her hand as she unstrung the bow. 'I know there was no intent to cause injury and had I appeared a moment later the arrow would have already found its mark in the target.' She nodded in response. 'I must be grateful that your aim was initially good enough so that it still hit the target when distracted at the point of release. Are you as good an archer as you are an angler?'

'I am accounted so, yes, sir,' she mumbled, feeling now just a little sick. A few inches to the left and—She must banish the thought from her mind.

'And I will have the ridiculous plank removed from across the gate. I take it that it was placed there upon the instruction of the late Lord Cradley. It seems excessive in the extreme.'

'Thank you.' She did not sound very grateful, but her feelings were jumbled.

'It is a pleasant walk from the house.'

'Will you dare come here, sir, when to do so risks life and limb?' She gave him a very shaky smile. Madeleine Banham would have lowered her lashes and dimpled as she said it, but Mary Lound simply looked unsure, a little shy. He found it peculiarly touching.

'I think I might, if you use the red warning and promise you will not actually take aim at me.'

'I . . . I promise that, Sir Rowland. It . . . it is rather early for a formal call, and coming through the gap in the hedge implies a degree of informality, to say the least.'

'It was a thing of impulse, not that I would describe myself as an impulsive man. My brother is applying himself to his Juvenal, and I thought I would take a walk about the park before the heat of the day precluded it. When I found the boundary and then the barred gate, I thought I might see if you and Lady Damerham were at home.'

'I am certainly at home, sir. Mama had, I believe, a disturbed night, and did not come downstairs early, but no doubt she has done so by now. If you would care to come into the house we would offer you coffee, or perhaps a glass of brandy to counter the shock of nearly having an arrow go through you.' She tried to make it sound less serious, but he saw her bite her lip when she had said it.

'Coffee would suffice, I assure you. I . . . I spoke intemperately, Miss Lound. I can only . . .'

'You were right, sir. I nearly killed you. In such circumstances "intemperance" is justified. I do wish, however, that you did not keep putting me in the wrong whenever we meet.' This was said more mournfully than resentfully, but there was a thin trace of annoyance. He failed to see how it was his fault that she had been so forthright by the lake, or for simply walking into the garden, but he let it go. She was evidently trying to be placatory, and he had a sense that it was not something she found easy or did very often. He was not a ladies' man, though he had three younger sisters and had learnt early in life that the female of the species thought in a different way to the male, and was thus frequently incomprehensible to a man. Perhaps she had always had to counter being called 'only a girl' by brothers, and assumed that he was the sort of man who thought women should only sew and play the pianoforte, and neither fish nor engage in archery. This was certainly not the case.

She led him round to the front of the house and preceded him into the hall.

'Let me take your hat and gloves, Sir Rowland. Atlow is cleaning the silver this morning, and it seems harsh to make him come upstairs to perform a task I can do in moments. He is not young, you see.'

'Aged retainer? Yes, I understand perfectly, Miss Lound. Thank you.' He removed his hat and laid his gloves in it as she took it from him. 'I take it he came with you from Tapley End, since there I found no butler upon my arrival.'

'Yes, and secretly I think he is the one person pleased to be here. There are far fewer stairs and no long passageways.' She spoke without realising how much she was saying. 'Mama may be—' Mary stopped as Cook came out of the morning room, and a guilty look crossed that dame's features. She dipped in a curtsey that made her corsets creak.

'Morning, Miss Mary. Good morning, sir.'

'Good morning, Mrs Holt. Could you send some coffee up, please.'

'Of course, miss.' Cook bobbed once more and slipped away downstairs, glad that the visitor meant that Miss Mary had not enquired why she and her ladyship had been in discussion on a day other than Friday, which was when the menus for the following week were determined.

They entered the room and Lady Damerham, who had been seated at an escritoire, looked up and gave a small start, as though, thought Sir Rowland, discovered in some dubious act. She flushed slightly as her daughter introduced him.

'Mama, may I present our neighbour and landlord, Sir Rowland Kempsey. Sir Rowland, may I present my mother, Lady Damerham.' It was very formal, and he was surprised to be termed their landlord. He was aware that he owned the dower house, but he did not feel that it was his. He did not feel like a landlord, but the situation clearly rankled. He made his bow to Lady Damerham, who came forward and greeted him with polite if disjointed phrases.

'I would not have you feel, ma'am, that I am as Miss Lound says, your landlord.'

'It could not be said otherwise, Sir Rowland,' remarked Mary, before her mother could answer. 'If, as I assume, you have taken a proper look at your inherited property, you know that the dower house and grounds are yours, but that my mother is to have the right of abode, without the payment of any rent, for her lifetime.' She looked at him squarely. There had been the faintest of stresses upon the word 'her' which he did not fail to notice. Without knowing how, Mary felt that his eyes asked the unspoken question 'And afterwards? What of you?' She gave a twisted smile but said nothing.

'I see. Yes, I see.' He did see, more than she thought.

'I have no complaint, Sir Rowland,' declared Lady Damerham, seeing the frown that appeared between his brows.

No, you do not, but your daughter does, he thought to himself. Small wonder I hear resentment in her voice, see it in her manner. She is cornered indeed.

'I sincerely hope that you do not, ma'am, and I can assure you that as far as I am concerned, you, both of you, have the right to use the park for walking, or for any other activity, quite freely, should you choose. The clumsy barring of the wicket gate, through which I, er, almost passed this morning, will be removed forthwith. To say that you may treat it as your own, when it was previously yours, may seem offensive, but no offence is intended.'

'Thank you, Sir Rowland. I myself am not a great walker, but Mary is one who needs fresh air and activity, and I am sure will take advantage of your kind offer.'

'I shall.' Mary glanced at him, and he thought she looked confused. Part of her wanted to fling the offer back in his face, for it was Lound land in all but legal deed, but it would be churlish in the extreme, so she was reticent.

The door opened and Atlow entered with coffee.

'Dear me, do please take a seat, Sir Rowland. What must you think of us!' Lady Damerham took a chair to the right of the fireplace and invited him to be seated opposite her. Mary very intentionally took a seat which meant that, if he wished to converse with her, he would have to turn slightly. She was not sure that at that moment she could face looking at him directly, though her practical inner voice told her that being missish was foolish and if she wished to engage his affections she must at least engage his gaze. Her mama felt only an awareness of some awkwardness, and in an attempt to prevent silences, chattered away volubly for some minutes. Sir Rowland made the most sensible answers that he could to questions that covered diverse topics and required an agility of mind to follow. Eventually he gave in and turned to Mary, with a look that pleaded for rescue. She took pity upon him.

'Do you intend to reside in Gloucestershire for much of the year, Sir Rowland?'

'I intend to make it my home, Miss Lound.' He said it with a smile but saw her wince before she smiled back. He was a clumsy fool. How must it sound hearing him want to make his home in what had been hers?

'I hope you will be very happy at Tapley End, sir.' The reply was mechanical, but she was thinking that it made her plan all the more logical.

'And your family, Sir Rowland? My daughter says you have a young brother with you.' Lady Damerham liked the idea of permanent neighbours rather than a frequently empty house.

'My brother Tom, ma'am, shortly to resume his studies in Oxford. My sisters are married, and my mama lives with her widowed sister in Richmond, at the edge of the park. She likes to be able to get to the Metropolis without difficulty.'

Lady Damerham talked about several visits she had made to London in her more youthful years, exhibiting a confused sense of the capital's geography, and finally Sir Rowland ended the conversation by extending an invitation to both ladies to come to dinner the following evening. Lady Damerham accepted with alacrity, feeling a little aggrieved that he could invite people without a thought to the expense, but also realising that in dining with him she could honestly say to Mary that the weekly budget need not be exceeded just because she was going to order a lobster from Gloucester for their own dinner party. He made his bow and departed to take a circuitous route back across the parkland, and with much to think about.

Mary was also thinking. There had been no mention of a wife. Somehow or other, she really, really did have to persuade him to marry her, but so far she had done nothing but alienate him, she was sure.

CHAPTER SIX

Mary was not such an outdoor woman that she was careless of her appearance, except when actually engaged in her outdoor activities, but she gave special consideration to her preparations for dinner the following evening. Lady Damerham, having dithered about going into dove grey with three days remaining of her full mourning, had been persuaded by her daughter that Sir Rowland would have no idea when Lord Damerham had died, and would care even less if she was a few days short of the required period of deepest blacks. For herself, Mary chose an old favourite, a soft, slightly grey-blue silk, which reminded her of summer evenings just after sunset when the sky blue deepened just a little, and the fish were rising. It also complemented her complexion and her fair hair, which she felt was insipid, although others would describe as a mellow, pale gold. She let her mother's maid dress her hair and clasp a pearl and aquamarine necklet about her throat. Her jewels were not numerous, but the necklet and matching drop earrings were good quality. She draped a spangled gauze scarf over her elbows, but then wondered whether it was worth risking goose pimples. The dining room at Tapley End was not a warm room, even with a fire lit in the large fireplace, and in late summer she would have worn a fine wool shawl, or perhaps a Norwich silk. Yes, there was a silk one in black with a grey fringe close enough in colour to the gown to be considered a match, not a clash, and it would go with her black gloves. It was so long since she had been dressed quite so fine for dinner that she had forgotten the best combinations.

It felt odd, drawing up outside the front of Tapley End and not being greeted by Atlow, and welcomed home. It gave Mary a disembodied feeling. Mrs Peplow met them, and was familiar, but not performing the role of butler. She did escort them to the yellow saloon, which was bathed in the early evening sunshine that would soon give in to a soft sunset. Mary stopped as she entered the room, and for a moment a frown appeared between her brows. Sir Rowland noticed it.

'There is something amiss, Miss Lound? I have not altered the arrangement of the room, not, I must admit, from any feeling that I should not do so but because those items I wish to bring to the house from Cumberland take a long time to come by carrier.'

'I am sorry, sir. It is just that . . . it sounds foolish, but the room smells different. For a long time it was used almost entirely by my mama and by me, two women. There was the pot pourri of roses, and, I suppose, a lingering hint of feminine perfume. One does not notice the smell of one's own house, until it changes, and the associations made by eye and nose cease to match.'

'Yes. It is something that I had not considered, but it is true. When I arrived, I was conscious that this was a feminine room and assumed it was because of the arrangement of furnishings, but what you say is true, if unavoidable.'

'There is no blame, Sir Rowland. It was an observation, and you did ask me.' She sounded defensive again, he thought.

'I did. Forgive me, Miss Lound, but would you "explain" this house to me?'

'Explain it, sir?'

'Yes. We, the Kempseys,' he extended a hand to include his brother, waiting patiently to be introduced to Lady Damerham, 'come to it afresh, observing its age and development, but having no knowledge of why or exactly when. The history of a house influences not just its look, but its feel, a bit like your awareness of the change in the smell. My brother and I have explored quite a few odd corners, and even a dead end, and since we wish to belong, it would be nice to know the history. It is patently close to your heart.' It occurred to Sir Rowland, in the manner of a revelation, that he would rather like to be closer to the heart of Miss Lound, though that might be a less than comfortable place to be.

'Am I so obvious, Sir Rowland?' She blushed, just a little, and he expected her to lower her eyes, but her gaze held his. Women flirted, even without thinking. He had seen his sisters do so with his friends, as well as being upon the receiving end of encouraging looks. The total absence of flirtation was, in itself, peculiarly attractive. She was totally unlike any woman he had ever met, and it fascinated him.

'Sir Rowland?' She repeated his name, and it was his turn to look discomfited, for he had stared at her in silence.

'Yes, ma'am, but that is no criticism. This is the home of your antecedents, perhaps from its first construction, I do not know, and it has meaning to you. There are things I would like to change, a little, and I will do so without asking your permission, but I would prefer to do so within the context of the house.'

It was a very reasonable request, in fact a very considerate one. It would also, she told herself, be a very good excuse to spend time with Sir Rowland, and yet her practical mind had her blurt out the wrong thing.

'You might learn much of the history from Mrs Peplow, sir. Her family has served the Lounds for some generations.' She did not mean it to sound like a put down.

'I could, but I would have preferred—'

'I did not say that I would not do so,' she interjected

hastily, attempting to retrieve the situation, and then thinking that she sounded rather desperate. 'I . . . I did not wish to sound as though I would instruct, like a governess.'

'You do not strike me in any way like a governess, Miss Lound.' He smiled at her.

'You think me ignorant?' She was doing it again, being defensive. It made things very difficult.

'No. Quite the reverse. I do, however think you more Artemis than Athene, shall we say. Your element is the outdoors, not a library and tomes.' It was a pretty compliment, and most women would have accepted it shyly. Mary Lound frowned, and considered it perfectly seriously.

'Yes. I see that. I do not deny that I find being indoors for any length of time constricting. Mama will tell you I am perfectly happy to go out even in inclement weather, though I am not so peculiar as to wish to rush out into storms and gales.'

'Getting wet does not worry you, ma'am?' asked Mr Kempsey.

'Not if one may return home within a short time and change one's clothes. It is, after all, merely rain. I would not advocate getting soaked to the skin, nor remaining in wet garments.'

'You are a pragmatist, Miss Lound, not a romantic,' declared Sir Rowland.

'I think that fair, sir. Yes.'

Lady Damerham looked at her daughter and Sir

Rowland and gave up. How a man was meant to find a woman attractive when she took things literally, and even frowned at him, she could not imagine. Poor Mary simply did not have the ability to set her cap at a man, and never in a hundred years would she succeed in getting an offer for her hand.

Sir Rowland presented his brother to her ladyship, but then turned back to Miss Lound. He spoke quietly.

'So you will come? Come over and show me around the house, Miss Lound?' Sir Rowland sought confirmation, for he guessed, correctly, that if she said that she would come, she would not renege.

'I will come, Sir Rowland. You have but to name which day, for my social diary is entirely blank, I assure you, excepting an appointment with your fish when the sun is not too bright.'

'Then shall we say tomorrow afternoon, fish permitting? At three of the clock?'

'It is agreed.'

He noted that she did not ask her mother's permission, nor request a chaperone as though entering his house put her at risk. He judged that she felt mature enough not to need one, and that one of the maids would be sufficient escort within the walls of the house, which she still felt was secretly 'hers'.

'Will you check with the fishes, Miss Lound, or shall my brother do so?' Mr Kempsey enquired with a grin.

'It depends, Mr Kempsey. Does Sir Rowland speak "troutish"?'

‘I do not. Indeed, my acquaintance with things piscatorial is at best loose,’ – Sir Rowland laughed, and Tom Kempsey glanced at his brother, a little surprised – ‘and I have never before possessed a lake.’

‘Then you really ought to become far better acquainted with it, sir. I sometimes think there are trout in it that know my methods and my tricks. It would do them good to have another try their hand against them.’

‘You think them clever, ma’am?’ Sir Rowland was still laughing, softly.

‘Oh not “clever” for they are fishes, but they have an animal’s fine sense of self-preservation, and it is the nature of things that it is the “foolish” trouts who end upon the dining table, because they have fallen for my pretend fly.’

‘Do you make your own flies?’

Lady Damerham groaned at the question.

‘Sir Rowland, please, do not pursue this conversation. When most ladies are hemming handkerchiefs or putting new ribands upon their hats, my daughter is to be found with an enlarging glass, scraps of fur, feathers and I dare not ask what else, and peering at illustrations of ghastly little insects.’

It was Mary who laughed this time.

‘*Mea culpa*. I will answer you, Sir Rowland, despite Mama. I usually purchase my flies, especially the ones I use the most, for it is more than frustrating when one loses the last of a particular fly that has been proving successful. However, I do like to make some of my own also. There is a fly local to this area not quite like those in the book, and I have endeavoured to replicate it, with my "secret" addition of a specific-coloured silk thread wound about it like stripes. I have found it very good in its season, which is the spring, when one recommences fishing.'

'And have you named it?'

'Of course. It proudly bears the name "Lound's Lucky".' She gave him a smile so genuine and from deep within that he was taken aback.

'Alternatively, it must therefore be "Trouts' Misfortune",' quipped Mr Kempsey, as Mrs Peplow entered and announced that dinner was served.

It was a very thoughtful Mary Lound who sat before her looking glass and carefully removed her earrings before she went to bed. She had enjoyed the evening, at least for the most part, having dreaded sitting in the dining room of her old home as a mere guest. In the event, she had forgotten that in the first few minutes, and settled into an easy conversation with Mr Tom Kempsey while her host listened to her mother with apparently rapt interest, but which was probably complete mystification. It took time to learn to follow Mama's train of thought.

She thought Tom Kempsey a nice boy, with a quick mind and a ready smile. He had expressed a desire to go into politics, or rather into the business of governance, and had aspirations within the Foreign Office. If his personable nature and high intelligence were anything to go by, he ought to do very well. He admired his elder brother, and had talked happily about his three older sisters, now married and living in Kent, Berkshire and Shropshire, respectively, and the mothers of enchanting infants, though this was their description of their progeny, not their uncle's view.

'To be frank, ma'am, babies are all squalling brats to me, and I cannot for the life of me discern the resemblances they claim to either side of the family.'

'I think with babies, Mr Kempsey, it is rather a case of "beauty lies in the eye of the beholder", and parental doting is part of nature. I am sure every cat with kittens thinks no other kittens were ever half so fine.'

He had laughed and agreed. Shortly afterwards, by the mutual 'dance moves' of dinner conversation, he transferred his attention to Lady Damerham, and Mary found herself engaged with Sir Rowland. For no good reason, she found it harder to be relaxed with him, and felt self-conscious. He had spoken of general topics, which had moved to art and his liking for paintings.

'Though I favour landscape, which is currently, according to the periodicals, not at all in favour among the experts.'

'So you do not account yourself an expert, Sir Rowland?'

'No, that would be presumptuous. I appreciate good painting, and by that I mean painting which represents the physicality of the scene, or thing, but also a sense of feeling.'

'Did you study art in any formal way, or has it been by your own interest and experience?'

'Oh, mostly the latter, though one of my tutors at Merton happened to also love pictorial art, and I learnt a little from him about what to see in a painting. I was at least spared the Grand Tour of my grandfather's day; the thought of being dragged about Italian frescos and Greek statuary in poor repair fills me with horror. The one good thing I will say about Bonaparte is he has made the Grand Tour impossible. Personally, I am more than content with "this sceptr'd isle". This shows that I am undoubtedly a philistine underneath, but there. It has meant a war, but . . .'

'My brother was killed at Sabugal,' announced Miss Lound, flatly, and though her voice held no tremor, an expression crossed her face that needed no explanation.

'Forgive me.' Sir Rowland's light-hearted manner had gone in an instant. 'I did not know . . . did not mean . . .' He had frowned, angered by his own clumsiness. It was as if a great stone had been thrown into a pool and its mirror surface had been broken by the ripples. Mary had fought with a sudden wave of loss, which she still felt sometimes as a physical thing, as if the breath had been knocked from her, as Sir Rowland tried desperately to think of something to say that would not sound crass or trite. When he did speak, his voice was quiet and low. 'Unlike most of Europe, we are spared the reality of war in our towns and countryside, and our army, being small in number by comparison with many, is in some ways forgotten by all who do not have loved ones within its ranks. What happens in the Peninsula is reported, but not "felt". I am truly and genuinely sorry, Miss Lound.'

'You did not know, could not have known.'

'You were close.' It was not a question.

'Very. Sir Harry Penwood, whom I am sure you will meet, has lately returned from Spain and sold out upon the death of his father. He and James and I, we were a childhood trio with James, the eldest, at its head.' She had looked at him, and in her eyes he saw a depth of sorrow that made him want to take her hand and reassure her. Yet to do so would have been impertinent, and there was no reassurance. One could not make such a thing better, by word or deed.

'Forgive me,' he said again, and then there had been silence between them for some minutes, neither knowing how to recommence the conversation without it feeling false. Eventually it had been he who broke it and asked, hesitantly, 'Are you still prepared to come here tomorrow, and show me about the house?'

The humility won her in an instant. He had not presumed that it would not upset her in such a way that returning when the memory had been so actively stirred would hurt, or that she might wish to keep from him. She shook her head.

'No, Sir Rowland. I said that I would come, and so I shall – not as a martyr, either. It is you who ought to forgive me. Some losses can be borne with surprising ease, some memories blur to nothing, but some wounds stay raw and open and nearly unbearable for so very long. It is not something that can be explained. That wound, for me, is one such, and you touched it without knowing. I cannot blame you, do not blame you, but I hurt.' She finished upon a whisper that held pain as acute as if it were physical.

'Then tell me something, anything, that might in any way take your thoughts from it. Tell me something unimportant, frivolous even; a like, or a dislike.'

She had pondered for a moment.

'I have an illogical fear of spiders.'

'I do not see that as illogical. Many people fear spiders, for there is something intrinsically frightening about them.'

'But those in England cannot do one harm, at least, not much. You would get a far worse bite from a pig, for instance, but how many people are afraid of pigs? Very few.'

'Ah, but could it be that many people are afraid of pigs but conceal it, in case they are mocked, and thus the percentage of the population who are terrified of them is underrated.'

It brought a smile, a small one, but a smile nonetheless, and gradually they had resumed a moderate degree of conversation, but it had clouded the evening, and lay between them as a barrier.

'And how has that in any way helped in my intention that he should ask me to marry him?' Mary asked herself as she laid her head upon the pillow. 'Not at all. He has seen me miserable. Men do not want miserable wives.' This was of course true, but rather stark. 'I could have shown emotion, perhaps with a hand across the brow, but not sat there looking distraught. But I was distraught and I do not play at emotions. Do I have to be false to get a husband? And if I do and I succeed, when and how do I reveal that it was not "me"? Oh, why is this so hard, and why do I like him more than the other gentlemen I have met, excepting Harry, who is as a brother? Should I doubt myself for such feelings, or am I trying to make myself believe that a union with him would work? After all, we have met but three times. I must approach this better tomorrow and not be silly, or I will never get my home back.'

Being a woman who believed in common sense meant that the upheaval occasioned in her heart and mind left her feeling as if sinking into a quicksand when she had always stood upon rock. It worried her, frightened her, and made her angry with herself because she was used to trusting her own good sense, and it had clearly flown out the window.

She tossed and turned, nearly tangling herself in the sheets, and when, eventually, she slept her dreams were full of James, and Tapley End being a mirage that faded to nothing, and being watched by a tall man with eyes that were not 'brownish', but definitely hazel.

* * *

'Do you like Miss Lound, Roly?' asked Tom Kempsey, stifling a yawn as they ascended the main staircase together.

'Yes, I do.'

'Odd sort of female in a way.'

'Not in the common style, I grant you,' admitted Sir Rowland.

'And unpredictable. Just when you think everything is going along nicely, she goes all prickly. I saw it at dinner. She shut up like a clam at one point, and yet had been quite animated beforehand.'

'I think one has simply to learn to understand her. I do not think her flighty or fickle.' If Tom had not heard what had passed between them, he was not going to elucidate.

'You really do like her.' Tom grinned. 'Well, you know your own mind best, but I think "learning to understand her" might be a long and even painful process. She looks the sort of female quite prepared to slap a fellow's face if she takes umbrage.'

'Better that than putting an arrow through his chest.'

'What?' Tom stopped upon the stair and turned to his brother.

'I did not tell you. She very nearly put an arrow through me yesterday.'

'Good Lord, Roly. Keep out of her way if she is inclined to the murderous.'

'Oh, she was not trying to hit me. If she had, I doubt very much I would be still breathing. It was an accident and not a wayward shot. I may tell you about it tomorrow, over breakfast. Now, I am for my bed, and you, yawning away, are obviously in need of yours.'

The brothers parted at the door to Tom's bedchamber, and Sir Rowland went to his own room and made his preparations for bed. Having finally dismissed his valet, he lay with his arms behind his head, not at all sleepy, but very thoughtful, and with all the thoughts about Miss Mary Lound.

He had been attracted to her at that first meeting, to her form and figure and to her personality, despite the fact that she was wearing old clothes for a practical purpose and with no attempt to make her look beautiful, and that she had shown spirit which might have led the critical to describing her as 'a termagant'. She did possess a sense of humour, which surfaced when she was not being defensive, but the problem was that she was defensive for much of the time. He wondered what had made her like that, and whether he might be able to prove to her that she had no need to be defensive when with him. He might be wrong, and she was genuinely the shrewish sort, but his instinct said otherwise. She was pragmatic and not romantic, she admitted, but then was a romantic female intrinsically one with whom he would wish to spend his life? The ones he had seen sighed a lot, and looked as if anything untoward would give them a fit of the vapours. Miss Lound would undoubtedly sniff at the possession of a vinaigrette, rather than at its contents. Her situation, it was easy to see, was unenviable. It looked very much as if she had no guarantee of even a roof over her head if her mother should die, or the means to live in any comfort. From what he had gathered from Mrs Peplow, the current Lord Damerham was not worthy of the name, and had sold the estate to the family's historic 'enemy' for a paltry price and left the country. His attachment to the family acres had been non-existent, but it was equally clear that Tapley End meant the world to his sister, who faced potential destitution. Was it surprising that, with her life having been turned upside down, she had a rather cynical view of the world? No, it was not. Well, on the morrow he would discover more, a lot more, about the house which he now owned, and the young lady who had grown up in it. He knew which was the more intriguing.

He fell asleep, and dreamt of a mermaid with long, mellow gold tresses, who rode side-saddle on a trout the size of a whale.

CHAPTER SEVEN

Lady Damerham found her daughter bright and cheerful next morning, and was suspicious. She was too bright and sparkling.

'Are you sure about giving Sir Rowland the history of the house?' she asked, nervously.

'Oh yes, and I did promise to do so. I think Tapley End deserves that he know its past, and I will give him credit for appreciating that he ought to do so. I am intrigued about the changes he mentioned.'

'You will not like them, dearest. It will upset you.'

'Not necessarily. I wondered for several years whether we were right to keep those high-backed oak chairs in the hall, for all that Papa bought them because they date from the time when Sir Robert and the Lady Elizabeth restored the house. It does not make them comfortable, or even safe to sit upon. To be honest, it was so unusual for Papa to buy anything for the house . . .'

'He did not actually buy them,' admitted Lady Damerham. 'He won them at cards playing against Lord Snitterfield.'

'My goodness! Well, I suppose that is more likely. I wonder what he set against them in the bet?'

'You would not like it, so I never told you.' Lady Damerham took a deep breath. 'Sir Robert's breastplate. He was, he told me afterwards, in his cups.' She offered this in mediation of the enormity of the 'crime'. Mary stared at her open-mouthed for a moment.

'He . . . he cannot have.' She was genuinely shocked. 'That is . . . well, a sort of sacrilege.' She had wondered if she ought to have removed the breastplate from the house with Sir Robert's portrait, but it felt too much part of the fabric, as though some things were not 'family' possessions but belonged to the building itself. Perhaps that was why she had never liked those oak chairs; the house 'tolerated' them but never absorbed them into itself. This was not something she could say before her mama, who would have thought it fanciful, if not peculiar, and Mary herself was rather embarrassed at feeling it, for it went against her pragmatic attitude to life.

'Sir Rowland and his brother do seem very nice.' Lady Damerham changed the subject, and was watching Mary carefully as she continued. 'When you said . . . I know you were funning of course but . . . And he is not married.'

'I was not funning, Mama, but I agree that I might have shied from it had he been an ogre.'

'Mary, casting out lures for him would be . . .'

'Difficult, yes. I am not entirely sure how one does so.'

'I was going to say it was unseemly.' It might be what she would have said, but Lady Damerham privately thought exactly as her daughter admitted. It would be hopeless.

'I agree, Mama, but he has Tapley End and in the long term, forgive me, I have no home at all. The logic is inescapable.'

Logic did not feature heavily in Lady Damerham's mind, so she could only look at her daughter and wonder at her.

'I blame your Grandpapa,' she said after a moment.

'Grandpapa? For what?'

'For giving you the idea that the Lounds and Tapley End are indivisible.'

'But he believed it, and so do I, at least in heart. I feel exiled, Mama.'

Lady Damerham sighed. She had been very impressed with Sir Rowland, but could not see how he might form an attachment with her wilful and plain-speaking daughter.

Mary knew just how long it would take to get from the dower house to the main house, but found herself hurrying a little, since she had spent too long deciding what to wear that would be suitable and show her off to best advantage. She might not know how to flirt but she was, she told herself, quite capable of making the best of whatever looks she had. She had chosen a gown of pomona green cambric, which was one of her favoured colours, though anyone with an eye to fashion would know it was so high-waisted as to show it five years out of date, but had looked at her reflection critically in both a deep cream kerseymere spencer with 'rifleman green' velvet-covered buttons, and an open pelisse in nutmeg-coloured twilled sarcenet. She finally opted for the spencer, and a chip straw hat with dark green ribands. She laughed at herself for taking so much trouble when in truth she was going to walk across the park and round the house.

'If this is the trouble girls go through during the Season in London, I am mightily pleased I never had one. Such a fuss, and all to catch a husband. Goodness, I shall be late!'

Her pace across the park was brisk and her cheeks were healthily flushed when she rang the bell at the front door of Tapley End. It felt as odd as on the previous evening. Mrs Peplow, giving her a maternal smile, ushered her into the great hall as Sir Rowland entered from the west wing and came towards her.

'You are but five minutes late, Miss Lound. That is very good timing.'

'I am actually probably on time, sir, for that clock,' she pointed to the timepiece upon a side cabinet, 'is notorious for gaining ten minutes a day. As a timekeeper it is poor, but it has a most pleasing face.'

'Then I bow to your knowledge and commend you for arriving upon the hour, ma'am.' He smiled as he took her hand and bowed over it. When he straightened the smile had faded. 'Thank you . . . after last night.'

'It is . . . forgotten. Besides, I owe it to the house to make a "formal introduction" between the pair of you.' A dimple peeped. 'You are, after all, now its new guardian, and it is in far safer and better hands than those of a Risley, of which the previous Lord Cradley was a classic example.'

'I confess I never met the gentleman, and am intrigued, for there is clearly what must almost be termed a feud between the Lounds and the Risleys, of which I am therefore glad not to be a part, excepting through the marriage of my great aunt.'

'It is a feud, which sounds silly in this day and age, for we are not mediaeval warlords, but it goes back to the Civil War and is in fact much connected to this house.'

'Then please educate me as you take me about the place. I take it that this hall is the earliest part, from its height and the beams, though clearly altered.' Sir Rowland was more than content to be 'educated' by Miss Lound, who looked, he thought, very pretty in that green dress.

'Yes. I shall begin at the beginning.' Mary began a little self-consciously, but soon relaxed as she told him about the origins of the house, and how, in 1415, Sir William Lound, knighted by King Henry V after the storming of Harfleur, returned to England in poor health and came to recover with his uncle in Gloucestershire. He fell in love with the landscape and one day came upon this house, a little dilapidated, and offered to buy it from its yeoman owner. The man was unwilling to sell except upon the condition that Sir William marry his daughter. Sir William thus gained a house and a wife. 'The newly married Sir William restored the main hall and had the chimney built instead of a hearth in the middle of the floor.'

'It is certainly an impressive size. It must take several whole trees over a winter.'

'Yes, but at Christmastide it comes into its own, and we still have a great yule log, which would be impractical in most houses. I remember very merry gatherings as a child. The Lound crest above it was a later addition. I am actually relieved it remains, for it would have been entirely in character for Lord Cradley to have had it defaced or indeed totally removed.' Miss Lound looked thoughtful. 'Now, follow me.' She gave a little laugh. 'I am sorry, Sir Rowland, that sounded peremptory. I ought to have said "If you would care to follow me".'

Sir Rowland denied she sounded commanding, and followed obediently, enjoying listening to her as much as learning from what was said. She was not trying to impress him, at least not with her own person. She was focused upon the house and that alone, as though introducing him, he thought, to a friend she was desperate that he like. She led him to where the dark oak stair ascended with broad, worn treads, and thence up to the first floor.

'This wide passage, which later became known as The Long Gallery, leads to the chapel that Sir William built, but I am sure it needs no explanation, and we need not visit it now.'

'Indeed. I recognised its age upon first viewing. I like the grisaille glass in the chapel's east window, by the way.'

'Yes, it is rather nice, and considering it is made up of the pieces that were collected by the housekeeper when all the windows were broken in the Civil War, it is amazing.'

'Clearly that period was . . . difficult.'

'Yes, but I shall not tell you about it just yet.' She halted in the gallery. 'Calling it "the Long Gallery" is rather grandiose because it is only fifty feet or so. I remember my brother James pacing it out when he was first able to make his stride one yard. Apparently, people would promenade up and down when the weather was inclement, but if so, they must have looked more like soldiers upon guard duty, marching up and down and turning at the end.'

'There speaks the lady who prefers the outdoors,' commented Sir Rowland.

'Very true, sir. I had not considered it, but that must account for my disdain for the idea. However, one must be fair, and if they were wearing those starched ruffs and stiff skirts and slashed velvet doublets, I can see why getting their clothes wet would have been most unpleasant. Can you imagine a limp and soggy ruff?'

'Not without laughing, Miss Lound.' He smiled and realised that he often had the urge to smile when he looked at her.

'This was all panelled, and the chimney in the gallery added, in Queen Elizabeth's time. Houses must have been very cold, and people really had to wear thick furs and layers of wool. One Lound went to sea with Grenville for one rather profitable expedition, which ended in them ransacking the Azores, and earned his share despite discovering early on that he was vilely seasick. His name was Valentyne Lound and there was once a Hilliard portrait miniature of him, but it was "removed" with the other contents that were plundered during the Civil War, and all that the family retain is a letter from Sir Robert to his son in the 1680s, relating the family history and describing the picture as he had seen it in his youth. Seasickness is not at all romantic, but when I was a girl, I thought any adventurer romantic, and several times drew rather inexpert sketches of a man with close-cropped, copper-gold hair and a neatly trimmed beard, a ruff, and a golden chain of plundered Spanish gold – and I was specific that it was plundered gold – about his neck. I do wish that, of all the old things, had been saved.' She sounded regretful, but then shook her head. 'It does no good to grieve over what happened over a century and a half ago.'

'I assume the portraits here now are all ancestors?' Sir Rowland, for all that he liked landscapes, had looked at the faces that stared from the frames, unconsciously seeking resemblance to the lady before him.

'Yes. Some of the men are rather grumpy, I feel, and I doubt that all of the ladies can have been as beautiful as portrayed. Not one is even "rather plain".'

Sir Rowland wisely forbore from commenting, lest he put Miss Lound upon her guard against compliments.

'This wing is much less used, of course, since the erection of the west wing, and the fact that several of the rooms are only accessible through the others is awkward.'

'Do you have any great attachment to the chair and little table by the window at the end, ma'am? Is it some Lound heirloom?' Sir Rowland enquired.

'No. I believe they were bought by my grandmother, but she tired of them and sent them into "exile" in this wing. Have you thought of something else there?'

'I am not a collector of sculpture, but my grandfather bought a bronze by an Italian called Soldani Benzi, a representation of autumn. I think the morning light on it there would be rather good. I have a *pietra dura*-topped table that it could stand upon.'

'Well, at least it would be a reason to go there rather than seeing an uncomfortable chair.' She glanced at him with a twinkle in her eyes. 'I do not think the house would be offended.'

'That is good. I am having those pieces, and some paintings, brought down from the house in Cumberland.'

'Has your family lived there many generations? I always think of it as cold and wet and in autumn colours.'

'As well you might! Actually, my father inherited Skillerslaw rather unexpectedly. As the younger son of the younger son it had not looked likely, and my father was in Holy Orders. What money we had came from my mama, and her connections, which was also how my father found himself with a very comfortable living in Berkshire, and a rectory that rambled. It seems that a rectory ought always to be described as "rambling", which leads one to wonder what vicarages ought to be.'

'If the vicar's wife is to be trusted, Sir Rowland, it is "leaking", prodigiously, through the roof.'

'Accurate, no doubt, but not alliterative, ma'am.'

'This I admit, sir, but do continue.' She felt light-hearted, and could not explain why, even to herself.

'My mama has suffered for many years with an arthritic complaint, which meant that travelling all the way to Cumberland was simply impossible, so although my father went up there once or twice, he never lived there. I would go more often, and we did what we could to improve the farmland, but it is in truth fit for sheep and turnips. The land here is so very much better, and one can get to Bath or London quite easily without night after night upon the roads. I want this to be my home, not an outpost to visit upon occasion.' He paused. 'I am sorry. It must gall you to hear another want to live in what was, and still must feel, yours.'

'In a way, Sir Rowland, though it grieves me, I would rather someone was living here who cared for it, and will love it, than Edmund, for whom this was merely a house and land from which to get rents.' In that moment Mary Lound forgot her plan, forgot her aspirations, and was filled with a deep and mournful realisation of what was actually the state of affairs.

Sir Rowland saw it, heard it and felt the generosity of it. This young woman was seeing the loss of four centuries of her family in this house, and through the bad husbandry of her sire and elder brother.

'Thank you. I will do everything that I can to be a good guardian.' It sounded very formal, but it was like a handing over of more than legal deeds. It was responsibility.

'I did not come here to make you feel weighed down by another's family, Sir Rowland.' She gave him a shaky smile. 'Let me tell you about what happened after Valentyne's time.' She led him back along The Long Gallery to the door and then into the great hall, where she halted. 'Valentyne's son was one of those whom James I raised to a baronetcy. The Lounds remained King's men even when the king might not show great sense. Thus, when Charles I raised his standard, there was no doubt that there would be a Lound raising troops for him. Sir Martyn Lound was not a young man, and one whose failing sight rendered him incapable of fighting, but his son Robert did so.

'There has been bad blood between the Risleys and the Lounds since the Civil War. Just as we were for the King, Lord Cradley, despite being elevated to nobility by King Charles for support over taxes, was very much a time-server and chose to support Cromwell. He did so with words and sending men to fight, rather than taking up arms personally.' She sounded scornful. 'Robert Lound, in contrast, fought at Roundway Hill and several skirmishes, before he inherited the title from his father. His breastplate is there upon the wall.' There was a touch of pride in her voice as she pointed to a very utilitarian piece of armour on the wall opposite the fireplace, set above a pair of crossed pikes.

'After King Charles was beheaded, Cradley made sure that the estate was sequestrated, and he profited by it. It was his steward who took over the estate, and took everything he could from it, in goods and in rents. That went straight into the Risley coffers. They were good at accruing wealth.' She spoke with disdain in her voice. 'Lady Lound joined her son in exile, sailing from Bristol with her jewels in her petticoats, and the most vital family documents in her maid's bodice. The poor lady did not live to see England again. Sir Robert married another exile, the Lady Elizabeth, and at the Restoration they returned to find this house little better than a farmstead, the chapel ruined, panelling damaged, anything of obvious value stolen. There were even holes in the roof, through neglect.' She shook her head at such lack of care.

'It is remarkable that it shows so little evidence of its years of peril,' remarked Sir Rowland. 'I take it at the Restoration it was itself restored?'

'The Lady Elizabeth used the family jewels and her own to fund the repairs. She and Sir Robert rescued the house, but it took time, and the family fortunes did not improve until their son, Sir James Lound, was made a baron by Queen Anne, rewarded for diplomacy during the Wars. I would not have said my grandfather was diplomatic,' mused Miss Lound, 'and nor was Papa. I can only assume that great-grandfather used up all the diplomacy in the family.' She did not seem concerned by this. 'He used his newfound wealth to build the west wing, which is far more comfortable and better organised for modern living. We use – used – that far more, of course. It has made the house almost in symmetry, a "C" shape not an "L". I think the fact that it was all of the same local Cotswold stone means that the outside has a pleasing unity despite that, and who actually paces out the size of a house?'

'Who indeed, Miss Lound.' Sir Rowland was enjoying hearing her views. Here, in 'her' house, she had lost all the anger at the world in general, and that look of being trapped in a nightmare not of her own making. She was honest and direct and no, would never be termed diplomatic, but she was a breath of fresh air to him. 'Was the first Lord Damerham the man who had the park designed, or enlarged? Its situation and shape seem too well formed to be entirely the work of nature alone.'

'Yes. He kept the formal garden to the front of the house, and enlarged it, but he saw the potential of the brook, and he was a fisherman.' Miss Lound evidently thought anglers a superior breed for she stressed the 'he'. 'Grandfather was equally keen, but the interest bypassed Papa altogether. Fishing is far better than playing cards, especially playing for large sums of money. I have never seen the sense, since however much skill is involved, there must be an element of luck also. Are you inclined to games of chance, Sir Rowland?'

'No, I am not, though I can spend a very convivial evening playing piquet with a friend, or my brother. I did as most young men do in London when I went there for the Season as a greenhorn, and tried the gaming tables, but it gave no pleasure. I like London for a few weeks, and then I wish I was back in the country. I was found to be a very boring fellow indeed.'

'A very sane fellow, sir. I never went up for the Season. An aunt, my papa's sister, was going to bring me out, but died quite suddenly two months before. I think I regretted it for all of one week, and then realised how much happier I was at home. I have attended the assemblies in Cheltenham, and some in Bath, and talking of nothing to people one does not know and having one's toes trodden upon by clumsy partners is not my idea of pleasure.' She had led him from the hall to where the grand staircase rose to the upper floor. Unlike his ancestor, Lord Damerham had not treated stairs as simply a way to reach the upper storey. This staircase was a statement, with carved newel posts and a sweeping oak banister either side of a broad stairway that could accommodate four persons ascending abreast, rising to a half landing which turned to the left. 'Since the upper rooms are bedchambers and dressing rooms, I do not think I need show you anything there, Sir Rowland, but the dining room, saloons and the library are noted for their fine ceilings and door pediments.'

'I would be most interested in your view of the furnishings, ma'am, since it is in this portion of the house I would wish to add a little of my own taste. I cannot simply add more and more and make the rooms cluttered. I wonder, if there are items and pictures of importance to you, which I would replace, whether you might like them for the dower house?'

'And thereby clutter that instead, sir?' She saw him wince at his own clumsiness. 'No, no, I am roasting you, Sir Rowland. It is a very thoughtful offer. Shall we see what you have your eye upon as surplus to your requirements?'

'Thank you.'

They went from chamber to chamber, Sir Rowland began a little cautiously, lest his wish to replace something appear to denigrate a much-loved piece, but gradually relaxed. In the drawing room was a pianoforte.

'Do you play, Miss Lound? This takes quite a lot of room and—'

'I am abysmal. Mama had it brought from

Cheltenham, in the hope that I would become accomplished, but I admit to you, sir, that I am remarkably lacking in accomplishments. I stumble over even country dance tunes, I cannot sing beyond humming to myself when in good humour, and my sketching is, er, "sketchy" and my watercolours . . .'

'"Watery"?'

'Decidedly.' She gave him a smile and a gentle laugh. It was not musical but low and very genuine.

'But you are a good angler, Miss Lound.'

'That cuts no ice at functions. A young lady is not elevated by her prowess upon the hunting field, or with rod and line.'

'You hunt, ma'am?'

'I used to, when I possessed hunters. They were both sold by my brother. I shed a tear at their loss, not just because I was attached to them, but also because it was another diminution of my life. I have but my old hack, who is a dear, but could not possibly hunt.'

'That must indeed have been a blow. How fortunate that he could not sell your bow or your fishing rod.'

'If he had thought they were of worth he would have tried, but I would have probably put an arrow through his leg if he attempted it.'

'Remind me not to thwart you, Miss Lound.' Sir Rowland laughed, and then made a request. 'You are free to fish here just as you always did, but I wonder, would you impart your skill to me? You see, I am no fisherman, but feel it would be a very pleasant way to spend a few hours, and that since the lake was designed to be fished . . . Would you, Miss Lound, be gracious enough to show me how?' It was an idea that had occurred to him during the course of the tour. It would mean spending time with this fascinating young woman in her natural environment, the open air, where she would be as she was here, fresh and direct, and unencumbered of spirit.

'Why, of course, Sir Rowland, though you will find me a hard taskmaster, or taskmistress. What begins as being thought through every time has to become instinctive through practice, as though one's limbs learn to do it like walking, where one's brain does not instruct one foot to be placed before the other, at least not consciously. And you must be warned now that there is but until the end of September in which to learn to fish as I do for trout, for thereafter they are left over the winter until the end of March.'

'In which case, may I request a first lesson at your earliest convenience?'

'The day after tomorrow, sir, in the afternoon, if the wind is not blustery, and if there are still rods in the house. I doubt not they remain. Let us go to the gunroom. Edmund kept my father's guns and took them with him, saying that Canada contained many wild beasts. It probably contains good fishing too, but he would not consider that.' She led him towards the back of the house, and to a door beside that which led to the servants' quarters. 'Oh, of course, I need the key.

If you have not been within, Sir Rowland, Mrs Peplow must have it.'

Mrs Peplow, who had followed them around the house a respectful few paces to the rear so as not to listen to their conversation too closely, coughed, and vouchsafed that in fact she did indeed have the key, and went off to bring it. A few minutes later Miss Lound entered a room she had come to feel was hers almost exclusively. The glass case in which the guns used to be was bare, excepting for an old fowling piece, which was too archaic to have been taken, but the fishing rods hung in their bags from a row of hooks, and Mary Lound went to them, touching them as one might stroke a pet.

'These have not been used since my brother James . . .' She swallowed rather obviously.

'If it distresses you . . .'

'No. What is a fishing rod if not for fishing. He would think as I do, that the lake, and the rods, need use.' She looked along the line, remembering the contents of each. 'This one ought to suit. It was James's first rod, ideal for a beginner, and will not have been put together in years. Let us see if the ferrules are still in order.' She unhooked the bag and opened it as if unwrapping a gift, untying the binding and laying the sections upon the deal table in the middle of the room. 'They look sound enough, but best to assemble it just to be sure.'

He watched her as she put the rod together with deft fingers and a certainty of touch. He had the feeling that she could have done it blindfolded.

'You began angling as a child?'

'Yes. How . . . oh, you must wonder at my lack of hesitancy. Well, I have been putting rods together more than half my life. It is natural to me now. There, that is all secure. I will not add the whalebone tip. I had forgot how nice a rod this is. There are boxes of flies in the drawer here, but we can select those when we see the weather.'

'I am looking forward to my lesson already, Miss Lound.'

'You may not feel that way once I have told you off for making a mull of it, sir. I really doubt my patience as a teacher.' She gave him her smile again, and he felt he would not care if she told him off if he also earned smiles like that.

'If we go to the library, I think we will find my brother at least attempting to study, and then, if you would like, we might have tea served in the morning room.'

'Oh, thank you, yes. Is your brother very studious?'

'Not unless pressed,' Sir Rowland laughed, 'but he knows the value of being ready for Michaelmas term after the long vacation when one becomes "rusty". A few days' work will pay dividends later.'

They left the gunroom, and Miss Lound handed back the key, then went to the library, where Tom Kempsey was furrow-browed over a Greek text. He looked very relieved to have an excuse to abandon his books, at least temporarily, and the trio went to the morning room, where Sir Rowland rang for tea. Miss Lound's impression of Tom was confirmed. He was open, pleasant, and just a little 'unformed' as yet. She liked him. When she left, a half hour later, it was in an uplifted mood, and she was halfway across the park before it dawned on her that she really had not done anything to make Sir Rowland favour her. This just proved how little she knew about men.

CHAPTER EIGHT

Lady Damerham did not know whether to be pleased or worried when her daughter returned from giving her tour of Tapley End. Having feared that she would be either melancholy or enraged at Fate, her ladyship was surprised to find Mary certainly preoccupied, but in no way low spirited. When asked about it, she was vague, saying that Sir Rowland had shown himself a man of sense, and that his brother was applying himself to his studies before returning to Oxford toward the end of the month. This struck Lady Damerham as decidedly odd, as was the way she blurted out during dinner, with a mixture of defiance and triumph, that she was going to teach Sir Rowland the art of fly fishing.

'That will be nice, dearest,' was all Lady Damerham could think of in reply, and then changed the subject to what flowers from the garden might be best arranged for the dinner table the following evening. Mary was so caught up in her own thoughts about fishing and Sir Rowland that she even opened her mouth to ask why dinner would be in any way special, and only then did she recall the engagement. Other than being glad to have Harry present, she could not say that she regarded the evening as one of entertainment, but rather of study. It was vital that she learnt the feminine arts, or at least the rudiments, so that she could begin to put her plan of campaign into effect properly. As she had expected, Harry Penwood had been only too eager to come to dinner, but his mama preferred to remain at home and write her letters, despite his entreaties.

Whilst Mary dressed with some thought, the thought was not actually about her clothing, but rather whether Lady Roxton still decided what Madeleine should wear or whether she was being given an element of her own choice to prepare herself for the spring. Mary did not want to be seen as a dowd, however long in the tooth Madeleine felt her to be, and so had selected the most modish of her evening gowns, which was to say it was only two seasons old. Her 'advanced years' did mean that where Madeleine would almost certainly be wearing pearls, she could be rather more showy. Her grandmother had left her a demi-parure of emeralds, drop earrings and a rivière necklace, but that was too grand for a dinner. However, she also possessed a pretty citrine necklace and citrine and pearl earrings, which would do very nicely with the gold vandyking on the cream silk gown. She let her mother's maid dress her hair, since Jane, the housemaid who acted as her maid to unhook fastenings and put things away, was not really very artistic with comb and pins. The overall effect was of a young woman with style and poise.

'You have youth and beauty, Miss Banham, such as I cannot match,' remarked Mary, studying her image in the looking glass. 'I will not even try, and tonight you will teach me new things.'

Harry Penwood arrived before the Roxton party, and Mary was privately a little glad, because if he was going to be drawn to Madeleine Banham, then at least until her arrival they could be as 'brother and sisterly' open with each other as normal. He looked, she told him, 'fine as fivepence', at which he demurred, though admitted it had taken him four attempts to get his cravat tied as he wished.

'I am rather out of practice with the fancier sort after uniform,' he admitted, 'and I thought I ought to make an effort for . . . my first dinner engagement.'

'Oh yes, very wise.' Mary pursed her lips and looked suitably serious, though her eyes danced. He laughed.

'You never pander to a chap's ego.' He shook his head in mock dejection.

'Ah, but that is because I have always found the male ego, er, self-panders, and needs no help from me.'

'Minx.'

It was her turn to laugh, but then her expression hardened.

'I met Lord Cradley when I went to deliver the invitation to Lady Roxton. He was paying a social call.' She sniffed derisively. 'Very fashionably attired, lots of polish, and as nasty a Risley as one could meet. If his predecessor was charmless, he is the opposite, but more dangerous. He thinks a lot of himself too.'

Even allowing for Mary's bias, this did not sound good news.

'Oh.' Harry was thinking of the effect of such a man upon an innocent young lady like Miss Banham.

'However, I can report that Sir Rowland Kempsey is not of the same ilk, although I initially mistook him. You will laugh at me, Harry, for I was convinced it was he who had splashed me upon the road because I saw the curricle leave ou—his gates, but it turns out that it was Cradley, who must have been paying a call. I went to fish in the lake as my revenge, only to be discovered by two gentlemen whom I thought visitors and turned out to be Sir Rowland and his young brother. I think you may rub along quite well with Sir Rowland.'

'Praise indeed. You must have been impressed.' Harry looked at her a little more closely than she would have liked. Well, he was her dearest friend, but she was not going to reveal her plan, for she felt he would not see it in the same light as she did herself, as one of dire necessity. It was, said a small but clear voice in her head, very fortunate that dire necessity took such a pleasing form.

'I was not unimpressed.' She sounded unemotional.

'And tell me about this splashing incident.'

'Alas, you will mock my misfortune.' Mary told the tale, and though he smiled at her narrative, he did not mock.

'Bad form all round, I would say. First of all, he was thoughtless about a lady pedestrian, and then he made an offer that must put a decent young lady to the blush.'

'Oh, I was too angered already to blush, Harry, I promise you. I cannot recall my exact words, but he drove on in no doubt as to what I thought about him.'

'That would give him something to think about. You have a sharp tongue, madam.'

'I do, don't I.' Mary grinned at him, and it was then that Lord and Lady Roxton were announced, with Miss Banham, and he turned from informal friend into ponderous gallant. To be fair to him, Mary could quite understand why his wits were addled by Madeleine Banham. She entered the room and seemed to shine. She wore no jewellery except a gold locket about her elegant throat, and a filet of pomona green ribbon, the colour Mary favoured so much, was threaded through her hair. If the colour looked good on Mary it suited Madeleine to perfection. Her gown was of white muslin delicately embroidered with sprigs of flowers, and simply cut. Miss Banham needed no fancy gown to make her draw all eyes. The red gold in her hair made Mary feel her own locks were instantly even more insipid. Life was not fair.

Lady Roxton looked regal, and her spouse proud, as well he might be. The degree of familiarity between the persons present meant that formalities were perfunctory, and Mary, not wishing to be an unwelcome third in a conversation, dutifully took it upon herself to entertain Lord Roxton until dinner, since the two mamas were happy to chat, and Harry Penwood was struggling to loosen the knots in his tongue to speak with Miss Banham.

Mary was quite able to talk about things that Lord Roxton found interesting, from the harvest to the prospects of the French being driven back over the Pyrenees, whilst observing Miss Banham putting her skills to work. What Mary found amazing was that it was so very natural. When she looked shyly at Harry Penwood it did not seem cloyingly coy, and even the way she had seated herself at an angle to him, showing off her profile, which Mary was certain would be termed 'enchanting', appeared mere chance. She had then turned her face to him and gave every indication of hanging upon his every word. Listening, even half listening, to their conversation was, of course, very rude, but Mary did so, to be educated rather than pry.

'. . . but it must seem so very dull back here in Gloucestershire, after all the dangers and excitement of campaigning, Sir Harry.' Miss Banham's eyes opened a fraction wider. Her mama's warning about captivating him was forgotten because he sounded so 'safe' and was not talking to her in the bashful voice her younger admirers used. Little did she know he was just as enthralled, but able to conceal it a little better, at least from one who did not know the grown man too well.

'Oh no, really, I would not say that at all. It is . . . different, you see, a different world.' There was just the tiniest hint of regret in Harry Penwood's voice. Mary picked it up from long years of close acquaintance, but so did Miss Banham, which surprised her.

'You see, you do miss it,' she smiled at him in a way which showed her pleasure at being right, and a ready sympathy. 'I . . . I am not quite sure why, of course, for it must be something that only gentlemen feel, that degree of companionship. I had friends at school, naturally, but I do not miss being a part of that life.' It was the nearest she could imagine, but it made his mouth twist in a wry smile.

'I think that is because whatever "privations" exist in a young ladies' seminary, they are not the sort experienced in the field, and there is, I hope, little risk in the classroom.'

'Ah yes, for we had nothing more dangerous than a sharp pencil, or an embroidery needle.' She gave a small, soft laugh and then became more serious again. 'Danger must bond men very much. You must be terribly brave.' There was nothing but youthful admiration in her voice, and he coloured and demurred. Mary thought that if she had said the same words, and privately she did think Harry a brave fellow, he would have believed she was mocking him. Had she become such a cynical 'old tabby' that everything she uttered sounded barbed? It made her think, and not happy thoughts.

'I think that back here, at home, it is easy to ascribe the actions of soldiers as brave, but much of the time it is simply getting on with things as best one can, though I have seen some very brave deeds, and some very foolhardy ones, over the years.' Harry Penwood's gaze, even when embarrassed, seemed fixed upon Madeleine Banham's. Had he said this to Mary, she would have pushed to hear the details, but Miss Banham put her kid-gloved hand to her cheek and said in a 'fluttery' voice that she was, alas, a poor weak creature, not up to tales of gore. This lowered her in Mary's estimation, but did her no harm in Harry Penwood's eyes. After all, the fair sex were not meant to be bloodthirsty. Fragility was, it appeared, appealing. Mary was not sure how to be fragile.

It was at this juncture that Atlow entered and announced dinner. Lady Damerham went in upon the arm of Lord Roxton, and Mary, seeing Harry about to offer his arm to Lady Roxton, took pity upon him and pre-empted him. She was not entirely sure if it was protocol, but she dismissed too much protocol as stuff and nonsense with families who knew each other well. Lady Roxton gave a slight smile that was brighter in her eyes. She had often wondered why Miss Mary Lound had never tried to attach Harry Penwood, and her conclusion was that she was one of those odd females who did not wish to marry. She did commend her generosity on this occasion. Whilst her ladyship might lie in her bed at night and dream of her beautiful daughter taking the Ton by storm and securing an earl or a marquess, she was also very close to her Madeleine, and the thought of her living in some distant part of the country did not fill her with delight. She had already discounted the new Lord Cradley as a suitable match, though Madeleine had been impressed by him, and she thought Harry Penwood was the sort of boy who would make a dependable husband if Madeleine developed a genuine *tendre* for him. Herself in a very happy and loving marriage, Lady Roxton wished that Madeleine might be as blessed. Marrying a man who was very nearly a neighbour, and one who lacked exalted rank or immense wealth, was not the stuff of dreams but . . . well, it was early days. Most probably his admiration would not develop, and Madeleine would simply gain a little experience of handling men before her come out.

Seating six persons about the dining table when the gentlemen were outnumbered two to one was made easier when one applied the impromptu rule that husband and wife should not sit together, nor mother and daughter, but father and daughter might do so. It meant that Harry was placed at one end of the thankfully modest length of mahogany, with Madeleine to his left and Mary to his right. At the other end, Lady Damerham had the Roxtons to either side, with Lady Roxton next to Mary. Harry was not so fixated upon Madeleine Banham that he ignored his friend, and indeed tried to make the conversation one in which he attended to both young ladies equally, though his eyes sparkled the more when he was speaking with Miss Banham.

What was it that Madeleine Banham did, besides look beautiful? That of course would provide the immediate attraction, but there was more. It dawned upon Mary that she made a man feel . . . valued? Respected? She certainly encouraged Harry to talk about himself, without saying anything so blatant. Mary had always got on with men by talking about the things they were interested in, such as horses, hunting, fishing, and the land, and in return she had been treated like a brother, or an honorary man. She put a man at ease, and Madeleine did not, but that was because she seemed to . . . well, in Harry Penwood's case at least, make him a trifle excited. There was no other word she could think of that fitted.

This did not bode well for the fishing lesson, for the last thing a fisherman needed was to be excited, but if she was teaching Sir Rowland to fish, then she was most definitely in 'honorary man' mode. It was most depressing.

It had to be said that Mary was quite pleasantly surprised by Madeleine Banham. She had assumed, because she was so pretty and innocent, that she was also fairly vapid, despite Harry Penwood's belief that she had more sense than most pretty girls. However, when they were sat together in the drawing room before the gentlemen joined them, Mary discovered that whilst she was not interested in the same sort of things as herself, and she had little knowledge of the world, she did have views, even upon gentlemen.

'You have added Harry Penwood to your list of conquests, I see.' Mary gave a wry smile.

'Oh, do you think so?' Madeleine looked unsure. 'You know him better than I do, of course.' She sighed and Mary gave her a puzzled look.

'Do you not want him to admire you? He is a very sweet-tempered and honest young man, and rather dashing, surely?' Mary was not sure he would like that description, but it was true enough.

'Oh, he is, I am sure of that, but . . .'

'But . . . ? Forgive me, I had thought a large number of admirers must be pleasing to a young lady.'

'They are and yet . . . Sometimes, Miss Lound, I wish some of them did not gaze at me as they do. When it happens every time, it feels as if . . . as if none of them are interested in me, just the way I look.'

'Goodness me, I had never considered that.' Mary thought rapidly. 'Do call me Mary, by the way. I know I am positively ancient compared to yourself, but we live close enough for us to be upon friendly terms. I think only your presence in the schoolroom prevented it before.' This was not entirely true, but not an utter falsehood. 'I have never had admirers, and never thought that if universal it might feel a lack of deeper thought than physical attraction. However, I am sure many marriages in Society are based upon just that.'

'But would they be happy? In the longer term, I wonder. A person's character, their attributes other than beauty or being handsome, are long-lasting. Beauty fades.' Madeleine sighed again. 'At least Lord Cradley did not treat me the way all the local young gentlemen do. I daresay that is because he is used to all the prettiest young ladies in London.'

Mary thought it was because he was far more experienced and had gauged that the beautiful Miss Banham would find it far more fascinating if he did not fall instantly at her feet and pay homage. She gave a non-committal answer, and then enquired as to what Madeleine might wish a young man to find appealing about her. After all, since she had made sure Harry Penwood had been invited to provide her with the chance to study Madeleine Banham's 'technique', she thought she owed it to him to find out a little intelligence that might advance his suit.

'I am not perhaps the right person to answer that question, Mi . . . Mary, for it might make me sound puffed up in my own esteem.'

'Not if it is honestly thought.'

'Well, I love music. I like to sing, even when I go about the house doing little things for my mama, and I play upon my pianoforte every day for at least a half hour, without fail. I was accounted the best singer in my school. That of itself does not mean very much, I know, and having a good voice is not as important as a good temper or . . . being kind, but . . . I used to have a poor temper when I was much younger, but Miss St Germans, my headmistress, taught me to curb it, and not to take a pet when I did not get my own way. I try hard to see the best in people, and I do not shout or stamp or throw things. And do you know, I have a love of arithmetic.' She giggled. 'I cannot expect a gentleman to admire me for that, but it does show that I am not just a doll.'

'You like arithmetic? Really enjoy it?' Mary was competent at it, far more so than her mama, but to her it was time spent in a task that needed to be addressed. She also found Madeleine's eclectic list of things she was good at, and personal qualities, very schoolgirlish.

'Oh yes. There is something so very pleasing in a complicated sum that is worked out correctly. I think it is one of the things I most look forward to about being a married lady, overseeing the accounts of the household.'

Mary could think of nothing to say, being both stunned at the thought of it being a highlight of the married state, and suffering what might just be a pang at the confidence, well placed, which told Madeleine that she definitely would be married. She had no doubts of it. Like her flirting, it was without intent or self-pride. She was beautiful and she would marry; it was quite simple.

Male voices announced that the gentlemen had finished their port and were about to join them. When they did so, the small party divided naturally into youth and maturity, and both mothers covertly observed their progeny, with very different thoughts. Harry Penwood was friendly towards both young ladies, but Lady Damerham was under no illusions; he was like a brother to Mary and always would be, whereas there was nothing fraternal in the quietly offered admiration he showed Madeleine Banham. Lady Roxton, sparing Lady Damerham a pitying thought, watched her daughter far more than Madeleine realised, and was generally approving. She was much more her natural self with Sir Harry this evening, less formal and cautious, but she had not behaved in a manner that might mark her as forward, and could not be said to have thrown out patent lures which might give the gentleman cause to think she favoured him to a particular degree.

The Roxtons departed a little before Sir Harry, having further to go, and when he had thanked Lady Damerham for a very pleasant evening, Mary took him to one side.

'I am glad you had a nice evening too, Harry. Er, do you like music?'

'Music? Well, I did not get to hear much of it in the army beyond fife and drum and the rather unrepeatable songs the soldiers sing. Definitely not material for round the pianoforte.'

'Madeleine Banham loves music. She told me she spends half an hour a day at the keyboard, and she loves to sing, but simply applauding her will not do. She says she thinks gentlemen praise her because of her looks. I suggest you cultivate an interest in music. Could you discuss some famous composers?'

'I have heard of Handel, and that Mozart fellow, but I

would not be able to sing you a tune by either.'

'You used to sing, I remember now, with James.'

'Yes, but those were just folk songs, not the clever stuff.'

'Well, I imagine folk songs are perfectly respectable "about the pianoforte", so brush up a couple and then if you are at a function where she plays, you can ask her if she knows such and such and sing with her. That would please her, I am certain.'

'You are the best of friends, Mary.' He leant, impulsively, and kissed her cheek. 'By the way, I am going to leave my card with Cradley tomorrow. I don't much like the sound of the fellow, from what you told me, but one has to be civil. I will let you have my opinion of him on my way home, if I actually get to see him.'

'Um, you might find I am not at home.' Mary flushed, and he raised an eyebrow. She would not do so if she was going to visit the indigent, or the parson.

'That look leads me to think you are up to something.'

'Not at all. I am . . . I am teaching Sir Rowland Kempsey how to fish for trout.' It came out in a bit of a rush.

'Why?'

'Because he asked me to do so. It seemed churlish not to agree.'

'Is he not the sporting sort, then?' Harry sounded disappointed.

'Oh, I am sure he shoots and hunts, but he said he had little experience with rod and line.'

'Then perhaps I had best call first upon Sir Rowland Kempsey, and make sure he is up to your weight. He might need warning.' Harry grinned.

'Don't be vulgar.' She paused for a moment. 'I do not frighten men off, do I, Harry?'

'You never frightened me, but we virtually grew up together. You might frighten Kempsey if you are a strict teacher.'

'Then best he attend to me well.' Mary looked prim.

Harry agreed, wholeheartedly.

CHAPTER NINE

Mary awoke in the morning, hoping that the day would not be wet and windy, and even slipped out of bed to draw back the curtains before summoning the maid. She saw, with relief, the puffy cloud that was moving lazily across the sky. She took a deep breath. Today she would commence her attempt to catch Sir Rowland Kempsey. She would not, she told herself, be diverted by his friendliness and air of understanding, and she would put into practice the 'arts' she had observed Madeleine Banham use so successfully upon poor Harry Penwood. This was despite the fact that when she had tried them before her looking glass before retiring they had, in her opinion, looked both obvious and frankly ridiculous. Since Harry was in most ways a very sensible fellow, it must be that the male of the species was simply incapable of seeing such ploys in the same light as women. Just for a moment she felt sorry for Sir Rowland, who did not deserve to be caught upon a fly that was no more lifelike than a very short strand of knitting wool on a hook. She liked him, just as she liked Harry. The inner voice that declared her 'liking' for the two gentlemen to be very different was firmly muffled. She did concede that had he been fifty, fat and with snuff stains upon his person, she would not be making the attempt at all.

Of course, she did have to wait until the afternoon before giving her fishing lesson, and patience was not a virtue she had in abundance. She was a clock watcher, and the more she watched, the slower the hands appeared to move. She spent a half hour with her box of fishing flies, wondering which she might sacrifice, for Sir Rowland was bound to lose some, and she could not be absolutely certain there would be suitable flies in the old boxes. She then surveyed her straw hat in a critical manner. She loved it, for it was part and parcel of her fishing world, but it was certainly very battered. The ribands were water stained, and there was even a green mark where some slimy weed had managed to adhere to one of the ends. It was not, Mary decided, something that Madeleine Banham would even touch, let alone place upon her lovely hair. However, Madeleine was not going to have Sir Rowland to herself for an hour or so this afternoon. Besides, being dressed in delicate muslin and lace would be perfectly foolish if one wanted to fish. If she turned up at the door dressed like that, he would be very suspicious. No, she must work this as she would fishing for the wiliest trout, taking her time and with no rushed movements or surprises. She sighed. If only the time would pass more quickly.

When Lady Damerham saw her daughter ready to depart at a little after half past two of the clock, she groaned inwardly. There was no way on earth Sir Rowland Kempsey was going to find Mary irresistible in that hat.

Sir Rowland was not, by nature, a clock watcher at all, which was why his brother grinned and mocked him when he very definitely looked at the face of the clock upon the mantelshelf in the morning room three times in half an hour.

'You know, I think I might need fishing lessons too, Roly. Do you think Miss Lound might teach me as well? I would also be the perfect chaperone.'

'No.' Sir Rowland was blunt, but smiled. 'Miss Lound does not need a chaperon to oversee my casting.'

'I was thinking it was you needed chaperoning.' Tom's grin spread from ear to ear. 'You had better be careful, brother mine. As a new single gentleman in the district, you are bound to be courted by the local spinsters.'

'What an unappealing term "spinster" is, to be sure. "Bachelor" has no such connotations. I doubt, very much indeed, if Miss Lound regards this as any more than keeping in favour with the man who owns the lake she wishes to fish in perpetuity.'

'You sound as though that is a matter of regret,' Tom noted.

'Perhaps. I do not know the young lady well enough to be sure, as yet.'

'But an hour or so by the lake would help matters, yes?'

'An hour or so, without the addition of your presence, very definitely.'

'Do not be cast down. You said yourself she has taken Lord Cradley in aversion, and since she is hardly in her first flush of youth, we may surmise that she has not been courted by the long-term residents.'

'Stripling! "Not in the first flush of youth" indeed! I doubt she is more than three or four and twenty, and if she is unwed, it is more likely that the local gentlemen have not met her requirements. As for Cradley, well, I agree with her. I would not trust the man an inch.'

Sir Rowland had ridden over to Brook House the previous afternoon to leave his card, and without any preconception of the owner other than he was not a man Miss Lound liked. However, when informed that his lordship was at home and would be delighted to receive him, he was able to make his own judgement. Upon being announced, and entering the library where Lord Cradley was lounging in a winged armchair by the fire, and with a glass of wine in his left hand, he halted in some surprise. The loose-limbed Cradley rose and advanced towards him, hand outstretched, unaware that his features were not unknown to Sir Rowland.

'Kempsey, good to meet you. I see we are to be near neighbours, and also possess some form of family connection.'

Sir Rowland responded rather automatically. He had not associated the name and the face in any way, but he ought to have, since Miss Lound had given the family name clearly enough.

'Cradley. Yes, quite near neighbours, but as to a familial relationship, it is but through a marriage which comes later than your branch of the family diverges. I think it tenuous.'

'No matter. We can claim it to be as close as we wish, eh?' Lord Cradley smiled, and Sir Rowland saw the calculation in the eyes.

As far as Sir Rowland was concerned, the link between them was non-existent. When his middle sister had made her come out, primarily under the aegis of his aunt, since his mother had been suffering from a recurrence of her ill health, there had been a 'hiccough' in the smooth transition from maid to matron, and some tears and stern words. Aunt Maria was no fool, and a forceful personality. When Elizabeth, a very pretty girl, had made her curtsey to Society, she had been courted by quite a few young gentlemen of impeccable lineage and character, and a few who were deficient, at least in the latter. It was almost bound to be that at least one of these silver-tongued gentlemen would impress her, and the man now standing before him was 'the one'. Sir Rowland wondered if Cradley had made the association himself or whether he made advances to so many young ladies that their names were forgotten in a Season. It was five years ago, and although Mr Jasper Risley had been pointed out to him, they had not actually met, Aunt Maria being very firm in saying that she could deal with the matter perfectly well without 'some hot-headed brother making a mountain out of a molehill'. What Aunt Maria had said was that the man was not the sort she would ever wish to see allied with her niece, for he had a reputation with women that was not savoury.

Elizabeth had been flattered, made very much the object of his affections for several weeks, and then he had been unwise enough as to hand deliver a note to the house which laid plans for an assignation. Unluckily for him, Aunt Maria had been in the hall herself at that minute and recognised his voice. She had demanded that the missive be opened by Elizabeth in her presence, and shown to her, whilst animadverting upon the foolishness of girls who accepted *billet-doux* from 'unscrupulous devils'. This had resulted in Elizabeth declaring her aunt a monster, and throwing herself upon her brother's chest when he came shortly afterwards to visit, but thankfully a very much more acceptable, and blatantly adoring, suitor had taken Risley's place within a couple of weeks. Sir Rowland had merely remained in Town and squired his sister at a few parties, and played 'guard dog' just in case. Elizabeth, now married to her adoring suitor, and the mother of two small boys, had put the whole thing very much behind her, and in truth, it was not some great scandal. She had been but eighteen and naive, and Miss Lound was far more mature, but Sir Rowland was glad that he would not feel duty-bound to warn her of the man's reputation.

His visit had been of short duration, and his response to the suggestion of friendship polite but cool. Lord Cradley put him down as a stiff-mannered bore, but consoled himself with the knowledge that he would scarcely be a rival for the smiles of the local ladies, Miss Banham in particular.

Miss Lound presented herself at the door of Tapley End at a quarter to three, having briefly diverted past the lake to assess the degree of sun and shadow. She was taken aback to find an unfamiliar face open the door to her.

'Oh. Good afternoon. I am Miss Lound, come to take Sir Rowland for a fishing lesson.'

'Good afternoon, madam. Sir Rowland is expecting you. If you would hand me your . . . equipment and be pleased to follow me.'

She handed him the basket and net, but retained a firm hold on the rod bag. She also resisted the urge to say that whoever he was, she knew her way about the house far better than he did, but obediently followed him to the yellow saloon, where Mr Tom Kempsey rose to greet her.

'Good afternoon, ma'am. My brother is just attiring himself suitably for things piscatorial.'

'As you have seen previously, Mr Kempsey, "drab and battered" is best. I hope he has scoured his wardrobe for things near to being thrown out.'

'Best you do not let his valet hear that, ma'am. He is always complaining that Rowland does not follow the fashions enough and wears things for too long.'

'I declare myself with Sir Rowland then, for I see no point in wasting good garments for the sake of what is in vogue. However, since I have never sought to cut a dash in Society, it is easy to say.'

As she spoke, the door opened behind her and Sir Rowland entered, not in near rags, but a pair of fawn breeches, and a loose, serviceable overcoat with horn buttons. His locks were topped with a low-crowned hat that could not match hers for dilapidation, but had signs of wear upon the nap.

'Good afternoon, Miss Lound. Behold me ready for instruction. I hope you approve?'

'You look perfect, Sir Rowland. The fish will ignore you wonderfully.'

'Anyone with sense would ignore someone dressed like that,' mocked Mr Kempsey.

'And what am I to make of that, Mr Kempsey, since I look worse?' Miss Lound quizzed him, and he blushed.

'You have a certain, er, *je ne sais quoi*, ma'am,' he offered, after a moment's thought.

'There speaks the putative diplomat,' murmured Sir Rowland. 'Now, ma'am, if we collect rod and line from the gunroom, shall we begin?' He held the door open for her, and as she passed she remarked upon the new butler.

'Yes, he arrived but this morning, with good

references, by which I mean he is some distant relative of Mrs Peplow and thus "trustworthy, competent and respectful". I would not be surprised if you are the first person he has admitted into the house. His name, by the way, is Hanford.'

'I shall remember it. I confess, Sir Rowland, to a little trepidation. I have never given instruction before and fear that I may appear positively overbearing. I am not a very patient person, alas, excepting when it comes to rod and line. You cannot rush a fish.'

'I promise not to be put into a quake.' He took a key from his pocket and opened the door to the gunroom, hearing her take a deep breath as she entered. It was not the sort of deep breath that preceded doing something arduous, but one of familiarity and contentment. 'I do not recall exactly which bag it was that I was to take.'

'This one, Sir Rowland.' Miss Lound went unerringly to a bag slung part way along the line of hooks. 'I have some of my own flies, but we will also take a selection from here. I do not think we need to take another landing net and basket today, since I will only be casting to illustrate the method and so we shall not both be fishing.'

'Besides, there is little chance that I shall catch a fish?'

'There is such a thing as beginner's luck, of course, but I would not set your heart upon it. The concept that one comes to water, casts one's line, and brings forth a fish from the depths each time is quite erroneous and does not necessarily imply any failing upon the part of the fisherman. One needs "angler's luck".'

'Then I shall not be downcast if we return without supper.' He smiled.

'Oh no, you really must not.' Her answer was made in all seriousness, and he found it hard not to laugh. For her part, she was focused upon what she must impart, and was suddenly aware that this might necessitate her being rather closer to Sir Rowland than she had imagined. It was oddly disconcerting, and thrust all thought of entrapping him from her mind for the time being. An air of constraint rose between them, and it was a silent couple, several feet decorously apart, who drew close to the lake's edge. There Miss Lound halted and set down her basket.

'We begin, Miss Lound?'

'We begin, Sir Rowland, and far enough from the water's edge that the fishes do not know we are here. Firstly, you must become proficient in putting your rod together. I would suggest that you try it in the gunroom, repeatedly, and eventually you ought to be able to do so without looking at the ferrules at all. It has to become an act more of nature than intent. If you would take your rod from the bag and copy my actions.'

He watched her dexterous fingers, and the way that they truly seemed to move without her thinking. For his part he fumbled a little, dropped the hazel end, and frowned in concentration when trying to attach the whalebone tip. She guided, her hand hovering close to his own, encouraging as one would a child. When he had completed the construction, she smiled and congratulated him.

'Now, take it apart, and do it all again, then I will show you how to attach your line and how the multiplying winch works.'

He obediently repeated the process, and then she showed him with her own rod how to run the line through, how to attach the multiplying winch and to tie on the short leader and then a fly. The fly being rather small, and the knot fiddly, he had, perforce, to be rather close to her when she did this. She then put a fly upon her own line, explaining that the choice of fly was dependent upon the month and which real insects would be available to the fish, and then advised him to watch her as she made a few casts without explanation.

He watched her, seeing a grace in her movements more than the execution of good casting. She sent her fly to within a foot of the same place three times in a row, and then turned to him.

'Now, if I tried it very slowly the line would not have tension, so you must simply understand that the twirl about the head is to give momentum to the line. It is the fly you are attempting to launch over the water, via the line, not throwing a javelin. Strength is unnecessary, merely balance and precision. Watch once more and then you must try it for yourself.'

She began to draw in her line, and as she did so, a fish took the fly. She had cast into shadow without thinking, and gave a little 'oh' of surprise. The fish ran from her, and she let it do so for a few yards, and then, without haste, began to reel it in, permitting it to exhaust itself in a series of ultimately futile runs. Once it leapt clear of the surface, the sheen of the water silvering its scales in the soft sunlight, and she dipped her rod, lest the force of the fish landing back in the water broke her leader. Sir Rowland took up the landing net, and would have scooped the trout up in it, but her hand went out, imperiously, and he gave it to her to perform the task. She laid the net upon the grass, a good-sized trout flapping about in it, then took what Sir Rowland saw was a short length of ash sapling, cut with some root ball to make a small club, and despatched it swiftly, before removing her hook.

'Nicely done, Miss Lound. I mean, even a novice could see the skill in that. Did you know where the fishes would be?'

'Not consciously, but I have fished this lake so many years it is perhaps, like casting, second nature. I had not intended to try for a fish myself. It is not very polite, I think, for a teacher to "show off", but I promise you it was mere chance.'

'Chance aided by knowledge, ma'am. Do not belittle the achievement. You will have to teach me to "read the water", but first I must master the cast. You make it look very easy, and I am sure it is not so.'

'We shall see, Sir Rowland. Let me put this trout in the basket and then we shall continue.' She pulled several dock leaves and laid the fish upon them in the basket, then dipped her hands in the water and rinsed them off. As she straightened, she smiled at him, an open, natural smile of one pleased with a small triumph. He thought it enchanting, and smiled back. There was something in that smile that made her blink, for she had not seen it in a man's gaze before. 'Take up the rod, then, sir, gather sufficient line, and see what you can do.'

He did as he was told, but in truth was thinking far more about his teacher than the instruction. He swirled the rod upright about his head and then flung his forearm back ready to throw the line forward, but it whipped out behind him and caught in the lowest boughs of a lime tree.

'Who put that there?' he complained, though with a laugh in his voice.

'Impressive, if you want to catch trees, Sir Rowland, but not cast for fishes,' remarked Miss Lound, and pursed her lips.

'I am not a very apt pupil, ma'am,' replied Sir Rowland, apologetically, laying down his rod and going to the willow to try and untangle his line from it.

'It is not a matter of aptitude, but of doing as I tell you,' she said with authority, and came to join him. He was all fingers and thumbs, and she shook her head at him. She was lost in the teaching, but he was lost in her closeness, the tress of soft, golden hair that had escaped from under her straw hat and hung in a slight wave before her right ear, the healthy glow of her skin, not tanned, but not the pallid look of those ladies who avoided the outdoors unless veiled, for fear of the sunshine. 'Now, we do it again. Your arm is too stiff, and you flung your arm back. It is not a javelin, Sir Rowland.'

'No? Well, that is something I really must remember.' His lips twitched.

'This is where you are stiff, sir, in the wrist.' Her hand took the offending wrist, and for a moment he held his breath. She seemed totally unaware of the 'intimacy', and then it was she who tensed, and, to his total surprise, gave him a look under her noticeably long lashes which in Madeleine Banham would have looked innocently coy, and which from Mary Lound appeared as though she had clumsily engineered the situation, which he was sure she had not. He frowned, and saw her withdraw, not just her hand, but her whole being.

'I am sorry, Sir Rowland,' she murmured, 'I did not intend to embarrass you.' Her voice pitched a little lower than normal, and he blinked. It was as though an entirely different person had taken over her body.

'You did not do so, ma'am. Please, correct my error.' He sounded calm but was in some confusion.

'When you are about to make the pass about your head you are making too great a movement and using too much of the arm. It ought to be like this.' She stepped away from him, and picked up her own rod, deftly performing the manoeuvre and sending her fly gracefully over the water. He thought it very good, but she knew it was not as good as she would normally achieve. He could have no idea that her heart was pounding, and that doing something so natural to her was as much to calm her nerves as to instruct. 'You see?'

'Yes, I do.' He saw the action but was in the dark as to why she had, for a minute, seemed to be imitating some femme fatale, rather badly.

'Try again, and relax the wrist and your whole body. You are not going to lash the water as if needing to get a team of horses to go at full pelt.' She was back in fishing mode, the prim teacher.

Had he imagined it? Surely not, for it was the last thing he would have expected from her, of all women. He tried again, frowning, but at his thoughts, not the action. It was not smooth, and the line, whilst going forward towards the water, landed with rather more line actually hitting the surface than was necessary, and looked ungainly.

'At least that was in the right direction,' Miss Lound sighed.

'Am I a hopeless case?'

'I hope not, Sir Rowland, for the sake of my own self-esteem.'

'You are not considering mine?'

'Not much, at least, not yet.' She gave him another look from under her lashes and dimpled. He was aware of a deep sense of disappointment. He had seen in her something different, something wonderfully natural and unfettered, but it was an illusion. She was just like other women after all.

'Perhaps it would be better if we abandoned the idea.'

His voice had lost the light-heartedness with which he had begun.

'Oh no, Sir Rowland. Do not tell me you would be so poor spirited. Perseverance is a virtue.'

'Like that of patience, which you claim you do not possess, Miss Lound.' The riposte was a little too swift to be meant as a jest. Her eyes registered surprise, and then resentment.

'I do at least try, and I am not sure that you have been trying, sir. It is not a game like spillikins.' There was no sign of a dimple now, and her lips compressed in a thin line. They were at odds with each other, and both were not entirely sure why or how, other than a dissatisfaction that had risen between them, one with the other. That it made neither happy exacerbated the situation.

'I think, ma'am, that I had best leave you to the fishes, with whom you can presumably find no fault. I believe I will be perfectly able to disassemble my rod back at the house. I wish you a good catch.' He touched his hat and gave her a nod without any emotion upon his face, picked up the rod bag, and stalked away across the park, leaving Mary Lound caught between wishing she could throw something at him and a strong desire to burst into tears with anger, frustration and regret. She had managed, on a couple of occasions, to act in a suitably feminine way and he had not even noticed, as she thought.

* * *

Sir Rowland, a man of generally very even temper, was fuming. What had he been thinking? He had been captivated by an idea that was an illusion. She was not some natural, slightly untamed beauty who would meet him upon even terms, but just another young woman trying to please a man, and since she had failed to please the others in the district and was not in her first or even second season, she was making a desperate bid to win him over. She—He stopped in his tracks.

'I am a damned fool.' He closed his eyes. 'I am right and wrong by the same measure. Until today she has never shown any sign of being coquettish, indeed it seemed impossible that she could, which was why she made such a mull of it. At the same time, it must have occurred to her that I may be her salvation, giving her not only the security of a roof over her head, but the roof she loves with a passion, and she has no experience in setting her cap at a man. What woman who had any experience at all would be so clumsy at it?' She had looked thoroughly uncomfortable, and it was patently alien to her nature. 'But before she thought of it, she did not in any way dislike me, even if she nearly put an arrow through me, and I have now put a stop to just the sort of encounters where she could be most natural, excepting her "acting", and we could be alone. Damnation!'

He resumed his return to the house, frowning, and once he had taken the rod apart, with an assurance that Miss Lound would have applauded, and hung its bag back upon the hook, he went to the library, and sat with his chin resting upon his steepled fingers for some time. It was there that Tom found him some half hour later with a blank sheet of paper before him, and a pen in his hand.

'Oh, I had not expected you back so soon. Were the fishes not biting?' He sounded in a good mood.

'No. Tell me Tom, do you know how to grovel without it being blindingly obvious?'

CHAPTER TEN

Mary could not face returning to the dower house, not in such agitation as she currently felt, and she could most certainly not fish. Instead, she packed away her rod and line and went to an old, old hiding place, a retreat she had used since childhood when she wanted to be alone. The boathouse, unused for years, had split boards silvered with age and knot holes like little owlish eyes, but was a sanctuary. There was no lock upon the door, merely a rusted latch, which she lifted, and stepped within. The soft gloom had a dusty smell that promised it would not reveal secrets to the outside world. There was, alas, the very real threat of spiders, but just at the moment she was too upset to do more than sweep a bough of willow, broken off with forethought, across the simple wooden bench seat that was placed along one side, and then sit upon it, prey to tumultuous feelings. She could not decide whom she blamed the more, herself or him. She was obviously so unattractive that even using 'wiles' would not encourage a man to look upon her as anything other than a sister, but he, he had evidently decided that her company was so unappealing that he could stand it no more. What had she done wrong? Was she too overbearing, too dictatorial, after all? Why could he not see she had never attempted to teach anyone anything before and was nervous? Why had he turned so cold upon her, and taken away the little laughter creases at the corners of his eyes, and the amusement in their depths?

It was hopeless. She would never catch him because she did not possess the right bait. She sniffed, sneezed at some dust, then covered her face with her very slightly fishy hands, and cried, heard only by a nervous mouse and a toad in a damp corner.

This weakness lasted only five minutes or so, and then she gulped and dried her eyes. What was she thinking to give up so easily? You could not guarantee catching a fish upon the first cast. She had got it wrong, somehow. If she could read the ways of the lake and fish, then how hard could it be to read a man? What had Madeleine done? She had made Harry Penwood feel that what he said mattered to her, had let him speak of things about which he felt confident. It could not be said that she had done the same with Sir Rowland. If men liked to feel in control and superior, the last thing they would want would be to be treated like a ten-year-old. She must have reminded him of a first governess before he was old enough for a tutor or school, and a man was scarcely going to become enamoured of someone who reminded him of his governess. However, she could not rectify this impression if he did not want to attempt fishing with her to guide him.

'And if things continue as they have, he will meet Madeleine Banham, and then I might as well become a hermit and live in a cave.'

She did not want to admit her failure to her mother upon her return to the house, but spoke very non-committally about 'difficult conditions', since Lady Damerham would have no idea what conditions were needed for fishing. Having left her lone fish with Cook, she went up to change her dress and do her hair, and looked at her image in the looking glass once again. No, there was nothing that would inspire devotion in face or features, especially under that hat. Add to that a tendency to speak her mind and act independently, topped with sounding like a strict governess, and she was essaying the impossible. For a short while she felt both dejected and rejected and wondered at her own folly in not being like other young ladies at eighteen, going out of their way to appeal to perspective husbands, securing their futures. Then she gave herself a mental shake.

'No, that is not me, was never me. Keeping my independence has made me think for myself, not become some puppet for a man pulling the strings. If I wed now, I would not become a puppet, and I would not deceive a man into thinking that I would. It would be both dishonest and unfair.' It occurred to her that although she had not developed any deep acquaintanceship with Sir Rowland Kempsey, he was the only man, other than Harry and her brother James, whom she had felt could even try and accept her for who she was. 'And I have alienated him in the space of under an hour. Hopeless!'

She rang for a jug of hot water, removed any vestige of fishiness from her hands and made herself presentable, but remained in her room, annoyed with herself, annoyed with him, and with life in general.

It was as she came down before dinner that Atlow presented a salver upon which was a letter delivered from Tapley End. For one moment her heart skipped a beat, but she managed to thank him as if it were a bill from a milliner, of no importance, and then, not wishing to read it, or even admit its existence before her mother, waited for Atlow to turn away and slipped the folded and sealed paper within the bodice of her gown. Throughout the meal she felt as if it was something warm and strangely heavy, for she was so aware of its presence, and it was only when she had wished her parent a fond goodnight and withdrawn to her bedchamber that she removed it, now indeed warm from contact with her skin, and opened it, with very slightly trembling fingers. Surely he was not going to berate her in ink? She sat heavily upon the side of her bed.

Dear Miss Lound,

I must beg your forgiveness for my ill-mannered behaviour this afternoon. I fell into the trap of masculine pride, resenting your very reasonable animadversions upon my lack of skill, and failed to either appreciate or applaud the generosity of spirit you showed in attempting to teach me an art of which you are clearly a mistress, but which you have not previously had to impart to another. Your intent was purely to help me, but I fear that I did not accept your strictures in the spirit in which they were made.

Mary took a deep breath. He was apologising to her, and that was something she did not expect from a man. She was not completely sure that she deserved so unreserved an apology, deep down. She had been angry at herself as well as him.

I do not deserve that you should grant me a second lesson, in view of my churlishness, but could you bear to do so? I cannot promise to be a better pupil in results, but I do promise that I shall be very attentive.

I remain, madam,
Your <u>obedient</u> servant,
Rowland Kempsey

She could not help but smile at the underlining. In the morning, she told herself, she would reply, and must sound not just gracious, but willing to admit her 'governess-like' manner must have been hard to bear. There was no logical reason why she should have put the note under her pillow, but she did, and slept better than she had anticipated.

Actually writing her response proved rather more difficult than she had thought when she sat at the little writing table in the morning room after breakfast, and it took her several attempts to find a form of words which she liked. Little did she know that Sir Rowland had himself cast aside three sheets of paper before setting his name to the fourth. She was frowning when Atlow knocked and then entered, announcing the man whose image was in her mind at that moment. She gave the slightest of starts.

'I am sorry if I have interrupted you, Miss Lound,' Sir Rowland made his bow, and had Mary not been dealing with her own emotions, she would have seen he looked a little tense.

Atlow withdrew, leaving the pair looking at each other. There was an awkward silence, then Sir Rowland opened his mouth to speak, only to find that they both began at the same moment.

'I felt that I ought . . .'

'I was in the process of writing . . .'

There could be times when a clash of speech might

result in slightly embarrassed laughter, but this was not one of them. Both parties coloured and said nothing for some moments. Then Sir Rowland cleared his throat.

'I am not come with reference to . . . yesterday, ma'am. It would be intolerable for me to put any pressure upon you, and—'

'As I tried to say, I was writing to you even as you were announced, and for my part, I too wished to apologise, sir, and to . . . begin again.' She coloured.

'I come with another request to lay before you, Miss Lound.'

'You do?' Mary's surprise was patent, but he took courage from the absence of any indication that her answer was going to be negative.

'Yes. You see, I was going to go about the estate today with Wilmslow, meet the tenants and so forth, but Wilmslow has sent me a note saying that he tripped over the cat yesterday evening, twisted his knee, and cannot walk or ride.' He gave a slight smile. 'It would seem unlikely that he will be able to get about for over a week and . . . you know your tenants and they know you. If introductions are to be made there is none better to make them. May I ask, if you are not otherwise engaged, if you would act as my guide? I am not suggesting that you are equated in my mind with my steward but . . .' His voice trailed off.

'I understand perfectly, Sir Rowland. I have no engagements,' she smiled, 'and it would take but fifteen minutes or so for me to tidy myself, change my dress and send for my horse and Silas, our groom. However, I would wish to let my mama know of the plan, in case she has any errands that she was intending that I fulfil this morning.'

'Of course.'

'If you would be so good as to wait, sir.' Mary rang the bell. 'And if you would care to take a cup of coffee or . . .'

'No, no. I am content to await you, Miss Lound.'

He would have been content to wait alone in the room, but a few minutes later Lady Damerham entered, having been advised of his presence by her daughter. Her ladyship considered his asking Mary to accompany him about the tenant farms as 'a good sign', but hoped her daughter would not appear as too efficient, for that was not, in her view, what gentlemen liked.

By the time that Mary returned, in her riding habit, Sir Rowland looked a little beleaguered, having had to perform feats of mental agility to follow Lady Damerham's train of thought. His face had a slightly dazed look, which Mary had seen so very often. Having grown up with a mother who made not so much connections of adjacent subjects as leapt like a squirrel from tree to tree, she had learnt to follow without, as it were, thinking.

Miss Lound in a riding habit was a sight Sir Rowland found very pleasing. She suited the stark lines and solid, dark colour. Like her, it was practical and without fuss.

'Did you leave your own horse with Silas, or did you walk over, Sir Rowland?'

'I rode over.'

'Then we had as well go to the stable as wait for the horses to be brought round.' It might also give her, thought Mary, the chance to explain . . . everything.

'I truly appreciate your letter. It was very . . . unexpected.'

'It was?'

'Yes. Men do not like to apologise. They see it as a sign of weakness.' She paused. 'I do not like to do so either, but I will. I made a mull of it, the teaching bit. I can think of very little worse than being treated as if you were in short coats by a woman dressed like a scarecrow and . . .'

'"Worse" is behaving like a fool. Miss Lound, may we completely forget yesterday?'

'Yes. I think we ought, though it might be advantageous if you just remembered the bit about moving the wrist.' She looked at him a little shyly.

'I shall endeavour to do so.' He smiled.

Sir Rowland felt his day had suddenly become joyous. She had forgiven him, would, although no day was set, be alone by the lake again with him, and today she would ride with him and show him the estate.

They found Silas tightening the girths on the old cob, which would be his own mount, and with Mary's hack ready and waiting. He would have thrown her up into the saddle, except that Sir Rowland cupped his own hands and did it instead. The trio trotted out of the little courtyard, and Sir Rowland relaxed, posing questions that would lead Miss Lound to inform him not only about the estate and its tenants, but also a little about her. There was nothing of the false siren about her today, only the open, straightforward young woman who had taken him about Tapley End, and it restored his faith in her and in his own assessment of her.

Mary was perfectly at ease. The day was fine, it was nice to ride with a companion with whom she could converse, and in a peculiar way it felt better 'handing over' the tenants to Sir Rowland than having them dragged from her and thrown at the feet of Lord Cradley. She had no doubt that the new landlord would be fair and considerate, and whether she had the running of the estate or not, these would always be 'her' people.

Sir Rowland listened, laughingly said that he ought to have brought pencil and notebook, and watched as the woman who could be rather stiff in a drawing room chatted with tenant farmers about yields of grain and the state of the markets for young stock, and was treated not as some interfering grand lady on a horse, but part of the land as much as every farmer and his wife. He might be the new landlord, but he too saw that these people and acres truly belonged to her. She told him about the woods and the coppicing, who took what and how many generations that family or this had farmed the same fields. She complimented the chubbiness of babes in arms, commiserated over the loss of an aged parent, accepted a jar of preserve from a girl who had just made her first jam on her own and had the little burn mark from boiling sugar on her hand as proof of her industry. Mary thought she was doing nothing; he saw just how much she did. She was, he felt, an admirable woman. He liked her, her looks, her outlook, and his admiration for her was growing upon every encounter. It was not more than that, but it held the chance that it might become more. For the first time in his life, Rowland Kempsey looked at a woman with the kernel of a question within him, a question which wondered what life might be like as a married man. He was not, he told himself, the sort who succumbed to a pretty face. What he thought he sought was . . . what Miss Mary Lound seemed to possess. Yet he was not sure, and what he wanted was time to watch, to listen, to explore her character. It was not perfect, as she herself had admitted. She was not patient, other than in fishing; she was frank to the point of being insulting; she lacked the 'social graces' that many regarded as the marks of a demure young lady. Life with such a woman would see sparks fly, at least from her, but that, he felt, was part of her vibrancy, which made a pretty face beautiful.

They had toured all the southern part of the estate and were walking, on loose reins, along a lane with Miss Lound telling him about how profitable the land had been in the time of her ancestors, who owned acres up onto the wolds above the scarp when wool was the wearable gold of the shire that had brought prosperity, and how down below the scarp there was good grazing for the local cattle, which she described in detail.

'They were common until the cattle plague in my grandfather's youth, but sadly much reduced in numbers now. But one of the bulls that survived was a Tapley End bull and he sired many of the calves whose descendants you see about you on the estate, both pure bred and crossed with longhorns. The purebreds give milk most suited to our local cheese. Have you tried it?'

'I have, ma'am. Mrs Peplow was keen that I do so soon after my arrival. A very pleasing taste.'

'I am glad you—' Mary stopped mid-sentence, and Sir Rowland thought he heard a very soft groan come from her. Trotting towards them were three horses, one ridden by a stony-faced groom, the others by Miss Madeleine Banham and Lord Cradley. If Mary Lound groaned, Sir Rowland took a deep and audible breath. Cradley was smiling, in as much as his mouth had lengthened and his teeth just showed, but his eyes glittered. He might well smile, for he was next to a girl who possessed the sort of beauty that made her shine like a star in the firmament.

Mary cast Sir Rowland a swift sideways glance and saw the look of 'shock' upon his face. Yes, that was the reaction of men to first seeing Madeleine Banham, she was sure. Miss Banham raised a gloved hand and waved, rather childishly.

'Mar—Miss Lound, good morning. Are we not both fortunate to have escorts to accompany us on our rides today?' She made it sound as if they rode every morning without fail. 'Lord Cradley has been so kind as to offer to ride with me, but you know he is a town gentleman for sure, for he has already pointed out to me an "eagle" that was a buzzard, and a "kestrel" that was a skylark!' Her eyes danced, and she gave Lord Cradley a look that Sir Rowland instantly recognised as the distant relative of the one Miss Lound had tried on him by the lake. The youthful beauty did not, however, look like a third-rate opera dancer trying to tout for business among the riotous gentlemen in the pit. She looked vivacious, charming, and so innocent he even wondered if she knew what she was doing. 'You have met Lord Cradley, yes? But do introduce me to your companion, dear Miss Lound.' Madeleine was not sure that calling her 'Mary' in front of these gentlemen was correct, but softened the formality.

'Good morning, Lord Cradley.' Mary managed to convey in the first two words that her morning was infinitely the worse for encountering him. Her tone was clipped, and she was as tense as a rod of steel. She nodded, but only very slightly, and in return he touched his hat with his whip and performed not so much a nod as an equestrian bow, very exaggerated and clearly mocking. Mary ignored him. 'Miss Banham, may I present Sir Rowland Kempsey . . . of Tapley End. Sir Rowland, may I present Miss Banham.'

'Your servant, Miss Banham. It is indeed a fine day to be out riding.'

'Especially when one has charming company,' drawled Lord Cradley, looking not at Miss Banham, but straight at Sir Rowland. There was something in his voice that suggested he was the one with the charming company, whilst Sir Rowland was far less fortunate. Madeleine Banham heard only the compliment to herself and blushed prettily, but Mary knew just what his lordship implied, and her eyes flashed. She was not a woman who concealed her emotions. It made Lord Cradley's eyes glitter the more.

'Indeed, Cradley, we are undoubtedly both very fortunate. Miss Banham can correct your faulty ornithology and Miss Lound has been educating me upon the estate and its occupants.' Sir Rowland sounded unaware of the implication, but he had noted it.

'I can see Miss Lound would make an excellent teacher. Perhaps you will be set an examination afterwards, Kempsey, to test your attentiveness.' Lord Cradley's barb was far sharper than he had imagined. After all the problems that her 'governess-like' manner had caused, this struck deep.

'Should she do so, I would strive to attain good marks, Cradley, for her praise would be worth having.'

There was just the veriest hint of an edge now in Sir Rowland's voice, but Mary was still reeling at being likened to a governess again, for however much it was said to hurt, it had sprung so swiftly to Lord Cradley's lips that it must have been reactive rather than planned. Her day lost the pleasure as if the sun had been hidden behind a large, dark cloud. Here was the reptilian Lord Cradley mocking her, already cozening the inexperienced Madeleine Banham, and worst of all, Sir Rowland had encountered her and been as stunned as every other gentleman. He had gasped, he had stared, yes, stared for several seconds at that beautiful face, and there was a tension between the two gentlemen which clearly indicated a rivalry. Lord Cradley was crowing that he was the one with the good fortune to be out riding with the glorious Miss Banham, whilst Sir Rowland had only 'a governess'. She was disappointed, angry, and felt suddenly as if she was an irrelevance.

'If we are to complete your rounds of the estate, Sir Rowland, we ought not to linger.' What did it matter if she sounded dictatorial now?

'Indeed, ma'am, I think that very true.' Sir Rowland looked at Miss Banham. 'I believe you were out visiting a friend when I called, Miss Banham. Do please convey my compliments to Lady Roxton.'

'I will, Sir Rowland, and it has been very nice to meet you too. I was so wondering what you would be like,' remarked Miss Banham, naïvely, which made Sir Rowland smile.

The two trios parted, and Madeleine Banham's gurgle of laughter at some sally by Lord Cradley did not please either Sir Rowland or Miss Lound. There was silence between them for a minute or so, then Sir Rowland spoke.

'You really do not like Cradley, do you, Miss Lound?'

'No more do you, Sir Rowland.'

'No, I do not. His behaviour is not that of a gentleman. It is most unfortunate that an inexperienced young lady such as Miss Banham should be exposed to a man of his cut when she has no more idea how to go on than a kitten.'

'Whereas I, "the old tabby" can well take care of myself?' There was bitterness in Miss Lound's voice.

'I neither implied nor thought that,' he replied instantly, looking at her. She had withdrawn into herself, and he felt it would be unlikely that she would emerge again upon their circuit of the farms and smallholdings. He wanted the Miss Lound that had set out with him, not this one. He consulted his pocket watch. 'It lacks but ten minutes to noon, Miss Lound. Did you breakfast this morning?'

'I . . . no, I did not, sir.' She had been so caught up in formulating her letter, and then he had arrived and there had been neither time nor thought for food.

'Then may I suggest we return to the dower house. We could arrange to cover the northern part of the estate tomorrow, if it is fine weather. I would not wish you to become faint through lack of sustenance.'

'You mean you cannot face any more "lessons" today, Sir Rowland.'

'I rather think of it as extending the pleasure, since I will have the advantage of anticipation, ma'am.'

'Very clever, sir.'

'Not clever, Miss Lound, just truthful.'

She glanced at him, her face questioning. He found

it strangely touching. She was considerably older than Miss Banham, and more worldly wise for certain, and yet in some ways even more innocent. She had no experience of being courted and complimented by a man, and could not believe such words, addressed to her, were genuine.

'I admit I am a little hungry, Sir Rowland,' she mumbled, and looked down, unable to keep eye contact.

'Then we shall not abandon our task, but reserve the second part for tomorrow. It will also enable me to make notes on what I have learnt today.'

'There is no test,' Mary replied, laying stress upon it.

'Indeed no, but what you have imparted to me is exceedingly useful, Miss Lound, and I ought to set the information down lest I forget important details. If there are any gaps, I will have no compunction tomorrow in requesting you to repeat things, thus showing up my inability to retain all I have heard. However, if we are to return to the dower house it must be you who lead the way, for one lane still looks much like another to me, and I can only get my bearings by the position of sun and scarp.'

'I will not leave you lost, Sir Rowland. This way, then.' She forked to the right where the main part of the lane turned left, and set off along a track, prey to jumbled thoughts, most of which were unhappy.

CHAPTER ELEVEN

Sir Rowland declined the offer to stay to partake of a luncheon, an offer that was made automatically by a Miss Lound deep in her own thoughts, and led his horse to the back of the dower house grounds and out through the wicket gate to lope easily across the parkland to his own stables. He also was prey to thoughts, but they were not as gloomy as those of Miss Lound, though muddled in parts.

The encounter with Cradley and Miss Banham had been in many ways unfortunate, and yet also illuminating. It did not take a genius to grasp that Miss Banham must be the beauty of the district, and fêted by the local gentlemen. Had Miss Lound, wondering how to make herself attractive to a man for perhaps the first time in her life, assumed that gentlemen were only attracted to the Miss Banhams of life? If only she knew, whispered an inner voice, that those aspects of character which so appealed to him were those which she thought might gain a friend but could not inspire the tender emotions.

'And that is what I am as yet so unsure of,' he said out loud, making his horse's ears twitch back to listen. 'Does she, will she, inspire the "tender emotions" in me or am I just enjoying the novelty of a very unusual female? Sometimes she thinks in such a way that I understand her as I might a man, and then she goes off at a tangent which leaves me wondering. Does she think her person unattractive as she does her character? Surely she cannot be that blind?' This question had to be rhetorical, and after a moment Sir Rowland followed a different train of thought.

'Why was she so upset the moment we encountered Cradley and Miss Banham? She and Cradley are openly at odds, and good for her, I say, but she did not make a sound indicative of anger, more of disappointment. Was this because our very enjoyable morning was to be disrupted? It could only be so for a few minutes. Or was it because she did not want me to meet the divine Miss Banham? Now, since I am the "fish" she hopes to hook, you might say, yes, you might, that it was simply that she does not want me to be distracted from her. At the same time, could it mean that she also looks upon me in a less calculating manner as well? What do you think, old fellow?'

Being a horse, the 'old fellow' gave no reply. It was a

not unhopeful Sir Rowland who handed his mount over to the groom and strode back to the house, where he met his brother emerging from the library with an open book in his hand.

'Ah, the studious student. Has the morning gone well, Tom?'

'Fairly well. You sound in good humour for a man I did not expect to see until mid-afternoon at the earliest.'

'I think I am.'

'*Cogito ergo sum*?'

'Er, not Descartes, no. The morning went very well as far as it went, and then it halted, and I decided it best to try again tomorrow. Miss Lound has escorted me about the southern portion of the estate and I know that Nathaniel Shaw's wife is expecting their seventh child, the tenant of Crossways Farm, and alas I have forgotten his name, has a shire stallion that is taken round half the county and brings him enough money so that he has built a new hay barn this year, and if Joshua Pilton ever tells me things are "not going so good" it means disaster must be right around the corner, because he is forever the optimist. It also appears that I am the proud possessor of the best estate in Gloucestershire, even though it is not the largest. In this, I feel Miss Lound was not unbiased.' Sir Rowland grinned.

'Did you get a word in edgewise?'

'Oh, I was more than happy to listen, and her tongue did not run away with her, I promise you. She knows an awful lot about the place, and I had already rather gathered that it has been she, rather than her sire, who saw to the day-to-day overseeing of the estate for some years, in part because he was a martyr to gout and did not get out much, and also because he was not very interested.'

'And she is?'

'Very. What is more, she has the respect of the tenants.'

'So, you will have an even tougher task in taking that place.' Tom pulled a face. 'Unenviable.'

'Perhaps.' Sir Rowland was caught between acknowledging that what his brother said was true, and admiring just how well Miss Lound epitomised the fair and thoughtful landlord.

Lady Damerham, who had been imagining how the morning ride had gone, almost interrogated her daughter over luncheon. She was concerned that Mary might have explicitly told Sir Rowland that she had effectively run the estate during her father's latter years, and begged her not to mention the quarterly accounts or 'anything about business'.

'Though I am now not sure I ought to have said that to you,' she paused while peeling an apple, 'for you know how it is when you know that you must not say something, dearest. It is always the thing uppermost in one's mind. Remember when your papa was most insistent that I should not tell anyone that he had sold my best jewellery and replaced it with paste and—'

'He what?' Mary gaped at her mother.

'Oh dear, of course you do not, because you were too young. See how things get out?'

'Your jewels are paste? The family jewels?'

'Well, I do not go anywhere grand enough to worry and everyone hereabouts has long forgotten, since it was ooh, fifteen years or so ago. Your Aunt Clarissa had just had her first nasty turn, when she found out about Hubert and that . . . female. You would have thought your uncle beyond all that sort of thing and no wonder he suffered with his back thereafter. Served him right in my opinion. But . . . where was I? Oh yes. You have the things your grandpapa left you, the things that belonged purely to your grandmama, and of course they are all still real. One should not,' added Lady Damerham virtuously, but with a tinge of regret, 'put too great a store on worldly goods. There now, it was that which made me reveal the details of my jewellery in the first place. It was all the vicar's fault for preaching about that the Sunday afterwards. I happened to just mention how it made me feel better, to Seraphina Calke, and whoosh, everyone knew as if the birds sang it from the treetops, though of course most songbirds sing from the middle of the trees, except that blackbird that was on top of the holly by my window all last spring and woke me at the most unearthly hours.'

Mary was left reeling by her mother's artless revelations, having as little knowledge of her uncle's indiscretions as she did of the substitution of fake for real in her mama's jewel case. For a while it ousted even her thoughts upon the morning, but then they crowded back upon her, not least because she looked back at her parents' marriage, which had been merely an acceptance of each other for many years, and thought, even upon a short acquaintance, that Sir Rowland did not look the sort of man who would betray his wedding vows, nor bring about near ruin upon his estate and family. Even without any other advantages, marriage to him would have to be infinitely more fulfilling than the one relationship with which she had had most contact. Mama had never talked of her own courtship, but Mary was almost certain that she had gone along with whatever had been suggested to her as a sensible course of action, and Papa, in his youth, had at least been quite good-looking, until good living had got the better of him. That was another thing. Sir Rowland did not have the look of a man who drank to excess. At this point Mary sighed. Dwelling upon his less than bad points was ridiculous if he was going to make a cake of himself like every other man over Madeleine Banham.

She tried to recall what exactly had passed between them all. Sir Rowland had definitely been dazzled by Madeleine's beauty, but then so was every man. She knew he had not taken to Lord Cradley upon introduction, but even in her own anger she had felt his hackles rise when the man had made a pointed comparison between his own good fortune in escorting Miss Banham and Sir Rowland's misfortune in having herself as a riding companion. His calm response was a veneer over his annoyance, and the fact that there was an irrefutable truth in what his opponent had said. What was telling was that he had said she was 'educating' him, which showed just how deep the impression of the governess had gone. His response about trying to 'attain good marks' had been clever, but no more, though there had been a touch of anger in his voice. He had also been as eager as she was to end the conversation, presumably since there was no way in which he might emerge the victor from the encounter.

'So now I have not only introduced him to the local beauty but been the cause of him being bested by a man he has taken in dislike. Is it even worth me bothering to try and impress him?'

From deep within the answer came in the affirmative, not because there was any great hope, but because she was drawn to him, and when he was with her she felt different. It was as though he lit a spark within her, a spark she had never before encountered, and which confused her. How awful it would be, she thought, if she was developing a real *tendre* for him even as he set out to court Madeleine Banham. It was bad enough that it would crush her practical aspiration to reclaim her home. She must keep her personal feelings under control and tomorrow she must show him that not only Madeleine could make sheep's eyes at men. She was not a girl to refuse a challenge.

* * *

The weather was even brighter the following morning, and Sir Rowland made his appearance in a patently good mood.

'I trust we will not meet with any distraction this morning, Miss Lound,' he declared, cheerily.

'Indeed, Sir Rowland. We have a larger area to cover, though a similar number of tenantry.'

Trust her to see the practical side, he thought.

'I was thinking it would be pleasant not to be interrupted. I very much enjoyed our morning together.' He did not think he could say more but wanted to reassure her.

'I am sure that it was most . . . instructive.' She coloured.

'It was, ma'am, but forgive me, you must not think that I look upon you purely in the light of preceptress. That is to demean yourself. Learning is not always a matter of teacher and pupil. If we learn nothing day by day we are ignorant. I have already learnt so very much from you and your generosity in imparting knowledge of Tapley End's history, of fishing, and of this estate.'

'You need not be effusive in your gratitude, Sir Rowland. I would not curtail today's circuit, even were we to encounter Lord Cradley again, though I would feel it a misfortune.'

'Any encounter with him is such, but I am not being "effusive". I am being honest. Do you find it so hard to even believe that someone may thank you and mean it?' He frowned.

She turned her head and looked at him, giving a twisted smile, but made no response. When she spoke next it was to tell him about the first tenant they were to meet, and her manner was friendly but with some reserve. He did not force the issue, since the previous day she had become more natural as they had progressed about the estate. Today it was not quite the same, and several times between the encounters she attempted the lowered lashes look and spoke in a purring manner that jarred. Yet he did not recoil from it as before, for he had not only seen what she was attempting to emulate, but understood her reasoning. So he smiled, not because he was taken in, but because her very awkwardness and ineptitude spoke well of her nature. Other than during these unnatural moments, she relaxed, and there was between them a pleasant camaraderie, which Mary attributed to him thinking of her in the same way as did Harry Penwood. Several times she took him on shortcuts across fields of burnt stubble that awaited the plough, and they cantered side by side, with Silas on the cob to their rear. She was, he thought, a very natural horsewoman, with good hands and an affinity with her mount. If the previous day he had mostly encouraged her to talk and then listened, today he prompted with far more questions, not all about the estate and tenants.

He asked her about the local hunt, and then mentally cursed himself, for he recalled that she had said she had hunted before her hunters were sold off.

Her response was honest, but held a touch of regret,

and it was obvious that she missed the activity.

'I ride as often as I can, but hacking about the locality on one's own gives the pleasure of the outdoors but not the excitement of galloping over the fields and jumping ditch and gate. I do not take Silas with me usually, for this is my . . . was my land and everyone knows me. It would be foolish to take fences, not only because if one were to take a tumble none would know where one lay, but because old Hector here is not up to it.' She patted the horse's neck. 'However, at least I still have him, which is a great blessing, and he is a dear old friend. It was heartbreaking to lose Orion and Molly, but I could not have borne it to lose Hector here, whom I have had since I was fifteen.'

He wondered, for a moment, what she had been like at fifteen, on the cusp of womanhood. He imagined her as a youthful Diana, trammelled by her skirts and the increasingly important aspect of deportment and being 'ladylike'.

'You make it sound aeons ago, Miss Lound.' He smiled.

'It sometimes feels it, Sir Rowland, though it is but a decade. We have a tendency to look back upon the past in some rosy glow. It was not an idyll, of course it was not, for there were pressures and problems that looked large to an adolescent and now seem minor, but it felt impossible that life would change as it has, that there would be so much loss.'

'I fear I have done it again, ma'am, dragged up

memories you would prefer to keep locked away.'

'You cannot refrain from broaching topics with me, sir, in case they might lead to sad memories. My brother James said . . . said when he went to Portugal . . . that life was to be lived, not tallied in years. It was what you put into it and got from it that counted.' She paused for a moment, gave Sir Rowland a tremulous smile, and then said, 'It was a very philosophical thing to say, and James was not a philosophical person. I have often wondered since . . . but . . .' She shook her head. 'One has to face what is, and do the best one can. I doubt not that Sir Robert and the Lady Elizabeth must have had times of great misery when in exile, perhaps struggling to make ends meet in a foreign land, and unsure as to whether they would ever see England, let alone the family estate, ever again. If I feel weak and low, I consider them.'

'You seem to have an affinity with them, considering they lived a century and a half ago.'

'I suppose it is because my grandfather spoke of them so warmly. He never knew them, of course, but his own father was very proud of what his parents had achieved, more so than his own elevation, and I used to go and look up at Sir Robert.'

'Look up "at" him?' Sir Rowland looked puzzled.

'His portrait hangs beside the fireplace in The Long Gal—' She halted, suddenly, aware of her mistake.

'Did he look like a Delft jug and an arrangement of fruit? How extraordinary, ma'am.'

Sir Rowland raised an eyebrow, but admirably controlled his desire to smile.

'No, he did not.'

'So, Miss Lound, is there any limit to your criminal activity? So far, you have essayed trespassing, poaching, attempted wounding and now, you admit, housebreaking.' Getting no response, he went further. 'I only ask that I may be assured you do not plan to murder me in my bed,' he added, evenly. 'My valet, estimable in every way, is upset by the sight of blood. Even a small nick when shaving makes him go pale. I think the sight of blood-soaked sheets and a dagger through my heart might give him severe palpitations.'

'Do not speak such foolishness. You only wish to mock me, sir.' Miss Lound looked away and made a dismissive gesture with her hand.

'You mistake me entirely. I thought that you would understand that I was in jest. Come, do not take umbrage, I beg of you. Perhaps you would show me his portrait, for you are clearly very proud of him.' The slightly cajoling tone won her over, and she assented, albeit in a mumble. They returned to matters concerning the estate for some time, and it was only when they trotted into the little courtyard by the dower stables that Miss Lound suggested that if Sir Rowland wished to see Sir Robert, and indeed the Lady Elizabeth, then he might do so before returning to his brother.

Sir Rowland declared himself eager to do so, and so, having thanked Silas, and made a fuss of Hector, she led him into the house and to the book room. The two portraits were a little large for the chamber, but Mary liked the fact that it was a place where she could be undisturbed and 'with' them, even if there was no supernatural assistance with adding the columns of figures in the accounting books.

'Here is Sir Robert. I almost feel I should make a formal introduction.' Miss Lound smiled and looked at the portrait with affection.

'He has a look of resolution to him, but a twinkle of humour also,' remarked Sir Rowland.

'Well, it was painted after he came home and made good the damage to the house and estate. I have often wondered how, and indeed why, he had a society painter immortalise them both in oils, but perhaps it was with the last of the Lady Elizabeth's money and it felt like a statement saying, "here we are, back where we belong, and Cromwell and the Risleys could not cast us down".'

'They are by Lely, yes?'

'They are. I know that Sir Robert is bewigged and clean-shaven, but I have often wondered if the wig echoed his real hair colour, and whether he had something of the look of Valentyne Lound in that missing portrait. In his letter to his son, he said – Sir Robert, that is – that there was a resemblance. I think that was what influenced my girlish drawings of Valentyne.'

'I am heartily glad that the fashion for wigs, of natural colouring or powdered, are consigned to the past. Hair grows naturally upon the head, and it seems ridiculous to me to have to cut most of it off only to put someone else's hair on top.'

'Oh yes, indeed. We have a portrait – yes, also "stolen" – of Grandmama in her panniers and heavy silks and tall powdered wig, and it all looks very constricting. It must have been hateful.' Miss Lound shuddered. 'That is the portrait in the drawing room. Here is the Lady Elizabeth. I think it was painted when she was in her thirties, but she is a very good-looking woman, and when you consider she had borne four children, and everything else that happened, she looks remarkably composed.'

The painting showed a lady with a glint in her eye and a proud head carriage, though the face was heart-shaped and the lips soft and with a hint of smile. It was the look of a woman who knew how men looked at her, and was perfectly content that they did so, but was cynical withal. Her hair was a mahogany brown and her skin creamy. Her shoulders were bare, but her voluptuous bosom was, if obvious, decorously covered with silk.

'We are fortunate that she is one of Lely's more clothed ladies,' said Miss Lound, matter-of-factly. 'Perhaps it was painted in winter.'

Sir Rowland let out a crack of laughter.

'Very pragmatic, ma'am.'

'Well, one has to be so.'

'She was very beautiful.'

'Yes, she was. I have always thought it was a good

thing that Sir Robert was not a courtier, because Charles II had a terribly roving eye, and one cannot but surmise that Sir Robert would have been put in a very difficult situation,' mused Miss Lound, without any embarrassment. Having had a sire who 'strayed' quite openly and frequently, she was not prudish about such things.

Sir Rowland was a little surprised, but not shocked.

'Er, yes, that is also a very pragmatic view.'

'Mmm. The problem with being pragmatic, is, however, that looking at it pragmatically, it is of little advantage to a woman.' She realised the sentence was convoluted, and added, 'If you see what I mean.'

'It is not, I own, likely to be the first term applied to a lady, but then comment is generally made first upon looks, not character, so you cannot have found it a disadvantage.'

Miss Lound coloured, unexpectedly, and murmured gruffly, 'I was not seeking compliments, Sir Rowland.' Then, realising that she was letting go an opportunity to cast a lure in his direction, she attempted to turn her embarrassment into a look that was both encouraging of more compliments yet maidenly modest, and lowered her lashes and dimpled. She had spent an hour of practice in front of her mirror the previous evening, but she was still not convinced it worked. To her own mind it was far too much like 'simpering', which she despised. It felt all wrong.

'No, you were not, but it is true, nonetheless. The

Lady Elizabeth handed down more than the ring that you wear.' Sir Rowland was not giving a compliment but voicing his true belief.

Miss Lound, forgetting all artifice, looked him full in the face, a small frown gathering between her brows.

'You noticed it?'

'The ring, and the familial similarity both.'

She found the realisation that he had studied her hands enough to be aware of the knot ring on her right middle finger made her pulse quicken more than the compliment about the resemblance.

'I always thought I had more of Sir Robert about me,' she said, with a touch of defiance.

'No, no, Miss Lound. I will admit to a straightness of the nose, but no more . . . in looks. You have the determination that was obviously present in both of them. You were right to remove them from the house. They would not have liked it in a Risley's hands, and I have to admit I am not only delighted to have inherited the estate, even from an unknown and not very pleasant family connection, but delighted also because my doing so has kept Jasper Risley's hands off it.'

'I do not think I could have borne it,' murmured Mary.

'No more than your ancestors, no. I have never, I have to say, seen myself in the light of gallant rescuer, and coming into the property was pure chance, but if you would like me to try on one of those old suits of armour I could at least assume the look of having saved you, noble damsel, from the dragon that is Lord Cradley. I hope you decline the offer, by the by, because I think being encased in all that metal would be rather claustrophobic.'

She laughed and shook her head.

'Since I always thought "damsels in distress" showed a marked lack of determination, I do decline your offer, Sir Rowland.'

'That is not to say I hope you will refuse every offer I ever make you.' The words tumbled out before he had time to prevent them, and as her eyes widened, he made a desperate attempt to pretend he was still in jest. 'After all, it would be very lowering if you never came to dinner again.'

'Yes, yes indeed, since it saves us the expense of dinner,' she responded, swiftly. Both laughed, though the laughs were a trifle forced, and when their eyes met again, Mary Lound looked down, and flushed in genuine embarrassment, aware of some frisson between them.

'I think the sun will be too bright this afternoon to actually catch any fish, Sir Rowland,' she said, changing the subject.

'Not that I am likely to actually get a fish on my hook,' added Sir Rowland. 'Would you prefer to wait until tomorrow afternoon?'

'I think so. I will be honest, sir. I think that too much of my domineering company in one day might give you such a dislike of me that those dinner offers would never be made again.'

'It is not domineering, Miss Lound. However, I would like to make my own notes upon the rest of the estate, and I feel that my brother might like a little of my company in these last few weeks before he goes back to Oxford. Tomorrow afternoon, at three, weather permitting, then?'

'Yes, at three.'

'Thank you.' He bowed over her hand and left her. She looked up at her ancestors.

'Well, what do you think?'

She received no reply, which was a good thing.

CHAPTER TWELVE

Sir Harry Penwood was in a thoughtful mood, and his cogitations were not entirely happy. He had encountered Lord Cradley when he 'happened to be passing' Hazelwood, the Roxtons' residence, and the gentleman had all the polish and address Harry knew he did not possess. The man clearly admired Miss Banham but had no problems in charming her with his conversation. His was one tongue that evidently never tied itself into knots.

It could not be said that Lady Roxton looked delighted at his presence; if anything, she looked watchful and guarded. However, Lord Cradley did not stay over long, nor say anything that might be construed as forward.

Miss Banham had been in a bright and happy mood,

which was wonderful as long as one did not think about whether it was Lord Cradley who had put her there. She did begin to tell the latest visitor what he had said and thought, until her mama had, quietly but firmly, suggested that Sir Harry did not want second-hand views.

'Oh dear, I have let my tongue run away with me, Sir Harry. Do forgive me.' The pleading look would have had ninety-nine per cent of men forgive her anything, and Harry Penwood was not in the tiny minority. Mindful of what Mary had told him, he did not try to compete upon silver-tongued compliments and worldly knowledge.

'Miss Banham, I would far rather hear your own opinions upon matters than Lord Cradley's.'

'You would?' Miss Banham even seemed to be able to frown without marring her loveliness. 'But I do not know anything. I cannot tell you who is the prime minister of Am—oh, they do not have one, do they!' She put her fingers to her lips.

'I am not talking of facts such as one might look up in an encyclopaedia, Miss Banham, and what you have told me of Lord Cradley's opinions are just that, opinions. I would rather hear if you have read that book which was all the rage this spring, *Pride and Prejudice*. One of my friends in the regiment had it sent in a parcel from his mother, with strict instructions to read it. He began it without enthusiasm but was soon absorbed by it. Several of us borrowed it from him, and though one fellow yawned over it and its lack of "action", I for one found it most diverting.'

'Soldiers read books?' Miss Banham clearly thought this a revelation.

'Indeed, ma'am.' He laughed, for she made it sound as likely as a dog playing the pianoforte. 'What a poor view you must have of soldiers.'

'Oh no, it is just . . . but how do you find time, between fighting battles and doing manoeuvres and such things?'

'The truth of the matter is that soldiers spend more time fighting discomforts, disease and boredom of mind, ma'am. One has always to be prepared for battle, but we encounter mud, rain, sunburn, poor food and fevers far more often.'

'Then why do it? I mean, you could have stayed in Gloucestershire.' It was a genuine question.

'I think young men fancy the concept of being a soldier because it appeals to the idea that they will be able to prove themselves, and that it will be an adventure. I suppose we dream of being heroic. The reality is . . . different. I do not think I have been heroic, but I have proved myself, to myself, if you can see what I mean. I have endured the discomforts, faced fear and overcome it, and, strange as it may seem, been part of a camaraderie one could not find as close as among men who have to fight alongside each other, for each other, and face injury or death. It was Shakespeare, was it not, who wrote about a "band of brothers"? Well, I have been of such a band, and . . .' He had trailed off, for Miss Banham's eyes were misted, and Lady Roxton was looking at him in a way he could not quite define. He coloured. 'My apologies, ladies. Not the sort of thing a gentlemen should discuss before the gentle sex. Lord Cradley has all the advantages, for he can discuss manners and fashions and I have spent the last six years in the army, which makes me unfit for delicate company.'

'You mistake, Sir Harry,' said Miss Banham, softly. 'Just because we do not know of such things does not mean we should not know of them. Oh, not the bloodthirsty things, but what it really means to be a soldier. It is humbling, and it is, yes, it is heroic. Men and women are different, but we can appreciate that a man needs to feel tested, as a man. At least,' she paused, thoughtfully, 'some men do.' It occurred to her that her older brother would not seek to test himself under privation and danger, and nor would Lord Cradley.

Lady Roxton, who had listened to his explanation from a mother's standpoint, and discovered a new respect for the composure of Lady Penwood, nodded.

'*C'est vrai*. It has always been so, that the man has need to show his *courage*, his . . . what is the word? Ah yes, his mettle. When men were savages, did they not go out to hunt the bear and the wolf, or fight other men? A woman, she does not seek such things, though she would fight to the death to protect her children.'

There had followed a silence, which was a combination of embarrassment on his part, and an awareness by the ladies that changing the topic to something inconsequential felt vaguely indecent. In the end, he had made further apologies and excused himself, curtailing his visit and feeling a fool. Cradley had brought out smiles and laughter and he had brought out frowns and introspection. Deep down it felt wrong that the man who had the silvered tongue and smooth looks should prevail over the one who had done the equivalent of 'hunt the bear', but Harry realised that was just a primaeval response. He had not advanced his cause with Miss Banham, and the more he thought about the softness in her voice and the film of tears in her eyes when she had heard him, the more he liked her.

It was therefore a rather despondent Harry Penwood who presented himself at the dower house, where his reception was always warm and friendly.

Mary, who was cobbling together, rather than darning, a moth hole in a favoured winter shawl, looked up with just the friendly smile Harry Penwood needed when he was announced, and Lady Damerham immediately ordered coffee and began to tell him how the weather was changing, even though it was he who had been outdoors and she had not gone further than looking out the window since church on Sunday. It took some minutes before she stopped speaking, by which time she was talking about her aunt's pug dog, which she remembered from when she was a child. Mary's eyes held his and exchanged silent laughter. It was one of those things they could do, understand the other without words, even though they had been apart for much of the last few years. As coffee and Mrs Holt's almond biscuits were handed round, he told them of his encounter at the Roxtons'.

'I am not saying he haunts the place, for I have no evidence of it, but I dislike him being too much in Miss Banham's company. He is all smooth words and not a hair out of place and . . .' Harry sighed, 'I suppose I am jealous because he is all the things I am not, and just what would attract a young lady.'

'Well, you are right and you are wrong at one and the same time, my friend,' declared Mary, firmly. 'He is certainly everything you are not because he strikes me as a crafty, coiled snake of a man, not at all honest in character, eager to wheedle and also to use clever barbed words to hurt, and that is the opposite of you. Sir Rowland and I met him the other day,' she did not make poor Harry feel worse by telling him that Lord Cradley was with Madeleine Banham, 'and he raised the hackles upon us both, for he intimated insults which could be denied if he was pressed, and he enjoyed every minute of it. Now, he repels me, but I agree that at first glance, an impressionable and innocent young lady might be impressed and overawed by his glamour, but Miss Banham is not merely a pretty face, and I have no doubt that as she sees him more, she will like him less.'

'Are you sure, Mary?' Harry sought reassurance.

'Utterly.'

'I have not myself met the gentleman,' said Lady Damerham, with an odd mixture of relief and regret, which was explained by her next words. 'You would have thought he would have had the courtesy by now to leave his card. Now, I am sure you will say he has not called upon you either, but in view of your mama being so recently into deep mourning that might be reasonable, but everyone knows it is over a year now and . . . do you think Lord Cradley, the previous one, left him a missive about the bad feeling between the two families?'

'Well, one must doubt it, Mama, since he was not on good terms with the current Lord Cradley either. One does wonder where that particular animosity came from, of course.' Mary frowned a little.

'Then why has he been so remiss? Not that I want to meet him after what has been said, but it is a matter of principle.'

'So, you want a man to come to see you, even though you do not want to see him.' Mary laughed.

'Yes. No. Yes. Oh, do not laugh at me, dearest, really.' Lady Damerham looked flustered.

'I am sorry, Mama, but it does sound droll, even though I do understand what you mean. Suffice to say that having encountered him now upon three occasions, I can safely say that if I never met him again I would be delighted.'

'I do not know whether to be pleased that my opinion of him is shared or concerned even more for Miss Banham,' sighed Harry.

'She has a mama who is no fool, and a papa who cherishes her also. I do not think that you need man barricades at their gates, at least not yet.' Mary smiled at him, but in a reassuring way.

'By the by, Sir Rowland has not left his card but did send my mama a very courteous letter, expressing himself as a gentleman ought with condolences that were neither cursory nor over effusive, since he never met my father. He also added that as soon as she felt she could attend small private dinners with friends, that he hoped we would both dine at Tapley End, and in the meantime he looked forward to meeting me when it was convenient. Very civil I thought it.' Harry looked at the clock. 'I had better get back to Mama for luncheon, since she thought I was only going to Hazelwood. I might go and see Kempsey this afternoon.'

'Well, you will have to have a very swift luncheon, for I am giving him another fishing lesson at three of the clock,' announced Mary, with a look that dared him to say anything. This of course meant that he just had to respond.

'Then I might make it tomorrow and give him time to recover.' He grinned, but then his expression changed, for Mary did not smile back. She frowned.

'Am I such a gorgon, Harry?'

'Oh, of course you are not. Come, it is not like you not to see when I am funning.' He gave her a quizzical look. 'Something has put you on end.'

'No, no, it is just . . . no, nothing. You are right, and I

was not thinking, or rather I was overthinking, I think.' She laughed, having made it a joke when she did not feel it as one. 'I promise he will not be some nervous wreck when you meet. As I said before, I think you and he will get on rather well.'

'I hope so. There are not so many of us younger fellows about the district, and having discounted Cradley . . . I really must take my leave of you both. Your servant, Lady Damerham, and yours too, Mary, despite all.'

He had risen, and now bowed to the two ladies, departing in a slightly better frame of mind than he had arrived.

Mary picked absent-mindedly at the food on her plate at luncheon, but Lady Damerham wisely refrained from asking if she felt quite well, since she could see that it was not so much a lack of appetite as mental distraction. She could not see how teaching someone how to throw a length of line into a lake and wait to see if a fish bit it was difficult, but perhaps it was more complicated than it looked. She would have been astounded to have found that her daughter was thinking about trying to land not a two-pound trout but a six-foot baronet, for she had decided that Mary was too pragmatic to waste her time attempting the impossible.

The truth of the matter was that the 'pragmatic' side of Mary had very nearly given up, and persisted only because a previously unknown part of her insisted. She had already given herself a shake for lying in bed that morning daydreaming about the man, which was a novel experience, for she had never been at all fanciful, and had certainly never sighed over a gentleman, except sighs of resignation at their stupidity. What was more, he had crowded into her thoughts as she fell asleep, the slightly amused expression in his eyes and his unhurried baritone voice lurking in her semi-consciousness. He was a restful sort of man, not a 'pond skater' forever flitting about, the sort who would make a good angler if he mastered the practicalities. That was where the daydream had taken over when she woke, for she had created in her head an image of a summer dusk and the pair of them by the lake, very content both with the fishes in their basket and with each other. They had dismantled their rods and were standing close together as the sun dipped below the western horizon, and those fish wily enough not to take their flies were rising to flaunt their survival on the mirror-smooth surface of the water. She would slip her arm through his and lean against him, her cheek against his shoulder, and they would walk very slowly towards the house, and by the copper beech tree he would halt, put down the basket and rods, and turn and . . . This is where the pragmatic Mary Lound had interrupted very forcefully. Was she seriously dreaming of being kissed? She had, naturally, only ever been kissed upon the cheek, and by relatives or, on a couple of occasions, by Harry Penwood, who was a brother in all but blood and name. She had never thought of anything more intimate, but here she was, wondering what it would be like, wanting to know what it would be like, if Rowland Kempsey kissed her. It was immodest, unladylike, and sent little thrills through her. She had been shocked at her own feelings, and therefore spent the morning very, very definitely not thinking about the afternoon, and the fishing lesson. Luncheon, however, meant that there remained only two hours before their appointment, and keeping it and him from her mind was no longer a possibility.

She went up to change still with a frown of preoccupation between her brows, and aware of excitement in the pit of her stomach, and set off rather early for the assignation, telling herself that she would linger by the lake a little on the way, both to assess the water and calm herself. It would not do to look too eager. Despite this, when she was shown into the hall at Tapley End the clock upon the mantelpiece assured her it still lacked five minutes to three, which must mean that she was in fact at least ten minutes early. She turned as footsteps sounded, and Sir Rowland entered from the west wing, his rod bag in his hand and dressed for the occasion.

'Good afternoon, Miss Lound. You see me ready for lake, lady and line. You would laugh if you saw my valet's face whilst watching me dress "down" for an appointment rather than "up". His soul is deeply offended.'

'Yes, I suppose it does go against instinct, but I have been doing that for so many years I have ceased to think about it. I have to admit I have reached the stage with several hats in the past that have become too disreputable and battered even for fishing.' She smiled at him, and if the dimple became rather forced, the smile had definitely begun as natural, and her eyes did not lie. A frisson ran through Sir Rowland. She was pleased to see him, possibly nearly as pleased as he was to see her.

They walked out to the lake together, not as close as in Mary's daydream, but perhaps closer than absolutely necessary, each trying to pretend they were not as aware of the other as they felt.

'You know, Miss Lound, I have been thinking how very fortunate I am to have you as a guide in so many aspects of Tapley End, for I feel remarkably at home here even after little over four weeks in residence. I have made copious notes so that I will remember my tenants and their holdings, and shall have them at my bedside – the notes not the tenants – so that I may commit them to memory quickly. I was told once that thinking about something just before one falls asleep lodges it more permanently in the memory, and it does seem to work.'

Mary thought of how her head had been full of Sir Rowland before she fell asleep, and how prominent he was in her mind upon waking, and did not challenge him, and her cheeks became very slightly pink.

'Have you also tried to remember my strictures upon your casting technique, Sir Rowland?'

'Er, I think so, but it would be foolhardy of me to say

yes, if I immediately prove that I have not. I shall remain slightly non-committal, if I may.'

'You may remain as you wish, sir, since we will see so very soon.'

'Is that meant to turn me to a jelly?'

'No, merely to focus your mind.'

'I promise you, Miss Lound, I am thinking of nothing other than here and now.'

She halted some dozen feet from the edge of the water and set down the fishing basket, laying her rod bag on top, then looked at him.

'Your first test, Sir Rowland. Can you put your rod together without hesitation?'

'Ah, that I can, Miss Lound, because I did as you suggested, and tried it several times in the gunroom. Observe my dexterity.' With which he removed his rod from the bag and proceeded to not only put it together but thread the tapering line through the rings and then attach the winch. At the completion of this exercise, he made her a small bow as at the end of a theatrical performance, and she laughed and gave a small clap of her hands.

'I am impressed, Sir Rowland, very impressed.'

'Put it down to the quality of the teacher, Miss Lound.'

'I shall not do so, sir, for it is the pupil who has put in the effort. Now we have to see how you manage actually making a cast. Remember not to free too much line to begin with.'

She watched him as he raised his rod and gave the

little twirl about the head and then looked back towards the trees as he flicked it forwards to land a few feet into the water with an audible 'plop'.

'How was that?'

'A distinct improvement, but you ought to be looking where you want your fly to land, not where you do not wish it to do so. The wrist was more supple, and you did not make too great a circle. Next time look at the lake, not behind you.'

He made another attempt, studiously staring to his front, but was concentrating so much upon that aspect that he let go of the line as he made the circle above his head and the hook was thrown outward by the action and caught in Miss Lound's straw hat.

'Sir Rowland! Be careful!'

'I am most frightfully sorry, ma'am. The hook has not gone through, has it?'

'No, but . . . I will remove the hat so that the hook can be extracted.' She untied the faded ribands and lifted her hat from her head and set it upon the ground, then knelt down beside it. Sir Rowland, much chastened, did likewise.

'Let me hold the hat so that you have both hands free,' he said, suiting action to words. Their heads were no more than two feet apart, and he could smell the scent of roses upon her. Her fingers trembled, very slightly. 'Have you ever jabbed a hook into your finger?' he asked.

'Twice, though I assure you it was not something I sought to repeat. It was exceedingly painful, and it is imperative that one does not attempt to pull the hook from the flesh, because of the barb. The only answer is to push it until it erupts through the skin at the adjacent point, and then cut off the barb and withdraw the metal.'

'I am surprised that you did not fall into a faint.'

'Would a gentleman have done so?'

'No, but . . .' He watched as she disengaged the hook and held it before him, looking him in the eye.

'We are not such weak vessels in physical form or in mental stamina that we must swoon at the slightest hurt, Sir Rowland. I do not say that should I receive such an injury as Sir Harry Penwood has seen upon the field of battle that I would be as sanguine, but for such an injury as this, the body must be commanded not to give in to an excess of sensibility. Besides, it is my sex which goes through the physical ordeal of bringing forth children, and I have yet to hear of a woman who spent her entire time of travail being brought round from continual swooning. We are a little stronger than you might think, than some men may even wish to imagine us.'

'I had never considered that, and will grant your example, of course, but why do you say than some men "may wish"?'

'Because it is not uncommon for gentlemen to wish to treat a woman as some precious, delicate object, and also one inferior in capacity of mind as in courage. There are some females who are weak of will, but then so are there gentlemen. I would hate to be treated like a piece of porcelain.' She spoke with some vehemence.

'I do not think you need fear such an eventuality, for I doubt very much that any man who wanted a "porcelain wife" would see your qualities, Miss Lound.' It was more than he had intended to say, but in that moment less than he felt. She was still looking at him and frowned, not so much in disapproval as confusion, as though the concept that she possessed 'qualities' of any sort that might please a man was alien to her. For a few moments she neither spoke nor moved, and then she stood up, and he scrambled to his feet, brushing off his knees. She went to her rod bag and opened it, and put her own rod together in silence.

'Have I given some offence?' he asked, quietly, and received no answer other than a small shake of the head. Only when rod and line were ready did she say anything.

'I think, Sir Rowland, that if you keep control of your line, we might now proceed to trying to aim the cast to a particular area, since the angler must "read" the surface of the water, the shadows and the weed, and decide where best to hunt for the lurking fishes.' It was as if the interchange had not taken place at all.

'What indications should one consider?'

'Well, fishes do not like to feel exposed to predators, so somewhere in a little shadow and where there is some cover under the surface is good. One must also watch for any telltale bubble or ripple where a fish surfaces. What you must not do is cast your own shadow over the water, since the fishes will comprehend that as a threat. It would be different in a river with proper currents and rocks and fallen boughs to give slack water and places to hide, but when the lake was created the bottom was not made totally flat, but with some humps in the middle that mean the flow, however slow, moves around them a little. Come the evening rise, the fish are often on one side or other but now they will most likely be nearer the banks, and this one is more shady. So you want to look about six to eight feet out and cast that distance or a little more. When the trout are not rising you must let your fly sink gently into the water, not try to tease the fishes by letting it land on the surface, for they will not come up. Let it sink a little over where they are lying. Fly fishing is in many ways the art of deception. When they rise, it is then we let the fly land just upon the surface.' She had been looking over the water but at this point turned to him, and smiled, and he watched what was very natural morph into something playfully flirtatious, yet without conviction. He did not want to betray his interest in her, so he simply could not tell her that she had no need of artifice, or indeed deception, with him. 'Shall we see if any fishes rise for us?'

The inclusive 'us' gave him a warm feeling, and he could have happily stood next to her and surveyed the surface without it breaking into the smallest ripple until the dinner hour without feeling bored. A fish was so disobliging as to make a very obvious appearance within three or four minutes, however, and it was impossible to deny having seen it.

He made a cast, but it fell short, and he took a step nearer the water's edge.

'No, no. If you do that you will soon be in view from under the water.' Miss Lound laid a restraining hand upon his arm.

'Yes, I am sorry. It was instinctive.'

'Curb the instinct and think.'

It was sound advice, and not just about the fish. His instinct when in her company was that marriage was no longer a vague prospect upon the horizon, but something he actively wanted, and soon, but it would be all too easy to take an irreversible step based upon a feeling, a frisson, an urge. He had not known her long enough to be sure, he told himself, either of the permanence of his feelings or whether she looked upon him as more than the route to security. He felt it, but again, it was simply a feeling.

'You are, of course, right, Miss Lound. I should let out more line instead.'

He cast again, a better length, but the fly was still not landing lightly.

'Do not worry about that as much, sir, for it comes with practice, a feeling as you cast. Once you achieve the fly "kissing" the surface, then you will learn to make it do so nearly every cast. I promise you, even experienced anglers sometimes have a fly that "crashes".'

'Do you ever fish for other than trout?'

'I sometimes used to go with James and Harry Penwood, and fish the river, for trout in season and the graylings a little later, for they too take artificial fly readily enough, but I have never enjoyed using live bait, both because it is messy and a little gruesome, and because standing with a rod, holding it and waiting for a passing fish has less of the hunt to it, for me. James caught a salmon in the river once, a very grand fish that was, and he was fêted for it for a whole week. My, what a fight he had with it, and several times I thought his rod would break with the strain.' She sighed at the memory.

'So if I now need to repeat my casts, over and over, will you fish with me?' Sir Rowland looked at her, his mouth not smiling, but his eyes doing so. 'If I lapse into error, you may still correct me.'

'I shall, sir, with pleasure.'

She picked up her rod, selected another likely spot lest their lines should become entwined, and for an hour they fished in an amicable silence, punctuated only by a clamour of rooks wheeling above the beech hanger that covered the base of the scarp nearest to the house, and an occasional recommendation from Miss Lound to seek a different patch of water. She caught a fish, but nothing took Sir Rowland's fly. Eventually, he took out his pocket watch and reluctantly admitted the hour was now twenty minutes after five.

'Then I think I must pack away my rod and return to the dower house, for I cannot sit and dine in this gown, Sir Rowland. It has been a very pleasant afternoon.' She paused. 'I think you do not really need lessons now, merely you should try and fish as frequently as possible to get the feel of what is right, and of course to catch a fish.'

'Ah, but should a fish bite, ma'am, it would be beneficial to be advised how best to bring it in to the net, for having watched you, it is not a simple matter of "pull fish from water".'

'You have observed and learnt from that.'

'But I think, perhaps, that fishing in the company of an experienced angler would be beneficial, at least until the end of the season, which is barely a fortnight away, and come the spring I may have forgotten the finer points. Besides, Miss Lound, fishing quietly with a companion is most enjoyable.'

'I have not fished other than alone since my brother James left England. I had forgotten "companionship", though I have never felt lonely here.'

'Then may I request, if not a lesson, then the pleasure of your company for an hour or so of fishing in the next day or so, if conditions are good? I will leave that decision up to you, and you could send a note over, or just come to the house, for I am not so often out in the afternoon. I would not take long to attire myself suitably.'

'You want me to pound upon your door and demand that you come out to "play"?' She raised her eyebrows, and her eyes danced, but she forgot to add the layer of 'coquettishness', which meant it had far greater impact than mere flirtation. It flooded his mind with the thought of 'playing' chase with her as children might play, but when he caught her . . . He swallowed hard before replying.

'I have learnt that however much it may be sport, fly fishing is not a game, Miss Lound. I would think it more a summons to attend the court of King Trout.'

'"King Trout"! Yes, I like that, sir, though the, er, "court dress" is somewhat unusual.'

'Then I await your choosing of a suitable time.' He wound in his line and began to pack away his fishing rod. The September afternoon was losing its warmth, and there were thick grey clouds emerging upon the western horizon.

'If those advance slowly, then tomorrow may not be a day to fish,' remarked Miss Lound, studying it. 'I draw the line at standing in the pouring rain.'

'As do I.'

They parted, each aware that they would rather have stayed together, and filled with a sense of quiet contentment.

CHAPTER THIRTEEN

Madeleine Banham was beginning to realise that life was rather more complicated than she had imagined. In her head she had thought she would emerge into the adult world, be courted by a delightful man whom she would adore as much as he adored her, in the manner of the mutual attraction of her parents, get married and live happily ever after. She castigated herself for thinking in terms of fairy tales. The adulation of the young men she had encountered up until now had been so universal that it had become not quite real, and lacked meaning, but now she was dipping her pretty little toes in the real world of grown-ups and serious suitors. She was not at all sure if Lord Cradley was a serious suitor or not, for there was something lurking in the back of his eyes that hinted at it all being an elaborate charade, a game. Mama, it was true, looked upon him with a jaundiced eye, though she admitted there was nothing definite that marked him in her books as 'dangerous'.

The visit of Sir Harry Penwood had given her food for thought, food which, had he known of it, would have cheered that gentleman no end. Sir Harry was at a disadvantage, since Madeleine could recall him as an unformed stripling, and familiarity, as they said, bred contempt. Well, she was not contemptuous, but she was not in awe of him in any way. He lacked the social cleverness of Lord Cradley, but then that also meant that he had an honesty to him that was rather sweet. He had said things which made her think about him the more. She had no idea what army life was like, other than bloodthirsty, and what he had said had made her see that he was not simply a young man who rode about with a sword in his hand, attacking the enemy. His honest words were also not some trite sop to the uninitiated but had been heartfelt. She had warmed to that. He had also asked her opinion on a book, which might sound nothing at all, and they had drifted from the topic before she had the chance to respond, but he had asked, and had read the novel himself. It was a sensible question, put to her as a sensible person. He did not talk at her, but to her. She sighed. He was not as tall as Lord Cradley, and not nearly as elegant, but if his features were not as aloofly aristocratic, they were pleasant, his smile was very genuine, and he did have lovely broad shoulders and a very manly bearing. Being admired by him was the same as being admired by all the other local youths, except, as her mama had said, he was not just a youth, but a man, and a man who may have fewer years than Lord Cradley, or indeed Sir Rowland Kempsey, but in those years he had seen much of both life and death and that made him rather more mature than age alone would indicate. Mama was right, she must take Sir Harry seriously, even though she had the prospect of a London Season come the spring.

Part of her was excited at the thought of London, and part found it too big and rather frightening. There was also a small but persistent little thought that daughters were treated unfairly in life. Her brother Marcus, who appeared to have a very generous allowance, rarely ever visited the ancestral acres and lived a life that revolved, as far as Madeleine could see, around his own pleasure, yet he had the knowledge that house, land and title would all be his in the fullness of time. She was, by contrast, an affectionate and indeed fond daughter, and at eighteen years old was on the cusp of leaving all that she had known. It was an adventure, perhaps, and Mama and Papa were keen that she have the security and comforts of being a married lady with an establishment of her own, but it still meant that there was little choice but to 'fly the nest' or face the sort of future Mary Lound had discovered, a tenuous hanger-on, dependent upon the kindness or otherwise of male relatives. She did want to be married, but at the same time felt a dawning resentment that she also had no other option. In her happy moments, Madeleine dreamt of the fairy-tale love and a mutual passion, but the cold reality she shied away from was that she needed to marry, and perhaps upon nothing better than 'quite liking' the man who offered for her.

Lord Cradley cast the letter from his mother aside and grimaced in distaste. He did not appreciate being told what he should do by her or anyone else. Coming into Gloucestershire to take possession of his estate as well as the title had been a perfectly logical and sensible thing to do, and remaining for a while, especially now there was the charming entertainment of Miss Banham to enliven what had at first appeared a very boring set of people, had its advantages. The first of these was that it would alter the image that his title created in people's minds. His predecessor had been a grumpy and rather unrefined man with a reputation for being anti-social and surly. He had certainly let his house become untidy and outmoded. As the new Lord Cradley, Jasper Risley wanted to excise that image and replace it with one of a Lord Cradley who was a man of discernment, the sort of fellow to whom one should apply as an arbiter of taste. In short, he wanted to be as big a fish in the local pond as possible. He also wanted to be seen by those he employed, so that they would know he was not a man to cross or dupe. If he spent the autumn and winter at Brook House, seeing it set in order and making his presence felt, he could return to London in the spring to enjoy all that being no longer plain Mr Risley on the edges of Society would mean. Doors previously closed to him would be opened, and he envisaged a very pleasant Season ahead. His 'obligations', a word his mama had underlined, were to his name, and here, not in the rather more modest residence in which he had grown up in Bedfordshire.

The day after Sir Rowland's second fishing lesson was, as Miss Lound had forecast, distinctly blustery, with frequent heavy showers, and he correctly surmised that there would be no fishing. He employed his time with making an inventory of the books he had inherited with the library, Lord Damerham having had no inclination to crate them all up and take them with him across the Atlantic. Sir Rowland thought that an awful lot could be learnt from the contents of a man's library, and not just from the pages. There were few works of recent date, and he assumed, correctly, that the ladies would at least have taken any novels of their own choosing with them to the dower house. There were a handful of novels remaining, but they were not the sort of book he could envisage ladies reading, and indeed he himself had no wish to delve into the *Memoirs of a Woman of Pleasure*. He doubted that either lady had any idea of their existence, since those particular volumes were tucked behind older books on astronomy. From what he could deduce, the last Lord Damerham had not been a man for books, lewd ones excepted, but the generations before him had been educated and thoughtful men, interested in the world, and both its history and physical properties, the sort of gentlemen who dabbled in science enough to know when they were out of their depth. They had possessed a healthy curiosity, which meant that there were not only the Latin and Greek classics which were currently of such use to Tom, but philosophy, in both English and French, expeditions to far flung lands, and the flora and fauna that had been encountered. He even found a first edition copy of Clarendon's *History of the Rebellion and Civil Wars in England*, annotated in a very neat hand with both approving and dismissive comments, which Sir Rowland guessed to be that of the first Lord Damerham, the one who was 'diplomatic', and whose father had seen action in that time of upheaval. There was an early edition of *The Compleat Angler*, and several books on fish, with very nice illustrations. As he turned a page of one of them a piece of paper fell out. It was not part of the book but showed a copy of one of the plates made by a child's hand. The fish was definitely a fish, but the colours were very bright, and if anyone ever hooked something that resembled it from lake or river, they would assuredly throw it straight back. Underneath the picture a large and laborious hand had written 'A Trowt, by Mary Lound aged 7 years'. He smiled. She had signed it the way little girls stitched samplers, and he was willing to bet she had far preferred painting this. Her proud grandfather had probably kept it as a memento. It did not show an aptitude for painting, but it did show an early interest in fishing. Sir Rowland wondered if she knew it was there, and went through the plates until he found the one of the trout, and carefully placed the juvenile artwork back in its place. He would not mention it, for he thought she would be embarrassed, but it gave him a little thrill of pleasure that he had been privy to a window upon Mary Lound as a little girl. He did not show it to his brother because he felt he had been let into a secret, and it was one he would keep.

The following morning, Sir Rowland braved a bracing start to the day and chose to ride, dragging his brother from his books to accompany him. Tom had not ventured much outside the perimeter of the park and found it interesting to set the estate in some form of geographical context. They had been out for about an hour when they encountered another horseman, a well set up young man on a dependable-looking bay horse. He was dressed without ostentation, but Sir Rowland still made a good guess as to his identity.

'Are you by any chance Sir Harry Penwood?'

'I am, and since I know you are not Lord Cradley, I venture to guess that you are Sir Rowland Kempsey, the fortunate new owner of Tapley End. You have been described to me by Miss Lound, and also there are rarely new faces in the district, so I was fairly certain.' Sir Harry smiled.

'If you were going by Miss Lound's description, which must be of an idiot who gets his fishing line caught in trees, I would be surprised if you made the association, unless of course I simply look an idiot.' The smile was returned. Both men, perhaps influenced by Mary Lound, expected to be pleased with the other.

'Not in the slightest, I promise you. Are you venturing anywhere in particular?'

'No, just becoming more familiar with the lie of the land. I want to get past that feeling every time I go out that I will have to ask directions to find my way back to my own home. The shape of the hills is very useful, but the lanes and trackways still have the potential to lead me astray.'

'And he has brought me along to experience getting lost too,' added Tom Kempsey, which gently reminded his brother that no introduction had been made.

'Sorry, Tom. Penwood, my brother Tom, who is shortly due to return to his studies in Oxford.'

'I surmised as much. Glad to have the chance to meet you before you depart, but you will be back for Christmastide, I take it? The hunting should be good if the ground is not like iron.'

'Which ought to be a hint that we should go to the best local sales.' Sir Rowland glanced at his brother and grimaced, then turned back to Sir Harry. 'The hunter I kept when young, back in Berkshire, is too old these days, and there was no hunting in Cumberland, at least there was, but on foot. I have not admitted to Miss Lound that I have not hunted for some years, since I think it would so lower me in her esteem that she might not speak to me again.' He gave a wry look.

'Well, I have no doubt she would be surprised.' There was a thought in Sir Harry's mind that he could not pin down, but since it evaded him, he continued in practical mode. 'There are good sales in Cheltenham, first Thursday of the month for horses, and you can obtain a decent animal for reasonable outlay.'

'Is that where you got that fellow?' asked Sir Rowland, eyeing the bay.

'Ah no. Crispin here is home bred.' He patted the horse's neck affectionately. 'He served my father well, and probably knows every lane and track hereabouts as well as the way from the paddock to his stable.'

'Ah, then my brother has but to steal your horse and we will not get lost,' suggested Tom, sweetly.

'Interesting. First my brother, very reprehensibly, recommends that I commit an offence which might well result in me being hanged, or at least transported, and secondly, he intimates that your excellent mount will be able to understand my plaintive pleas to take me back to Tapley End by the most direct route. Would you like a brother, Penwood? I have one here, free to a reasonably good home. Give him access to Thucydides and feed once a day and . . .'

Sir Harry burst out laughing, which made even the reliable Crispin jerk up his head, and raised a hand.

'Very kind offer and all that, but I could not supply the Greek texts. I bumbled my way through the Latin at school, but Greek was as good as impenetrable to me. I make no pretence to being very learned, and it was one of the attractions of the army. Nobody ever expected me to quote Hesiod at them in the original.'

'Ah,' said Sir Rowland, 'but in that instance you have missed a very apposite phrase. Hesiod wrote that "A bad neighbour is a misfortune, as much as a good one is a great blessing", and I feel confident we shall be good neighbours.'

'*Works and Days*, line—'

'Yes, thank you, Tom. Please note, Penwood, I cannot quote by line number.' Sir Rowland gave his brother a look which intimated that flaunting his book learning was not desirable.

'Observe me, chastened,' sighed Mr Kempsey, meekly.

'Well, I never thought I would find myself agreeing with an ancient Greek, but he was absolutely right, and I too think we will be good neighbours.' Sir Harry's face lost its cheerful look for a moment. 'My mama is not yet up to more than church and an occasional female friend – oh, and thank you for your very considerate letter to her, but if you would like to come over to the Hall some morning, I would be very pleased to see you.'

'Best you give us directions, then, or we might not reach you until afternoon,' murmured Tom.

'Hmm, he speaks true enough. I know the vague location of your property, but directions would indeed be an aid,' Sir Rowland admitted. 'I have a reasonably good memory for places, so once I have found you the first time, I should have no further difficulty.'

Sir Harry readily supplied the directions, which Sir

Rowland repeated back to him, and they parted, both in very good humour.

It was only as he was the better part of his way home that the elusive thought struck Sir Harry as a realisation. He and Sir Rowland Kempsey, who seemed a jolly decent sort, had never met before and yet the connection that Kempsey had brought up several times was Mary Lound. He was pretty sure that Mary would have described his own person very much in fraternal terms, and there was nothing to suggest Kempsey viewed him as a rival to be warned off. The stunning thought was that in fact the man had been indicating his interest as he would to her brother, not quite seeking permission, but certainly advising him of intent. Harry Penwood let out a slow whistle, which made his horse's ears flick back. So, Mary had an admirer, and a serious one at that. He wondered if she knew, because she might not recognise the signs, and hoped for Kempsey's sake she did not regard his admiration as some form of affront. You could never tell with Mary. Upon consideration, as long as the fellow learnt to fish well enough, he thought it might be the ideal match, and . . . A second amazing thought occurred to him. If Mary accepted an offer from Kempsey she would be mistress of Tapley End. Could she . . . would she . . . No, surely not? He arrived home in a brown study and his mama enquired if everything was all right. He answered in the affirmative, but to be honest, he was not entirely sure.

* * *

The Kempseys returned, with only one minor 'detour', to Tapley End in time for a light luncheon, and Tom said that he would hide away with his books for the afternoon, once he had written a letter to a college friend. Sir Rowland also sought the library, but to take down the Hesiod, which he recalled from discovering the day before, and left Tom to his studies whilst he sat before the fire in the drawing room, testing his rusty Greek for half an hour. He sought the quotation he had used without recourse to Tom to tell him the exact line. He turned pages, not quite idly, and then stopped. He read a passage twice to make sure he had it aright, and then apostrophised the book.

'I am at least attempting to do as you say, you old Greek.' He then read the lines out loud, translating as he went. '"Bring home a wife to your house when you are of the right age, while you are not far short of thirty years nor much above; this is the right age for marriage." Well, I am certainly that, which is good. "Let your wife have been grown up four years, and marry her in the fifth." The trouble is that deciding when a woman is grown-up is not simple. If we say nineteen, then she must be barely more than five years older, since she said she was fifteen ten years ago. We shall say that this also fits. "Marry a maiden, so that you can teach her careful ways, and especially marry one who lives near you, but look well about you and see that your marriage will not be a joke to your neighbours. For a man wins nothing better than a good wife, and, again, nothing worse than a bad one".'

He sighed, and grimaced. 'She lives as near could be, but the rub lies in the last bit. Would my neighbours think anyone marrying Miss Mary Lound is a fool? Perhaps, but then I doubt they have looked beyond the surface of the independent and prickly young woman who speaks her mind. I am not sure I could teach her "careful ways", whatever they are. I am tempted, yes, I most certainly am tempted, but it is not something one rushes. Six weeks ago, I had never even met her.' It occurred to him how these six weeks had flown past, and telling himself that it was because he was in a new place with much to take in did not quite work. She was not, he told himself, faultless. He tried enumerating her 'faults'. She spoke her mind to the point of rudeness; there would undoubtedly be occasions that heated words would be exchanged if he married her, and she would never be a 'submissive little wife'. 'But I do not want a submissive little wife,' he said to himself, 'and she has wit and brightness to her.' She was unconventional, and some might even say mannish, though he felt it was more that she had not left behind wanting to prove herself as good as her brothers. It was also true that fragile femininity would help her and her mother not at all in their current situation. 'Life has not dealt her an easy hand, but she has not crumbled but grown stronger. Living with such a woman might not always be easy but it would be worthwhile.'

He stared into the fire, with a private smile on his face, imagining, and it was as he sat thus that Hanford entered and informed him that Lord and Lady Roxton were in the great hall, with Miss Banham, and hoped that he was at home.

'Good gracious, yes. Show them in, Hanford, and go and tell my brother that we have visitors.' Sir Rowland stood and went from the library, glanced briefly into a pier glass to ascertain that his cravat was not askew, and then stepped forward to greet his unexpected guests.

'I trust we do not disturb you, Sir Rowland,' said Lord Roxton, once the civilities had been exchanged.

'Not at all. I have been sat with a book and contemplation and am only too delighted that you have come to call upon us.' He indicated a chair that was close to the fire and invited Lady Roxton to be seated. 'For unless you had a hot brick at your feet, ma'am, you will have cold feet from riding in the carriage.'

Her ladyship acknowledged that her extremities were not warm and thanked him. It was then that Tom Kempsey entered the room and froze. He had no idea that a vision would be sat upon the slightly faded brocade of the sofa, a vision that took his breath from his body. His mouth was suddenly dry and words evaporated for several seconds before he spoke.

'Forgive me, I . . .'

'May I present my brother, Mr Thomas Kempsey. Tom, Lord and Lady Roxton, and their daughter, Miss Banham.' Sir Rowland, who had forgotten his own brief surprise at the looks of Miss Banham, found it strangely reassuring that Tom, who was rarely at a loss for words, and clever words at that, could be bowled over in an instant by a beautiful girl. However, he was also pleased that his studies would be removing him from her vicinity in the near future, since guiding his young brother through the anguished highs and lows of calf love was not a prospect that filled Sir Rowland with joy.

Tom recovered his composure enough to make his bow, and if his cheeks were a little pink, then the reaction was common enough among young gentlemen encountering Madeleine Banham for her not to think it odd. He was bashful, but controlled it, neither stumbling over his words nor trying to impress too much. He observed without staring, which made Lady Roxton think him very prettily behaved, and he noticed the glance that Miss Banham gave the pianoforte in the corner of the room.

'Do you play, Miss Banham?' he asked.

'I do, Mr Kempsey. I am a poor needlewoman, my fingers seem always to be being pricked, but I have put many hours into my music.'

'Then perhaps you might essay something for us upon the instrument here. Neither I nor my brother play, all thumbs in my case, but we like music and it seems a shame that the pianoforte has become just so much a piece of furniture.'

Sir Rowland kept a straight face. He had been discussing with Tom the removal of the unused and rather unwanted pianoforte to one of the less used chambers in the east wing, and the difficulties of its dimensions, only the evening before.

'If you would honour us with a song, perhaps,' he added his own entreaty, earning a grateful look from his younger brother.

Madeleine looked to her mama. She did not want to look as if pushing herself forward, but of course a young lady with her advantages never needed to do so, since eyes were drawn to her naturally. She received a small nod of approval, but prepared her 'audience' for errors, since she had no music. Mr Kempsey immediately drew her attention to the canterbury that was placed out of the way and beside the instrument, and invited her to see if there was anything with which she was familiar. A first glance did not look promising, since Mary Lound had dutifully worked through arpeggios and a few rather dull songs where the accompaniment had been reduced to simple chords, but just as she was about to give up Miss Banham found a piece, clearly barely touched, that she knew, and which had an accompaniment worthy of her proficiency. It was a well-known song, and she sang in a clear and melodic voice. Part way through, Mr Kempsey, very daringly, joined in with the harmony. He could not play a note, but he sang quite creditably. The combination of voices worked rather well, and at the conclusion he begged her play something else, but Miss Banham, very aware that there was nothing else worth playing in the collection, and not wishing to show off too much, lowered her eyes and refused, gently but firmly.

* * *

Mary Lound had watched the weather all morning, aware that there lurked within her a level of excitement that was not, however much she enjoyed the activity, founded solely upon the thought of fishing in the lake in the afternoon. It was with no small degree of relief that she detected a drop in the wind, since she was sure that a novice fisherman such as Sir Rowland would be disheartened by his fly landing nowhere near where he had aimed and being unable to compensate. It was something which came with experience alone. She donned her fishing attire, took up her rod bag and basket, and set off across the park with the same sensation as she might have for some treat as a child. She was greeted by Hanford, who went to inform Sir Rowland of her arrival.

As the butler opened the door that led to the west wing of the house, Mary heard the sound of a pianoforte, and voices, singing. One was a soprano, very sweet, and the other a baritone. She caught her breath. Regardless of the fact that she had never shown any aptitude for the instrument, and it had been sold with the house, she felt as though another woman was using 'her' pianoforte to charm the man for whom she was forming a . . . liking. Even as the door closed, she heard a voice, one she believed to be Tom Kempsey's, entreating the musician to play another song, and she heard 'Miss Ban . . .' which identified the usurper. She felt as if she could not breathe, and stood statue-still, with the sound of her own heartbeat pounding in her ears. At this very moment,

Madeleine Banham was charming him with her beauty and here she was, dressed in old clothes that, indoors especially, made her look little better than a scarecrow. She felt out of place.

Sir Rowland entered, and he was smiling, looking very happy.

'Miss Lound. Now, I did wonder if conditions would be suitable this afternoon, but I am unable to ready myself for fishing immediately, since Lord and Lady Roxton have come to visit us. Do come through and—'

'Be laughed at?' Miss Lound interrupted him, her voice low and impassioned. 'Miss Banham might be polite enough not to do so out loud but you can be sure she and her mama will have plenty to laugh over when they leave. "What on earth was she wearing? I am sure I have thrown out gowns in better state, and as for that hat . . . Was it ever a hat at all?" You think just because I lack the feminine graces that I have no feelings? Well I do, so thank you so very much for your kind invitation but I would far rather drown myself in the lake. Good day to you, Sir Rowland. Oh, and I can sing, but not nearly as well as Miss Banham so a duet with me is out of the question, at any time.' With which she turned on her heel and strode out, very nearly slamming the great oaken door behind her.

He stood rooted to the spot, taken aback at the violence of her response, annoyed and perplexed in equal measure. He had come to her, eager to be with her and regretful that he might not instantly go and change, and she had turned on him as if he had intentionally invited the Roxtons so that they would see her dressed for fishing. It was ridiculous, and now she had flung off in some tantrum. He ought to return to his guests and let her sulk. He paused, muttered under his breath, and headed after her.

A normal young woman, he thought, would not have gone far, but Miss Lound was striding away at a very unladylike pace. He would not run to catch her up, but he did have to lengthen his own stride and walk briskly. Hc did not call after her, and his footsteps made little sound upon the grass, so he was within twenty feet of her when she heard him. She spun round and glared at him.

'Go away.'

'That is rich, since this is my land and you are the one leaving.' His own temper was rising at the injustice of her reaction.

'Leave me alone.'

In response he came closer.

'Stop sounding like a petulant adolescent and behave like a sensible woman.'

Rather than calming her, this added fuel to the flames of her wrath.

'A sensible woman like the divine Miss Banham?'

'I never mentioned Miss Banham.'

'You did not need to. I heard her singing, with you.'

'She was not.'

'I heard her, heard the duet. Can you not even have

the decency to be honest with me?'

'I am being honest, and you have no cause to rip up at me.'

They were both very loud now, and a crow flapped from an oak branch and wheeled away, cawing its disapproval.

'I came to fish with you and find you entertaining the Roxtons.' She made it sound an underhand thing to do.

'Who happened to pay a call. What the devil do you expect me to do, put up a sign at the gates saying "No visitors please. Miss Lound may possibly be coming over to fish with me"?' He was thoroughly exasperated because she was making all the wrong assumptions upon very little evidence.

'How dare you use bad language in front of me.'

'In the face of being treated to a display worthy of a nine-year-old in a tantrum I think I may be excused.'

'You may not.' She actually stamped her foot, lending weight to his description, and he did the worst possible thing. He laughed. It was not a nice, inclusive and convivial laugh, but jarring and bitter.

She stepped forward and slapped his face, or rather she attempted to do so. He was too swift for her and grabbed her at the wrist before any contact was made with his cheek.

'Go home and calm down, Miss Lound,' he instructed her, coldly. 'You do yourself no favours by letting your choler have the better of your normal good sense. Calm down, and you will realise that you have leapt to conclusions that are erroneous. I did not invite the Roxtons, I did not seek to see you mocked.'

'You looked so pleased,' she almost wailed.

'I was pleased to see you. Heaven knows why. Good day to you, ma'am.' He turned from her before she could reply and began to head back to towards the house. It was the best exit he thought he could make in the circumstances.

She stared after him and did not move until he reached the gravel paths and knot garden in front of the house.

CHAPTER FOURTEEN

If the Roxtons accepted his explanation of a small household crisis which had required that he abandon his duties as a host, and they did not see anything out of the ordinary in Sir Rowland's demeanour, his brother did, even though he was mesmerised by Miss Banham. However, Tom also knew better than to probe. Rowland was the best of brothers, but just occasionally he could shut the doors and keep one out of his thoughts. This was one such instance. Instead, upon their departure, Tom went into raptures about the 'Gloucestershire Aphrodite', and Sir Rowland let him gush at length, not listening to more than one word in ten. Eventually he raised a hand to halt him.

'Yes, yes, she is undoubtedly the most beautiful girl you, and half the shire, have ever seen, and she does not appear to be puffed up in that knowledge. I doubt you will have your mind upon your Greek translation, but might I suggest that you return to your books if you want to complete all that you set yourself as a target before dinner time.' It was a very polite way of saying 'Go away. I need to think.'

Tom took the hint, though his brother was right, and he spent more time sighing over Miss Banham than tricky grammatical constructions.

Left alone at last, Sir Rowland rubbed his hand across his frowning brow and sat down in the chair in which he had read the Hesiod, which lay on a small table to one side. He grimaced.

'Well, Hesiod, old fellow, not only neighbours would laugh at me saying I wanted to marry the woman from whom I have parted in such a bad temper. What on earth possessed her? She is in so many ways the most sensible, pragmatic woman I have ever met and then she—' He stopped. 'Good grief. It was thinking that I was singing with Miss Banham. She thought I was happy about that, and she was jealous. Jealous!' He said it with almost an air of triumph, not because he wanted her to be jealous, but because it showed that she cared about him, and because it meant that her outburst, howsoever much based upon a distortion, made sense at last.

She had heard the pianoforte, an instrument she had told him she had never really mastered, and heard 'him' singing with Madeleine Banham. Well, she was not to know that Tom sang in a baritone too, a little lower than he generally spoke. In fact, Sir Rowland thought his speaking voice had not quite found its final timbre. He had then come to her, all smiles, and invited her, in her disreputable clothes, which were, he admitted, very out of place in a drawing room, to come and see the reason for his delight. She had snapped. Well, she always said she was not a patient woman, and the fuse on her temper was not long, so this should not be a surprise.

'But I have not done wrong, not this time, Mary Lound. I shall not write a grovelling apology for your misunderstanding of the situation. I told you why I was happy and you chose not to believe me. It is therefore up to you to decide what to do next.' What worried him was that she might seek to break contact beyond the formal exchanges outside the church door of a Sunday morning and occasional public encounters. He did not wish that to happen, for all that she had angered him, tried to hit him. She had displayed the very faults he had tried to enumerate earlier, and to a marked degree, but now that he comprehended why, he felt . . . He realised why he had cut away from her so quickly. It was not just the best way out of an increasingly painful argument, but what he had really wanted to do was not let go of her at all, but pull her into his arms and hold her to him, soothe her, feel her anger and pain, for there was pain in her expression too, now he came to think of it, and reassure her that Madeleine Banham was nothing to him, and that she was more and more with every passing day. For one lingering moment he imagined it, feeling her against him, kissing the flushed cheeks, kissing the anger from her mouth. He had wanted all that, deep down. He still wanted it. 'Mary Lound,' he said softly, staring at the flames in the hearth, 'do not sever what we have between us, because it is, or at least could be, something very precious.'

Mary made her way back to the dower house more by instinct than anything else, blinded not by tears but by confusion. She had gone to Tapley End so eager, excited even, anticipating an afternoon of companionship and that strange extra special feeling that had wound through their last meeting, and it had all collapsed about her. He might deny all he wished, but she had heard the singing, the male and female voices joined, and she had seen his face. He could not have looked so happy just at seeing her, so heaven knew why he had tried to use it as his placatory lie. The only time anyone had ever looked at her like that was when James came home on furlough after eighteen months absence with his regiment in Ireland. And what man who thought about her at all would have invited her to step into his drawing room, with guests, in her fishing garb? Out of its context, her clothing looked a shabby mess, and, in her angry mood, she had no doubt that it would have been halfway round the shire in days that the 'peculiar Miss Lound' paid calls dressed as though she were on the parish and in dire need. That neither Madeleine Banham nor Lady Roxton would have ever spread such gossip was immaterial. Just at this moment the entire world was out to belittle, mock and deceive Mary Lound and she felt very alone.

She went straight up to her room and changed, her fingers trembling slightly, then sat upon her bed and tried to calm herself. She realised that what hurt so much was the feeling that Sir Rowland had played fast and loose, being one day affable and approachable as though nothing were more important than the hours they had together, and had then made a complete about face as soon as Madeleine Banham had, as she must surely have done, enchanted him with smile and voice. She ignored the fact that he had met Madeleine before. Why had he come after her, though, if he did not care? Ah yes, because she had shown spirit, and he did not want to feel bested by her, that was it. He had accused her of immaturity, of childishness. Well, he need not be exposed to it any more. She would avoid him, be cool and aloof in public encounters, and show him she did not care.

The trouble was that she did.

It was two days later when Harry Penwood came to see them, focused, at least initially, upon his own problems. Lady Roxton had mentioned, when he had 'chanced to visit', that she was already making her first preparations for a ball before Christmas, at which

Madeleine, though not officially out, might make her first real steps into the adult world among friends and neighbours. It was Harry's concern that Lord Cradley, suave member of the Ton, would eclipse him on the dance floor and gain further ground with Miss Banham.

'I am a clunch not to have considered it before. I am not even sure I recall all the steps of the boulanger,' he opined, 'so if there is more than the simplest of country dances, I fear I am lost. Can you remind me of the figures, Mary?'

'Yes, but . . .' Somehow, telling him that he need not only be concerned about the ascendency of Lord Cradley but of Sir Rowland Kempsey felt like kicking a puppy.

'But what? You must know them better than I do.'

'Well, perhaps, but you know I am no great dancer.'

'I know you have no especial love of it, not that you have two left feet. Come, aid me, dearest Mary.' He pleaded, his grin accompanied by begging eyes.

'Oh well, I suppose I shall have to do so,' she replied, grudgingly. 'I do not think Atlow ought to be moving furniture, though, not with his back, so if you desire a dancing lesson you will have to move the chairs about yourself.'

'No sooner said than done, if you do not object, ma'am?' He looked to Lady Damerham, who smiled, and shook her head.

'But do be careful not to trip over the edge of the carpet or forget a footstool. If you are going to have a short dancing lesson, I will leave you for a while, since I really must send a reply to Mrs Lissett's note, dear boy.'

She left them disarranging her morning room, and within a few minutes there was space enough for a single couple to perform the moves of the dance without risk to furniture or ornaments. Firstly, Mary interrogated her partner as to what he did remember. It was definitely a case of reminding rather than teaching afresh, and he was only very vague about two 'manoeuvres', as he termed them. Once he had tried them a few times he suggested going through the whole dance just once. As they began, he asked her how her fishing pupil was getting along.

'Seemed a jolly decent fellow when I met him and his brother. Quick-witted, or at least quick-tongued, is Mr Kempsey.'

'Yes, a nice boy, and ought to be well suited to the Foreign Office, which is where I gather he would like to go after his studies are complete.' Mary carefully avoided answering the question, and managed to sound sufficiently disinterested.

'Oh, is that his aspiration? Yes, I would think he would suit that. But you were right about Kempsey and our likelihood of getting on well. Took to the fellow straight away, and not just because I felt you would expect me to do so.' He gave her a quizzing look.

'I never said that.' She coloured this time.

'Not quite. You must be glad that it is he and not

Cradley at Tapley End.' He was watching her closely.

'Of course. Anyone would be better than a Risley, and that Risley especially.'

'Oh, be fair. Kempsey is not just an "anyone". You could do a lot worse, an awful lot worse.'

'What do you mean?' she exclaimed, tensing.

'Why, as a neighbour. What else did you think?' Harry Penwood looked innocently at her, but she had already given him the information he wanted. 'He is happy for you to fish the lake, looks just the sort to stand to in an emergency and be neighbourly and . . . you do like him, don't you?'

'He is indeed a – good neighbour.' She coloured.

'Just that, Mary?' His eyes narrowed. 'So why the blush?'

'I am not blushing. It is merely the dancing.'

'No it is not. Do not forget I have known you since I was in short coats, and I know when you are trying to pull the wool over my eyes.' Harry's tone softened. 'You know, Mary, gentlemen do not grow on trees.'

'I saw enough "young gentlemen" fall out of them when we were children.' She did not look him in the eye.

'But we are grown up now. You understand me, Mary. I am not telling you to be mercenary, but think, my dear, and do not raise barriers just to prove your independence.'

'I do not need to "raise barriers" to repel men, I assure you, Harry. I can do that perfectly well just by being me.' She sounded bitter. 'All they ever want is prettiness and patience, and I have neither in abundance.'

'Ah, so—'

'And since when have you been such an expert on . . . on affairs of the heart? You are the one who said they did not sigh over females until you saw her.' The 'her' was not difficult to comprehend.

'Ah', repeated Harry. So that was it. Well, the impression he had from Kempsey was rather different to Mary's view, but then, the girl had no experience of men showing interest in her.

'What do you mean "Ah"?' Mary sounded cross.

Harry just shook his head. She was impossible in this sort of mood.

'Well?'

'I tell you straight, Mary, if you are determined to fold your arms and defy all the male gender to find you attractive, you will succeed. Are you afraid?'

'Me, afraid? Of men? Goodness no,' she snorted.

'No, not of men, but of falling in love. Do you fear being that vulnerable? Lacking control over your feelings?'

'I do not know what you mean,' she lied, and looked at the floor.

'You do, but I will not press you upon it, just suggest you think about it.'

'I cannot hold a candle to Madeleine Banham,' she muttered.

'Stop thinking that you have to do so. You are a practical woman. There is one Madeleine Banham and many gentlemen. We, they, cannot all marry her or wear the willow thereafter.'

'You want me to wait for her cast-offs?'

'No. I am just saying not every man who looks at her and "sighs" will not be able to form an attachment to another woman.'

'Does that apply to you, Harry?'

'I . . . I think I would be very disappointed if she married a man like Cradley, and would be over the moon if she felt . . . but the chances are slim, and I am sure, in time, I would find someone else. I have to be sure.' He gave a twisted smile.

'I am sorry.' Mary closed her eyes for a moment. 'I did not mean . . . or rather I did mean and ought not to have . . . Forgive me, Harry. I do not deserve good friends like you when I treat them so badly.'

'Do not talk fustian. Now, we have completely lost where we were in the dance, and I need all the help I can get to impress Madeleine Banham.'

When Lady Damerham returned some ten minutes later, Mary and Harry were putting the furniture back in place, and the only change that she saw in her daughter after the visit was a tendency to frown as though unravelling a very knotty problem.

The ensuing week was one Mary would choose to forget. When the dower house ladies attended church, she felt as though some magnetic force made her aware of Sir Rowland's presence in the 'lord's pew' where she had been used to sit, set apart from the rest of the congregation by the sturdy oaken panels and opposite the pulpit rather than in the main part of the nave. She gave him one glance only as he and his brother entered, and thereafter kept her eyes lowered to the page of her hymn book. She could discern the sound of that baritone voice from among all the rest of the congregation, that voice that had sung with Miss Banham. It freshened her feeling of despondency and ill-usage, and then, by ill fortune, she found he was standing outside the porch, speaking with the vicar's wife as she and her mama left and exchanged words with the vicar. She responded to his salutation without looking him in the eye, gave a cool 'Good morning, Sir Rowland. The weather is indeed colder', before passing on hurriedly.

She had given what Harry Penwood had said some thought. She did not think she had been afraid of 'losing control' until after the fact. However minor her *tendre* for Sir Rowland, and she told herself, frequently, that it was only minor, finding that he did not reciprocate her feelings had wounded her, pride and heart both. Now she regretted being so foolish as to let herself be hurt. She had set out to catch Sir Rowland and had failed. Well, one did not always fish successfully, and she had long ago learnt not to be too disappointed at returning home with an empty basket. If she had kept to that intent and not let her silly emotions get tangled in her 'line' she would not feel so miserable.

She was torn with regard to the 'real' fishing, for the days remaining of the season could be counted in single figures, and she would have months without her favourite pastime. Yet she dreaded encountering him. Having put it off for five days, and been told by her mama that moping about the end of September was no use, she decided to brave the park, but devised a way in which she could fish without being at all visible from the house, and indeed from the place where she and Sir Rowland had previously made their casts. If she 'skulked' on the far side of the old boathouse, only the most keen-eyed would notice her rod and line. It did mean that she felt for the first time as though she really was a poacher, creeping in to remove his fish illicitly, and she was almost relieved that she came home with an empty basket. It had not improved her mood, and in fact she felt worse. It was as though standing by the lake heightened her thoughts of what could have been, if only Rowland Kempsey had not been ensnared in the net of the beautiful Miss Banham.

Mr Tom Kempsey walked over to the dower house a few days later to take his leave of the ladies, since he was returning early to Oxford and his studies. Lady Damerham, who found him 'a lovely boy', if rather too quick-witted for her, sighed, and remarked how lonely his brother would be all alone in the big house.

'"All alone" with the servants, Mama, and it is not

as though he will suddenly be isolated.'

'No, dearest, but servants do not really count, do they?'

'I am sure my brother will survive my absence, ma'am, but be kind to him, and make sure he does not pine,' pleaded Mr Kempsey, with a grin.

'You are very wicked, Mr Kempsey,' murmured Mary, with a slight, wry smile.

'So I am told, most frequently by my older brother. I bring, incidentally, a message from Rowland. He asks if you would be so good as to accept a couple of barrels of apples. The crop is proving very good this year and—'

'We are not a charity case,' interrupted Mary, a little stiffly.

'No ma'am, you are not, but this is the dower house to Tapley End, and I note there are no apple trees in the gardens. This cannot be chance. The dower house is linked to the main house, and it must always have been that apples from the orchard came here. Besides, it would be you being charitable. There are only so many ways one may eat an apple, and even though some will be used below stairs, I think my brother will be unable to face another fruit if he has weeks of baked apples, apple pie, apple fritters, apple cakes and . . . apples. Be merciful.'

'Is it not irritating that one longs for a good crop of fruit and yet when one is blessed, then it is suddenly a burden?' remarked Lady Damerham. 'It was the same with raspberries the year before last. I confess that I saw so much raspberry preserve that year I could have thrown it at Atlow, and last year it was the plums. I never thought they were as versatile.'

'For throwing, ma'am? Surely, they would have been better.' Tom Kempsey grinned.

'Oh, Mr Kempsey, you are too droll. I declare one would have to rise very early in the morning to outwit you.'

'Well, the Greeks and Romans outwit me week upon week, so I make no claim to swiftness of mind. It is mostly for that reason that I am going up a whole week before the beginning of term.'

'Yes, but those people lived centuries ago.' Lady Damerham beamed at him, and he blinked. He was not at all used to her thought processes.

'Er, yes, they did.'

Mary might usually have been amused at his confusion, but this day she gave but the briefest of small smiles.

'If we are doing Sir Rowland a service, then please tell him he may send his surplus apples to us, for we can find good use for them. Thank you, Mr Kempsey. You will be returning at the end of term, for Christmastide, yes?'

'Yes indeed, Miss Lound. I am rather looking forward to our first Christmas at Tapley End.' She winced, and he cursed himself for his lack of tact. 'I . . . I am sorry. That was inconsiderate, ma'am.'

'No. It was honest, and what should I answer, that I hope you are not happy in the house? That would be more than inconsiderate, it would be vindictive. I – we – have simply to accept the reality, and since we cannot be there, I am glad it is you, Mr Kempsey, and . . . your brother. You at least wish to be "part" of it.'

'We do, ma'am, very much.' He paused for a moment. 'With regard to Christmas, I – Miss Lound, do you think it would be impudent of me to purchase some music for Miss Banham as a Christmas gift? Just as a neighbourly thing, of course. You see, she played the piano when she and her parents paid a visit to us, and we sang a song together. I asked her about her tastes in music and she mentioned a couple of pieces which she did not possess but had heard and liked.'

Mary froze and paled. He had said '. . . and we sang a song together'. It was not Rowland Kempsey's voice she had heard. He had denied it being him and in her shock and ire she had not believed him. She had ruined everything.

'You think it would be wrong?' Tom, seeing her face, thought she was shocked at his suggestion.

'No, oh no, Mr Kempsey. I am sorry. It is a very thoughtful idea. I was just taken aback at the thought of the pianoforte at Tapley End being played, for I was no pianist.' It was a weak lie, but since Mr Kempsey was relieved that he might make Miss Banham smile, he did not scrutinise it.

Mary's responses thereafter were a little mechanical, for her mind was in a whirl, and she was quite glad that Mr Kempsey did not remain for long. When he left, she found an excuse to leave her mother, who was full of how kind a boy he was, and went to her bedchamber, where she sat for some time, her hands clasped tightly together, going over her intemperate behaviour and how she had both ruined all her hopes of the future and also lost a friend. It was all her own fault.

It was a thoughtful Tom who returned across the park, where the changing leaves were bringing tints of gold and copper to the trees, and reported to his brother that Miss Lound did not seem in high spirits and was more distant than usual. Sir Rowland did not know whether this was a good or bad sign.

Whatever was open to conjecture, the date was not, and with the last day of the trout fishing season looming, a day with light wind and soft white clouds was very tempting. In both Tapley End and the dower house there was thought of fishing, tempered by other thoughts.

Sir Rowland wondered, looking at the weather, if Miss Lound might be tempted, even if she was avoiding him, for it did look a perfect day. He himself felt the urge to try his hand one last time for a fish.

'And why should I not, for it is my lake, and they are my fish, and I cannot hide away in case my presence should frighten off the lady.'

'I beg your pardon, Roly?' Tom looked up from gathering the books he must pack for the Michaelmas term.

'I was talking to myself. You know, I think I will go fishing this afternoon.'

'Hoping to catch a lady?'

'That, I fear, would take a far better angler than I, Tom. No, I simply want the chance to cast before the last day of the season, and for all we know it might be wet or very windy over the next few days and leave no opportunity for fishing.'

Therefore, mid-afternoon, Sir Rowland took rod and line and went, not to the spot where he had fished with Miss Lound, but upon the further side of the lake. He surveyed the surface for some time, and, very tidily, made his first cast. After the first few he relaxed, even to the point where his mind was not upon the fishing at all, but full of a woman who was stepping ever further back from him just as he wished to be closer. He had been fishing for an hour when, rather to his own surprise, his line became suddenly taut. It was not a huge trout, but it put up a decent struggle which took his concentration, and as he landed it, and looked down at it in his net, he sighed.

'Are you a portent, trout, that the best way to succeed is not to try too hard, and just let things happen? I wonder if she would be pleased with me for this, at least. I dare not send you to her kitchen, lest she take it as some insult, me saying "look what I can do without you". The trouble is, I do not want to do without her.'

Below the boathouse, Mary Lound, who had indeed succumbed to what she feared was the last chance to fish for the season, and had caught a glimpse of her erstwhile pupil at the head of the lake, was pleased and also disappointed as she saw indications that Sir Rowland was reeling in a fish. She told herself it showed her instruction had been good, but it also showed he no longer needed her. She lost the heart to fish and packed up her rod, but did not leave, for the afternoon had a warmth to it that would soon be absent, and the grass beneath her feet felt very much 'hers'. She removed her hat and lay upon the grass, eyes closed, her hand almost caressing the grass, and the disturbed nights of sleep caught up with her. She drifted off.

Why Sir Rowland chose to walk around the lake rather than go directly back to the house he did not know, for it was a whim. Perhaps it was because, for the first time, he felt intimations of connection, of true ownership, rather than being on 'her' land. He walked slowly, listening to faint sounds of the rooks gossiping in the beech hanger beyond the house, and was taken aback to see the figure lying upon the grass. For one moment he feared something terrible had happened, and his heart beat faster. He approached and saw with relief the slow rise and fall of the bosom of her pelisse. What he wanted to do was stretch his length beside her, look down into her face, a face at peace, and wake her with his kiss, but that was for fairy tales. If she awoke like that she would be frightened, and a frightened Mary Lound would not scream but fight. Yes, she would strike out at him, and with due cause.

He dare not even remain and watch her, for if she roused from slumber to find him staring at her she would be embarrassed. He permitted himself one lingering look, committing it to memory, and retraced his steps, though not heavy-hearted, for his head was filled with delicious dreams of seeing her thus, not upon the banks of the lake on a September afternoon, but with her head upon the pillow beside him, ready to be woken with love. When he reached the house his throat felt tight, and he did not wish to speak with anyone. He went to the gunroom to hang up his rod, but if he felt her in all the house, she was even more present there, and unfulfilled desire was replaced by an aching of heart.

CHAPTER FIFTEEN

Tom left for Oxford, leaving Sir Rowland to attend the horse sales in Cheltenham the following Thursday with his groom, and with some vague description of the sort of animal he would like. Sir Rowland missed him as he always did at the very beginning of term, for, despite the age difference, they got on very well. As for the hunter, Tom had been honest with him, grinned, and said that since Rowland was buying the horse it was only fair that he select it also. As long as it looked of good temperament, was sound, and not too raw boned, he would be very grateful. Armed with these requirements, Sir Rowland went to survey the livestock that would be trotted round the ring. Whilst a proportion of the horses were for carriage work, and there were even a few heavy horses, he still had quite a large selection from which to choose. He and Sam Barnsley, his groom, were fully occupied for a good hour and a half, by which time Sir Rowland had a list of four possible animals, any of which, if not excessively priced, should suit his brother well. For himself, he hoped to purchase two horses, since he wished to hunt regularly, and Tom would not be home very much during the season. He and Sam then took up a good position by the ring and waited. Two hours later, very pleased with his first and third choices for himself, and the first choice for Tom, Sir Rowland sent Sam Barnsley off to a local hostelry, with instructions on getting the horses back to Tapley End, and himself went to The George for luncheon. As he was about to step within he was hailed by name, and turned to see Sir Harry Penwood.

'Penwood, good to see you. I have been increasing my stable, thanks to your advice. You were right about prices, for I thought most very reasonable.'

'Got what you fancied, then?' Sir Harry enquired, confident of an affirmative answer, judging from Sir Rowland's expression.

'Yes indeed. You must come over and take a look at them some time soon. Are you pressed for time? I was about to take luncheon and would be delighted to have good company rather than eat alone.'

'There is nothing that cannot wait a little. Thank you, I will join you with pleasure.'

The two gentlemen entered together and bespoke a

table. Conversation was friendly, and initially about horses and hunting, but as the covers were removed, Sir Rowland broached the subject that had been upon his mind.

'Have you seen Miss Lound this last week?'

'Yes.' The response was cautious.

'Is she . . . well?'

'She is not confined to her bed, but that is not what you mean, is it?' Sir Harry looked straight at Sir Rowland.

'No.' Sir Rowland sighed. 'You know her better than anyone, at my guess. Women, in my limited experience, are never easy to fathom, but she . . . I thought we were going along rather well, and then there was . . . a misunderstanding. She probably knows it was such, but is avoiding me.'

'I know it must sound impertinent, but have you a thought to fix your interest with her, Kempsey?' Sir Harry was perfectly serious, and his normal light-hearted demeanour was absent.

'Yes. At least I am pretty certain. I . . . sometimes I am entirely sure, and then I wonder if I ought to be confined to Bedlam for wishing it. She is a one-off.'

'Oh yes, not at all in the usual style, but rather wonderful withal.'

'That is what I think. But we are at an impasse, and I, for one, am not sure how to resolve it. I am not even totally sure that she wishes it to be resolved,' he added, gloomily.

'I can set your mind at rest on that one, at least. I will be frank. Mary, and I am not going to keep referring to her as "Miss Lound" in this conversation, is not happy at all. In fact, I have never known her as low in spirits, except when her brother James was killed and when Edmund first said he was selling up. In part I know the events of this summer, losing Tapley End, the economic constraints – and Lady Damerham is no more organised than a headless chicken, nice woman though she is – have weighed upon her, but there is more to it. She has changed these last couple of months, changed since you arrived. She has not said anything, and I am breaking no trust, but there was a sparkle to her I have not seen before, a sparkle that has been absent in recent days. She looks lost, and Mary has always been sure of everything, known where she stands, and where she wants to be.'

'I cannot see how I can go to her, that is the problem. The misunderstanding . . . well, if we are being frank . . .' Sir Rowland explained what had happened on the aborted fishing afternoon. Sir Harry, for his own part, was relieved to hear that Kempsey was not romantically inclined towards Miss Banham, for it would feel mean-spirited to resent a fellow who seemed to be jolly decent doing what he himself had done, and falling for the girl.

'I see how it must be awkward. Even if you apologise to her, she will know that you have no reason to do so, and it is she who . . . How about you try it without an apology but are just honest with her as you would be with me, or another man?' Sir Harry lifted a hand as Sir Rowland opened his mouth to speak. 'Yes, I know she is not a man, but she can, at times, be just as straightforward. It can make things remarkably simple, or extremely complicated. She does not know the "moves" of interacting with a fellow other than as a friend, which makes her the most wonderful sister to me, who never had a sister, but must make it deuced difficult now she is not thinking like a sister, and I swear she is not. Just ask to wipe the slate clean because you cannot both go on as you are, living cheek by jowl but with a huge great void between you both.'

'That is what I said when there was a far less grave misunderstanding, and it worked then. But I am not at all sure it will do so a second time.' Sir Rowland frowned.

'It is the best thing I can suggest.' Sir Harry paused. 'Would you object if I prepared the ground a bit?'

'In what way?'

'Well, if I say I met you today buying horses, and we came here, and I thought there was something on your mind. You know, hinted that you are not exactly happy as a grig at present? She might get the idea. Just at the moment I think she feels not just unloved, but unloveable, but looking you in the eye and saying she was jealous as hell, well, not exactly in those words, but showing her hand, what she feels, exposes her to greater hurt, not to mention acute embarrassment, because she will have convinced herself that you now regard her coldly.'

'Just how does a man without sisters get to comprehend women that well?' Sir Rowland raised a quizzical eyebrow.

'Not "women", alas, just "one woman", and one I have known since . . . forever. I love her dearly, and if I did not think I could trust you, Kempsey, I would not be telling you all this, because if any man trifled with her affections, well, her good-for-nought brother may be thousands of miles away, but she is not without a man to protect her.'

'I understand, and thank you. If there is anything I can do in return . . .'

'Keep a wary eye out for Cradley bamboozling Miss Banham,' murmured Sir Harry, his voice gaining a growl. 'I would not trust that fellow an inch, and she has no more worldly wisdom than a kitten.'

'I agree, on both counts. For what it is worth, I do not think Cradley has serious intentions, for he will marry cold-bloodedly, for advantage, but he may attempt "bamboozling" just to entertain himself. I cannot stand the man.'

'Well, it is no better for that, other than the thought of Miss Banham becoming Lady Cradley, living close by and forever being out of reach, would be a torment.' Sir Harry sighed.

Sir Rowland had a sudden thought. What if that had occurred to Mary Lound? Not with reference to Cradley, but to Miss Banham becoming Lady Kempsey, living across the park in 'her' home and with the man for whom she had developed a . . . distinct preference? It would crush her.

'You can be sure that I will do what I can to keep the wolf from the lamb, my dear fellow. I was heartily pleased to find Mi . . . Mary took against him at first meeting, but then she is a very unusual "lamb", in some ways so very worldly wise and yet in others a total innocent.'

'Thank you. I am glad we bumped into each other today, Kempsey, very glad. I will do what I can, and wish you every success. I want her to be happy. Lord, that does sound as if I am her brother!'

'She could do a lot worse.' Sir Rowland smiled, but gravely. 'She misses her brother James intensely, does she not?'

'Yes. I do too, to be honest. He was the best of good fellows, and my best friend also. She idolised him when small, adored him when older. They were close, but then we were a triumvirate . . . Except, of course, that Mary was not a man so the word is not right. "Trio" sounds too much like three musicians.'

'And she has told me she is no musician.'

'Very true. Half an hour at the keyboard working on her music would drive her into a very bad humour, mostly from frustration. She once said she wished she could take an axe to the instrument.'

This made Sir Rowland laugh, and the two gentlemen parted upon the best of terms.

* * *

True to his word, when next he saw Mary, Harry Penwood brought the subject round to his encounter with Sir Rowland.

'He has bought a hunter for his brother, and two for himself. I did not see them, but he seemed very satisfied.'

'No doubt. Were you looking for a horse?' Mary seemed keen not to talk about Sir Rowland.

'Oh no. I met him near The George and he invited me to partake of a luncheon with him.'

'Very friendly of him,' she said, with acerbity.

'Yes, it was, actually, so I see no need for you to sound waspish. He is a jolly decent fellow, and here you are snapping at him as though he was on a par with Cradley.' Harry was stung on behalf of the man he felt he would come to call 'friend'.

'He is not, and we both know that. I have never suggested . . .'

'I think he is settling well, but it was difficult to tell exactly,' continued Harry, ignoring her last comment. 'Seemed a trifle preoccupied, even a little blue-devilled.'

'Perhaps that was because his brother has just gone back to Oxford.'

'No, really, that won't fadge. I mean, a fellow does not look like that because his brother heads off to the university for eight weeks or so.'

'You never had a brother, Harry,' Mary reminded him.

'I know, but . . . No, it was not his brother's

departure, I would swear to that.' Harry shook his head, but left it at that, fearing to push too hard might set her back up. Better to leave it as a hint and let her consider the import of it in private. 'You are not exactly looking in plump currant yourself, my dear. Not ailing, are you?'

'No. I . . . I will miss the fishing over the winter, and I have no hunting to distract me this season. I fear being cooped up, or reduced to aimless walks.'

'You never termed your walks "aimless" before.' He looked questioningly at her.

'Well, not aimless, then, but . . .' That was the nub of the matter, really. Everything felt 'aimless' at this moment, for she had no aim in life other than to exist from one day to the next. There was nothing hopeful upon her horizon. One might argue nothing had changed since July, but it had, for Rowland Kempsey had appeared in her life, and there had been a glimpse of more than existence and penny-pinching, a glimpse of something previously unimagined and that filled her with a glow of excitement. That glow was extinguished, totally. No, not totally, for if Harry was right, and the man who haunted her dreams was in low spirits, could it be . . . just possibly be . . . that he—

'Mary?'

'Sorry, Harry, I . . . suddenly remembered something Mama asked me to tell Cook to order.'

Harry did not for a moment think that the truth, and

so, when he left, he felt he had sown the seeds of doubt in fertile ground. What either party made of the first green shoots was up to them.

Sir Rowland was a man of patience, but in this instance his patience was being eroded. He had thought, just once, that Mary Lound had looked at him as he took his pew in church on Sunday, though he had caught the turn of her head only from the corner of his eye. Yet when he left the church, he found she had exited with the clear intention of not encountering him outside. He did not know if Penwood had seen her as yet, of course, but . . . the face he had glimpsed was pale, and her skin normally had a healthy glow to it. Could she not see a way to break the impasse between them? He could not face this going on and on, so it looked as if he must do something, somehow. He must do as Penwood suggested. Mary Lound was straightforward, one who spoke her mind. He must be open with her, at least part way. If he told her that he felt her friendship withdrawn from him, and that it was all come from a misunderstanding that they could excise from memory, and request they start again, would she not grasp the chance? It would not mean apology or looking weak or foolish. Yes, what had happened, or not happened, between them since Miss Banham played the pianoforte in the drawing room should be forgotten, every last bit of it, and then . . . If he felt like this, was it not a sure sign that his feelings were not transient, that life without

Mary Lound in it would be a lesser form of existence? If he married her, if she chose to marry him, there would be stresses and strains, but if she never felt unloved or rejected they would not cause such a rupture in their closeness as had happened over this.

He wanted to be logical, even as his heart tried to dictate to him. How could a woman who had never been courted by a man, was thinking herself almost beyond marriage, see that she could be cherished above a patent beauty? It was her lack of self-belief that had made her think him false, and if her heart had not been touched, then she would not have been as angry and upset. He wondered, for a moment, if he ought to simply make his declaration immediately. She could be in no doubt then of his feelings. Since he was still rather mystified by the female way of seeing things, however, it was possible that she would be too surprised to say yes, would make up reasons in her head why she ought to refuse him, even if her heart was eager.

'One step at a time, Rowland Kempsey, one step at a time. First, we return to the easy friendship, and from that work to convincing her of the strength and durability of my love for her.'

It was easy enough to say, and far more difficult to put into effect. He was not aided by the following morning bringing a cloudburst in which only a madman would venture out of doors, and the heavy, black clouds were echoed by his frown. He paced about the house like a beast caged, and was uncharacteristically curt with a maid who, seeing his scowl, did not so much walk past him as press herself against the wall and pretend she was invisible. He told her not to be foolish, for he was no ogre, yet did so in a manner more like one than she had ever encountered before. Mrs Peplow and Cook had to give her a strong talking to, and a cup of tea to calm her.

Thankfully for the peace of mind of master and servants, the afternoon saw the skies lighten, and if it was not a fine day then at least it was now dry. Sir Rowland decided to ride across the park, which felt in some way less informal than walking over to the dower house, and when Atlow opened the door to him he requested that his horse be stabled and asked to speak with Miss Lound, privately, upon a matter of importance. He looked almost stern, and Atlow, who was rather shocked that he should request to see the daughter of the house alone, told himself that it was some matter concerning the estate, and certainly not 'personal'. He therefore showed Sir Rowland into the book room, where Sir Robert and the Lady Elizabeth looked down upon him, rather censoriously, he felt.

It was some minutes before Miss Lound entered, and he did not know the indecision that had delayed her. She had swung from being firm that she would not speak with him, and the next moment determined that she must face him. Atlow had watched her in some consternation, since this was far from her normal behaviour. When she did step over the threshold she was composed enough, her chin a little raised, her lips compressed. She looked unapproachable, but Sir Rowland was not put off.

'You wished to see me, Sir Rowland, about something important?' Her tone implied the wishing was all on his side.

'Yes, Miss Lound, I do.' He faced her squarely, and his face wore a serious expression. 'I shall not beat about the bush. The situation that has arisen between us is intolerable. We are the nearest of neighbours, and I take the liberty to say we have been on friendly terms, and I value that friendship highly, very highly. However, this last week there has been a chasm between us, one not of my desiring and, I hope – believe – not of yours either, one that developed from a . . . misunderstanding. I have not come to apologise, nor do I seek any form of apology, for it was something that simply "happened", and the breach occurred before either of us could prevent it. There is no blame attached. What I ask, most earnestly, is that we consign this breach to oblivion, as though it had never arisen. Would you be so gracious as to do that, Miss Lound?'

She stared at him in silence for what he felt was an age, but he did not know how fast her heart was beating, nor how she was struggling to untangle the thoughts in her head. It was a solution, and leaving things as they were was indeed intolerable. He was also correct in that they had been 'upon friendly terms' and she too liked that, but he had stressed 'neighbours' and 'friends'. That was how he saw her. It was how she might have been content to be when they first met, but now . . .

'Sir Rowland, it is you who are being too generous and gracious. Once before we set aside a misunderstanding, and that was what it was. The "chasm" you speak of is of my creation. I am at fault, but have been too ashamed to admit it, even to myself for a while. I was intemperate, insufferably rude, and I would not even listen to the truths you told me.' Her voice was steady, but the words came slowly. 'If you would be prepared for us to being good neighbours and – friends – I would be very grateful.'

She stepped closer, her hand held out as a man would shake the hand of a friend, or another man with whom he had concluded business. He took it in a firm clasp, and his eyes did not leave her face. He held it far longer than was necessary, and her lips parted slightly, and she breathed a little faster. She could not explain the sensation that ran through her, but it was strong, positive and, dare she even think it, promissory? It was as if he had read her mind and his grip was telling her that she was wrong, and the restoration of friendship was 'demanded' of her, but was not all that he desired from the relationship. Even as she doubted, eye and hand asserted.

'Thank you,' he said, quietly, but with feeling, and then turned her hand within his and lifted it, and kissed it, his lips just brushing the skin. Only then did he let it go. There was an awkward silence, for inconsequential conversation after something of such import felt all wrong. Then Mary heard her mother's voice outside in the passage.

'I agree, Sir Rowland,' Mary said in a calm, firm voice. 'Ah, Mama, Sir Rowland has come to enquire what have been the Christmastide customs with the tenants. Sir Rowland will be wishing to open his doors to his,' there was a fraction of a second pause, 'neighbours, and make a good impression.'

'Oh yes, of course.' Lady Damerham, alerted to Sir Rowland's presence, had not been sure why he would wish to be closeted privately with her daughter, but this, to a mind that did not think deeply upon things, seemed a plausible reason. It would not stand up to any scrutiny, but Lady Damerham did not scrutinise.

Sir Rowland gave Mary a glance which commended her quick thinking.

'And I must say that despite my fears, none of them – the tenants – ever ruined the carpets with muddy boots.' Lady Damerham smiled. 'But this is hardly being social, standing in the book room, for the fire is not even lit and we would be much better in the drawing room. Will you take a glass of wine, Sir Rowland? Did you walk through the park or ride this afternoon? I declare the weather this morning was so awful we had as many candles lit as if it were evening.'

'Thank you, ma'am, I will, and I rode.' He smiled at her, and then looked at Mary, whose heart thumped. Was it her imagination, or did the smile change, just a little bit? Sometimes she found her mama's conversations irritating, but this afternoon she was profoundly grateful, for she needed time to regain her equilibrium. She had swung from misery to a mixture of excitement, joy and a strange frisson that left her dizzy. She was glad to sit in the drawing room, her hands folded in her lap, apparently serene, as she attempted to regain her inner balance. Wine was brought for Sir Rowland, Lady Damerham's mind flitted from topic to topic, and eventually she paused. Sir Rowland turned slightly.

'Miss Lound, I have a question, and I wonder if you could furnish the answer?'

'I will attempt to do so, sir.'

'You told me about the portrait of Valentyne Lound being described in a letter from Sir Robert to his son. I remembered when I was awaiting you in the book room and was studying the image of Sir Robert. Did you yourself read that letter? If you were rather young, I wonder if you took all that could be gleaned from it. I have been thinking about your Tudor ancestor and wonder if I might see the letter for myself, if you possess it?'

'Oh! I do not! How odd that I should have forgotten. Sir Rowland, the letter is in the house.'

'It is? You are sure, forgive me, that it was not thrown away by the previous Lord Cradley or even your brother?'

'No, no, it could not have been, because Edmund never knew the secret.'

'A secret? You intrigue me.'

'It was Grandpapa who showed me the letter. Edmund and James were away at school. I had been asking about Valentyne, because Grandpapa told wonderful stories about him, no doubt altered for a child's ears and expectations. He took me to the library, and showed me the secret compartment by the chimney breast. It was constructed upon the command of the first Lord Damerham, when he had the west wing built. Grandpapa said to me that his papa had grown up in a time of uncertainty, even for kings, and believed that it was wise to always have a place where one's enemies would not find documents that were either important or indeed incriminating if the order of things was overthrown. I think Grandpapa admired his sire's forethought. By the time Grandpapa showed me the place, such things were in the past. Nobody would seek to steal such a thing as an old family letter, but I think he liked the idea that it was where a Lound had placed his treasures.'

'Goodness me, you never told me of this, Mary!' exclaimed Lady Damerham, clasping her hands together at her bosom. 'Do not tell me there were priests' holes and secret passages and . . .' She shuddered.

'No, Mama, not that I ever heard of, at least, and do not forget this is in the west wing, built after such things. All Sir James desired was a safe place for documents and treasures, not a place to hide himself or others.'

'Do you recall the exact location of this "hiding place for treasures", Miss Lound?' Sir Rowland was interested, but also saw that this was another opportunity to spend time with her.

'Yes, pretty well, although I could not say behind one particular panel. I know it was on the right side of the chimney breast, and into the chimney breast itself, not the wall adjacent.'

'But you would remember if you saw it, looked for it?'

'I am sure I would.'

'Then may I request that you both do me the honour of dining with me, informally, tomorrow evening, and perhaps then we might see if we can find Sir Robert's letter?' He looked at Lady Damerham and then Mary, who had the impression that her mama was not going to be dragged to the library to observe their investigations, and would, in fact, be rather in the way.

'I do not believe we are otherwise engaged, are we, Mama?'

'No, indeed, and we would be delighted, Sir Rowland.'

'Might I suggest that you come rather early. I dine at six, but there is still enough natural light at five, and it might be advantageous to at least commence our search by daylight rather than candlelight.'

'That sounds very sensible, sir. May we, Mama?'

'Yes, that is perfect, for it also means Silas is at least driving us there in the light. I know it is a short distance, but there is but a waning moon at present, for I noted it last night as I went to bed, and that does not give a great deal of light.'

'Then we will come for a quarter hour before five,

Sir Rowland, to be sure of the light.'

'I look forward to it.' He rose, aware that it was a natural point at which to make his departure, and also that he wished to have time to think upon what had happened within the last hour, and how it changed his view of the weeks ahead. He bowed to both ladies and left with a feeling of elation.

'She felt it as I felt it,' he said, knowing his horse would not reveal secrets. 'And she did not dislike it when I held her hand. We have closed the chasm, and not gone back to the beginning, but to the point at which it appeared, and I have let her see a little of what I feel.' He felt that at this moment she might be rather overwhelmed if she was made aware of the full depth of his feelings for her. In truth, it rather overwhelmed him also.

CHAPTER SIXTEEN

Maintaining a casual air the following afternoon was surprisingly difficult, so Sir Rowland shut himself up in the library, and did a little reconnaissance. He studied the panelling about the chimney breast and concentrated upon the right side. There were small bosses at the intersections, and although he could not see any obvious line about a panel, if the thing had not been opened in years it would have been concealed by dust. He tried several bosses, which were at a height that was reachable without standing upon a chair, and on the third attempt one did twist. He carefully turned it back, heard a click, and, by pressing towards the other end, the panel swung open on a pivot. His first thought was to leave the rest of the discovery for later, secure in the knowledge that ultimately Miss Lound would not be frustrated. However, he wondered if it contained more than just a family letter. If it did, well . . .

The ladies from the dower house arrived punctually, well wrapped against the chill, and he met them in the great hall as their cloaks were being taken from them. He was glad to see that Miss Lound had a better colour and her eyes were brighter. This had also been noted by Lady Damerham, who had wondered, dismissed, wondered, and then become totally confused.

'Do tell us, Sir Rowland, will there be a wide selection of apple dishes upon the dining table this evening?' asked Miss Lound.

'Apples?'

'Yes. Your brother told us that you were positively knee deep in them.'

'Those were not his exact words, though,' interjected Lady Damerham.

'Ah, I see.' Sir Rowland laughed. 'I confess they may appear in some form, but I promise that they are not the main component of the meal, and nor did I invite you in order to diminish the glut. It has been a very good year for them, and I hope the barrels sent over to the dower house will last you well into the winter.'

'Oh yes, Sir Rowland. Very kind it was of you to donate so many,' gushed Lady Damerham.

'Or practical. For all we know your storeroom is piled high with the fruit and Mrs Peplow is at her wit's end wondering what to do with all the other harvested supplies.' Miss Lound pursed her lips.

'Well, I cannot displease Mrs Peplow, now, can I?' His eyes met hers and the laughter was shared by both of them, though silent. 'There is a good fire in the drawing room, Lady Damerham, and I thought you might like to sit with a glass of sherry whilst we go treasure hunting?' He hoped that she would not be too assiduous a chaperone, for, after all, her daughter was scarcely a wide-eyed ingénue of eighteen, and he thought he exuded the air of 'dependable gentleman' rather than 'wolfish seducer'.

'That sounds very nice, Sir Rowland. Thank you.'

He saw her ladyship comfortably seated and provided with a good sherry, and then, as casually as he could, invited Miss Lound to show him 'the secret of Tapley End'.

'Well, after all this, I do hope I can correctly remember the place, or you will think I was telling you faradiddles, sir.'

'Never, Miss Lound, I assure you. If you will excuse us, Lady Damerham.' He bowed, and then opened the door for Miss Lound. As he followed her, he could not help thinking of her like this, walking about the house but as its mistress, not a visitor. True, she had been as good as its mistress even six months previously, but . . . He wondered if he felt so attached to the building already because he was so attached to her. They went into the library, where the light was still sufficient to examine the woodwork closely.

'Is your memory restored, looking at the panels?' he enquired.

'Only in as much as I know without a doubt that there are bosses that turn, and I recall that I was not able to see inside the cavity, for it was above my head height, but then, I was but ten years old.'

'At least it means I do not have to grovel upon my hands and knees, and if your grandfather opened it without standing upon a chair, then we have but two likely panels. Do you wish to essay the turning, or shall I?'

'You do it, Sir Rowland, then if they fail to budge it cannot be put down later to my being a "feeble female".'

'I doubt anyone would ever call you that, Miss Lound.' He reached to a boss, but not the one he knew would turn. Neither it nor its neighbour moved in the slightest. 'Then it must be that the four bosses above are the ones we need,' he said, and then paused. 'When the house and contents were sold, you accept that your brother probably had no idea that this secret hiding place existed?'

'Oh, I am certain.'

'Then will you agree to accept that if anything is within, it is yours, because it is what your antecedents put there, and whatever the law may say, morally you should be the custodian?'

'I . . . yes, unless that means you want to give me spiders.' Mary had stepped a pace back. 'If it has not been opened for fifteen years there might be tribes or colonies, or whatever you account spiders in.' She did sound a little nervous, and he laughed.

'Agreed. Anything living belongs to the house. Now shall we see what there is inside? This one or,' his hand moved down one panel, 'this one? Ah!' The boss moved, a little reluctantly, but the panel remained *in situ*.

'I recall Grandpapa pressing a part so it swung outwards, Sir Rowland.'

He glanced behind him at Miss Lound, but she now had her eyes tight shut, presumably to avoid seeing arachnids. His hand moved to push the panel and it opened, slowly.

There was no immediate evidence of spiders, but of a simple box-shaped recess in the wall, about two feet wide and tall, and about eighteen inches deep. There was a rolled parchment, slightly dusty, and two tin boxes. He withdrew the roll first, blowing the dust from it, for the tiny chamber was well sealed and really quite clean.

'Do you know what this may be, Miss Lound?' he asked, turning to her.

'Oh, yes, I had completely forgotten it. It is a long family tree that goes back beyond Sir William Lound and the creation of Tapley End. I remember now that it had little heraldic shields upon it.'

He handed it to her, suggesting it be unrolled upon the desk, and then took the two boxes, not at all dusty, to weigh the parchment and prevent it rolling up again. The family tree ran the length of the substantial desk and was written in a very neat hand, with, as Mary had recalled, the arms of the families who had become allied by marriage to the Lounds, where applicable.

'It is rather splendid,' he remarked.

'I was only interested in the heraldry, because of the colours, and the devices. You see here,' she leant forward and her finger hovered over one where a fierce red boar's head was shown in profile. Sir Rowland, himself leaning a little, was more interested in the less fierce profile of Miss Lound. 'I always thought seeing that on a knight's shield in battle would frighten the enemy.'

'And I have found Sir Robert and . . . you did not say that the Lady Elizabeth was the daughter of such an illustrious house as that.'

'Well, it was a long time ago and just before they gained the dukedom. However, I think Sir James, as he was before his elevation, found it useful having a duke as an uncle. It opened doors.'

'I have no doubt of it. And to have your ancestry traced back as armigerous to 1236 is not to be sniffed at.'

'Oh, I have never sniffed at my ancestors, Sir Rowland, I promise you.' She grinned at him. It was the first time since that unfortunate afternoon in the great hall that she had done so, and he felt as if a great weight had been lifted from him.

'Now, shall we see if that letter is in one of these boxes?' He lifted a box and rolled up the parchment. When it was once more tied with its worn binding, he opened the first box, and Mary gasped. There was paper within, but not letters. Sir Rowland removed a bound bundle of notes.

'My goodness!' exclaimed Mary.

'Let us see.' Sir Rowland began to count. 'Some of these are for fifty pounds, others for twenty.' He made two piles. 'Well, Miss Lound, you are precisely eight hundred and sixty pounds the richer.'

'No, no, you cannot include money, Sir Rowland.'

'But you agreed, and it is most certainly not alive.' He concealed his delight, since he had checked the boxes beforehand, and that was why he had made his offer. 'It is not charity, Miss Lound. This money belonged, presumably, to your grandfather, and whilst one could possibly argue that it ought to pass to your brother, he is not in the country, and to be frank, I feel he appropriated some things which really ought to have been yours, such as your horses. Undoubtedly, ma'am, this does not belong to me. For me to retain it would be impossible.' He handed her the bundle. 'Now, what else is here?' He wanted to distract her.

He opened the second box where there was a collection of folded letters, the seals long ago broken.

'I think you should peruse these, not me.'

'Well, I will do so, but if we do but look at the style of the hand, we will more quickly be able to deduce any that are of great age, for the style of forming the letters was very different a century and a half ago.' Mary opened the first letter, shook her head and set it aside. He took a small pile and opened them enough to see if the writing was more archaic. It only took a few minutes to reduce the likely epistles to a heap of five. Mary checked them one by one, and on the third gave an exclamation of triumph.

'Here, this is it! The writing is a little difficult, and some spellings . . . well, I suppose those may have changed. It is dated the 12th May, 1682, and it is definitely from Sir Robert to his son, James. Now, where is the passage? Yes, here it is.' She cleared her throat, and began, slowly but not ponderously. 'He says "You asked me about my grandsire, Valentyne Lound. I have some small recollection of him as an old man, but he died when I was but seven years of age. However, there was a portrait of him, a miniature by Hilliard, and accounted a very good likeness, painted in 1586, after his time at sea. He was a man of lithe",' Mary frowned, 'I think that says "lithe", well we shall account it so. Yes well, "lithe build, with copper-coloured hair and a close-cropped beard in the manner that was popular at the time, and he had about his neck a chain of Spanish gold, I remember right well, for my father told me that. He was dressed very fine, in green and gold, and held his head proudly. It was painted the year of his marriage, when he was eight and twenty, and I think he was well pleased with his life then, for he had wife, wealth and a good name, and had even been commended by Her Majesty. Sad I am to say that this picture was stolen during the dark years of the Regicide Cromwell, as was so much of quality from this, our house, to our great sorrow and distress. Howsoever,

I am pleased most mightily to hear of your diligence in your studies, and hope that you will be able to advance the name of Lound in the service of your king and your country".' She sighed. 'Sir Robert died before James was elevated by Queen Anne, of course, but I think he knew that his son was indeed doing as he had instructed.'

'I have looked at the books in the library here, and it is clear that your great-grandfather and grandfather were interested in far more than just the acres upon which they lived. I have found books upon the sciences and philosophy, and travel and history, well used.' Sir Rowland smiled at her.

'Yes. Grandpapa was an interesting person. I think he was disappointed in my papa, who was very unlike him in character. Papa was interested only in . . . Papa.' Mary said this without emotion, but simply as a fact. 'He spent much of his time, and money, in London, until he became ill with the gout, and then dropsy. One should not be glad of ill health, but it did mean that during his last years he was not so able to deplete the estate.'

It occurred to Sir Rowland that her relationship with her father was not one which would lead her to see the married state, legally subject to a man, as a good thing. Her sire and her elder brother had been very fallible, if not culpable, and the best relationships she had had were with a brother and a man she clearly treated as a brother. Unfortunately, his feelings towards Miss Lound were not fraternal, and he would regard her treating him as a brother as a huge disappointment.

'Do you wish to take the letter and the other documents back with you to the dower house?'

'Oh no,' she exclaimed, 'they may be "mine" but they are also of this place. If . . . if you do not object, when I have read them, I would like to place them back where they belong, where they have been kept for generations.'

He felt immeasurably cheered by this, for it indicated that she had no intention of breaking her bond with the house. If he had his heart's desire, there would be no question of it.

'Then shall we take the notes to the drawing room, and put the letters and family tree back? Or would you prefer to come at your leisure and read the letters here in the library? You are now assured that the cavity is without spiders, and do not need me to open it. To replace them.'

'But a spider might enter, unbeknownst. I . . . I would prefer it if it was your hand not mine that was placed in the dark.' She looked at him, a little shyly, and there was no attempt at a flirtatious coyness. She was simply a little embarrassed at the depth of her dread of spiders.

'Consider me always ready to defend you from eight-legged foes, Miss Lound. It is not exactly dragon-slaying, but I hope you will consider it a knightly gesture.'

'I might consider it silly if you did so in full plate armour,' she replied, though her cheeks gained added colour.

'Er, yes, it would seem excessive.' He glanced at

the clock. 'I think perhaps we ought to rejoin Lady Damerham, lest she think we have been grappled by giant spiders, or become lost in skeleton-infested secret passages.'

'Could one have an "infestation of skeletons"?' wondered Miss Lound, as he replaced the letters in their box, and thence into the secret compartment.

'I doubt it.' He secured the panel, turning the boss to catch the mortice behind, then he himself turned and smiled at her. She smiled back. It was but an exchange of smiles, they each told themselves, but it was as if they had touched. The only reason Sir Rowland could find for this phenomenon was that neither now had any defensive barrier raised, and the magnetic attraction that he felt was in some ways reciprocated.

It was a light-hearted pair who entered the drawing room, each trying to find the best term for a large number of skeletons in one's house. When Lady Damerham heard them, she shuddered.

'Do not, I beg of you. Horrible things, skeletons, not that I have ever seen one, thank heavens. I am not even sure it is proper to look at a picture of one, for after all it is the human shape, without any clothing.'

Both Sir Rowland and Miss Lound looked rather taken aback at this statement, but Miss Lound, successfully controlling the urge to giggle, managed a response.

'I think, Mama, that the usual depiction of skeletons in art form is emblematic, symbolising the transience of life.'

'Well, emblematic is all very well, I suppose, but I am not entirely convinced.'

It was fortuitous that at this point Hanford entered to announce that dinner was served, and all mention of bones, articulated or not, ceased forthwith.

Sir Rowland, with a lady upon each side, was a relaxed and attentive host, pressing such dishes upon them as he thought might be to their taste, although Miss Lound did murmur at one point that she felt he was treating her like the Christmas goose.

'For if I ate the half of what you urge, Sir Rowland, I would be too replete to even climb the stairs to my bed, and in no time at all I would cease to fit any of my gowns.'

For one very fleeting moment, Sir Rowland imagined her, not unable to fit in a gown, but simply not in one, and promptly choked upon a mouthful of curd tart, so much so that Miss Lound, casting propriety to the winds, thumped him forcefully upon the back. She then chastised him.

'That, sir, is the penalty for imagining a lady so rotund as to be the shape of a ball. Your eyes are watering. Do, I beg of you, take a sip of wine. There, now you look recovered.'

It was another minute before he could thank her for her practical assistance. He drank but a single glass of port in solitary state at the end of the meal, and then joined the two ladies, who had both been feeling the oddness of the situation, sitting together as they had every evening in this very room, as though nothing had changed in the last few months. Lady Damerham looked somewhat stunned, for Mary had revealed, once they were alone, the sum of money that had been discovered in the secret hideaway. Her ladyship was caught between delight that it would mean they could live for the better part of two years without eating further into their meagre capital, and the fear that having that much money in the carriage on the way home would make them liable to be held up by strangely omniscient highwaymen. Only when Sir Rowland suggested that they take but a small portion of the sum and that he would escort Miss Lound personally to the bank in Cheltenham at her convenience, was she in any way relieved of worry, but it had an adverse effect upon her train of thought, which became so obtuse that Sir Rowland was reduced to smiling and nodding. Miss Lound, seeing his desperate state, suggested that the tea tray be brought in early, and thus they parted a little after half past nine, with Lady Damerham chatting animatedly to her daughter, and not noticing that the replies were vague. Whilst she said that she would not sleep a wink for the excitement, her warmed bed soon proved her prognostication wrong, but neither of her dinner companions did so, though they were not unhappy. If anything, they lay awake until the midnight hour, wondering, wishing, hoping, and finally dreaming.

If the first part of October had felt interminable and dismal, the latter part passed, Mary felt, as quickly as the scudding clouds across the frequently stormy skies. It was not that she encountered Sir Rowland every day, but that on those that she did not she was aware of disappointment and then anticipation. Initially, Sir Rowland was circumspect, and his 'reasons' for coming over to the dower house or inviting Mary to ride with him had validity, but it was too intoxicating, and they soon became patent 'excuses'. He did realise that visiting his tenants too frequently might seem odd, and since Silas could always accompany them, simply inviting her to ride with him was not improper. He therefore suggested that, weather permitting, she might do so several times a week. To avoid gossip, and to enjoy the outdoors while she could, Mary also rode alone.

On one of these rides, she encountered the local 'weather seer', an aged individual known to all as 'Old Matthew'. This worthy shook his white locks over the winter to come, and warned her it would be 'a bad 'un'. Since he was often correct in his foretelling, she passed on the warning to Sir Rowland.

'Do you give much weight to doom-laden utterances?' He looked sideways at her.

'Not in the general way of things, no, but one has to be practical, and Old Matthew has had an uncanny knack of being right far more often than wrong. You had better not mock, sir, for as Old Matthew himself said "woe betides them as does not take heed".' Her rustic accent, which was very accurate, was too much for him, and he let out a crack of laughter, which made her horse toss his head at the sudden noise. He was laughing a lot these days, his spirits buoyed and each dawn greeted with anticipation.

The sober baronet within him told him he was moonstruck, but the rest of him simply agreed and declared how wonderful it was to feel this way. He put up no resistance to falling head over heels in love, and revelled in the slight madness of it all. They had, he told himself, learnt what it was like when they fell out, and it was too terrible to think about, so each would work the harder to ensure that any disagreements between them were of short duration. They did 'argue' over some small things, but never seriously, and if they did not come to a swift accommodation, agreed to differ, very happily. He was absolutely certain that he wanted to marry her, and he was increasingly confident that she would accept him if he offered for her, and not for the sake of living in Tapley End. Part of him was so eager, he would gladly make a declaration immediately, but there was also the idea of Christmas Eve and the yule log. She had mentioned it when she first showed him about the house, and it clearly meant a lot to her. He could imagine it, her lighting the log, even if there was nothing from the previous year with which to start, and then he would propose to her, in the great hall, beneath the armour of her ancestors. Yes, it would be more meaningful than in a field, on horseback, on a damp November day, or whisked into one of the rooms in the dower house. The only small difficulty he faced was that the more often he was with her, the stronger the urge within him that wanted to hold her, feel her in his arms, murmur sweet nothings in her ear, and kiss her.

The last leaves had been prised from the trees that stood embarrassed in their nakedness, the temperature had dropped, and then there were gales for nearly a week. Even riding was out of the question unless it was a necessity. Sir Rowland walked over to the dower house on a couple of afternoons but felt that most of his time there was spent in warming up ready to return, and there was not the intimacy of being alone which they had when out riding, except for the unemotional presence of Silas, who rode a respectful three horse lengths to the rear.

Upon his last visit he revealed that he was leaving Tapley End for ten days or so, and visiting his mother in Richmond, spending a couple of days in London and then returning via Oxford, where he would collect his brother at the end of term. He was gratified that this was greeted with a surprised 'oh' from Miss Lound that held disappointment, although she thereafter sounded very calm. Visiting one's invalid mother before the Christmas season was very understandable, and then to return with Tom was practical. One could scarcely decry such a plan. She therefore agreed with Lady Damerham that fulfilling filial duty was admirable, and hoped that the poor weather did not mean that there would be delays upon the post roads from fallen trees. It was only as he rose to leave that she said, softly, 'We will miss you, Sir Rowland.' Her eyes told him that what she meant was 'I will miss you.'

'I shall not be absent for very long, Miss Lound. Tell me, is there anything that either of you ladies would like brought from Town? Some delicacy that Gloucestershire cannot provide?'

Lady Damerham, taking him at face value, frowned, and looked thoughtful. Miss Lound laughed.

'Since I have never been to London, sir, I have no notion what "delicacies" are to be found there. You make it sound as though exotic provisions are sold upon every street.'

'Hardly that, but there are some excellent perfumers, and grocers with the finest sweetmeats.'

'A perfume is a very difficult thing,' remarked Lady Damerham, 'for it seems to change according to the wearer. I have always used lavender water, but Mary turns her nose up at it as fit only for keeping moths at bay, and dabs attar of roses upon her person.'

Sir Rowland, very wickedly, thought he would love to dab anything at all 'upon her person', but wisely said nothing. He knew she had smelt nice whenever he had been close enough to be aware of it. It was not often that he found Lady Damerham's utterances of use, but he gave her silent thanks for revealing her daughter's preference.

'And Mama has a fondness for sugared almonds, Sir Rowland.' Miss Lound did not know quite why she felt a blush rising, but she did.

'Sugared almonds. I will make a note and go to Gunter's in Berkeley Square.'

'Now even I have heard of Gunter's, famed for its ices.'

'But if I brought ices back, Miss Lound, you would not be at all pleased with a gelatinous pool.' He smiled at her.

'Indeed no. And I cannot think that travelling in a post-chaise with it would be very pleasant either. Confine yourself, dear sir, should you wish to purchase a gift, to something that will not melt.' There was laughter in her voice, but what he caught was that she had called him 'dear sir', not simply 'sir'. He wondered if she had even noticed.

'Observe me obedient to your commands, Miss Lound,' he said, with a flourish, and bowed over her hand, which gave him the chance to give the very faintest squeeze to it.

'Well,' declared Lady Damerham, when he had gone, 'just to think of it, sweetmeats from Gunter's. How our neighbours will be envious.'

CHAPTER SEVENTEEN

Harry Penwood, knowing both Mary and of Sir Rowland's intent, watched his oldest friend with a mixture of delight, amazement and a twinge of jealousy, for his own 'matters of the heart' could not be said to be progressing as well. Madeleine Banham always received him with a smile and soft words, but she was a girl whose smile came unbidden, and for whom soft words were normal. Had Lord Cradley not been 'hovering' in the vicinity, he might have thought himself in with a chance, but the man was, and whether intentionally or not, Miss Banham would frequently preface statements with 'Lord Cradley thinks', or 'Lord Cradley says', which was enough to get a fellow in the mood to throttle said peer on sight. Harry had done as Mary had advised, shown himself interested in more than Miss Banham's looks, and genuinely admiring of her other, less visible, charms. He had ridden in to Cheltenham and purchased a piece of music she mentioned hearing sung at a music evening she had attended in the town, and a new sable watercolour brush when she had been so foolish as to leave it on a chair, and her papa had sat upon it and snapped it in two. He was attentive without being toadying, and in fact, she was both flattered and charmed by his devotion.

The problem was that Lord Cradley had a certain something about him, vaguely dangerous, yet never going beyond that which a young and innocent lady might find pleasing. He sometimes praised and adored, and at others seemed vaguely uninterested, which was frustrating and intriguing at the same time. He came to Hazelwood often but ostensibly to see Lord Roxton, and he fell short of 'haunting the place', whatever Sir Harry Penwood felt. Had anyone asked Madeleine Banham if she was falling in love with Lord Cradley she would have said, quite definitely, no, but . . . It was the 'but' which kept her from considering that her youthful heart could happily reside with Harry Penwood.

Lady Roxton had some very private, and none too gentle, words with her spouse, suggesting that he drop Lord Cradley hints that he was knocking at their door too often, and that Madeleine was too young to entertain serious thoughts of marriage.

'But, my love, is that not just what we are doing in the spring, launching her into Society to see her comfortably established? It is but a few months hence and, to be frank, warning the fellow off now would look peculiar. Besides, you have not said I should warn young Penwood off, and he is about the place more than as a casual friend.'

'That is a matter entirely different. There is something about Milor' Cradley that I distrust. You must trust me upon this, *absolument*.'

'Of course I trust you, my dear, but that does not mean I can tell the man to keep away.'

'Why not?'

'Because . . . oh, you do not understand.'

'No, it is you who do not understand. Me, I understand very well that to let a wolf into one's field is bad for the lambs.'

'What? Ah, no, you cannot say he is a wolf.'

'I 'ave just done so.' Lady Roxton could sometimes retreat very neatly behind taking the English language literally, and it was always the point at which her husband gave up trying to persuade her of anything. Despite this, he did not actually go as far as suggesting to Lord Cradley that he need not call as often.

Mary was resolute that she would not cross off the days of Sir Rowland's absence, nor would she mope about the house and show her mama the depth of her regard for the owner of Tapley End. If her mama was still not quite sure if Sir Rowland would offer for her hand, there was also still just a shadow of doubt in her own mind, a shadow cast only by her feeling so certain that he would, yet distrusting that certainty. What did she know of men that meant she could feel this sure that he loved her? Could she not be deceiving herself because he had touched a heart that had effectively lain dormant? When she was with him there was no doubt, could be no doubt, but when alone . . . She did not think he was less than genuine, only that she was misreading matters. Sometimes she told herself it was just that she dreaded being disappointed, for the dream was so wonderful. When he entered the room, it made her heart race; when he smiled at her, it took her breath; when they touched, however briefly, she tingled. Tantalising her was the thought that her life could be spent with him, a life in the only home that she had ever known, since the dower house felt like some hiring, and yet it would be a new life, more exciting and vibrant than the one she had known there in the past.

So she set about practical tasks, preparing for Christmastide, since this year, out of mourning, they would entertain a little, and also making preparations for bad weather. She watched the skies as avidly as Old Matthew, fearing that snow would come early and keep Sir Rowland Kempsey from returning as he had planned. After the gales came rain, but it was so cold that often there was sleet within it. Harry Penwood rode over to see them and arrived with a coat that steamed in the warmth of the hall, and a face that told before he spoke a word that all was not well.

'What has happened, Harry?' Mary frowned in concern.

'Madeleine Banham. All I did was warn her, as any decent man would and . . . she told me it was none of my concern.' He looked both angry and dejected at the same time. 'What can I do?'

'You can explain just what happened, Harry, but first come and sit and get warm, and I will have coffee brought. Mama is in the small parlour and will be delighted to see you, as always.'

Once he had done as she suggested, and been persuaded into a chair by the fire, Mary asked him to start at the beginning.

'I went over to Hazelwood yesterday afternoon. Cradley was there, as so often, and the moment I was engaged in conversation with Lady Roxton he was trying to whisper things in her ear, since her mama was distracted. Calculating, that was what it was. Madeleine did not say anything, but she blushed and smiled. She has no experience of a man of his sort, how could she, and no defences. I do not blame her, of course I do not, but . . .'

'It would be a lot easier,' declared Lady Damerham, 'if a man's character were clear from his looks. Thus, all libertines and seducers would be repellent of form, and unsuccessful.'

This stopped Harry Penwood in full flow, and there was a brief silence, before Mary replied.

'Yes, Mama, I can see that it would simplify matters, but we all know that life is not simple.'

'Young girls should listen to the wisdom of their

parents,' added Lady Damerham, 'for I am sure Lady Roxton will have warned her daughter about cozening gentlemen. A mother knows best.'

This silenced even Mary, who had rarely found her mama's advice even pertinent. The coffee was brought in, and Harry only resumed his tale when the three of them were alone again.

'All I did was say to her, very gently, that her innocence left her vulnerable to the unscrupulous, and she became positively stiff and stern with me. What else should I have done?' He sounded hard done by.

'Kept your own counsel, and left remonstrance to her mother,' said Mary, not unkindly.

'But . . .' He looked both dejected, and a little sulky. 'So I have ruined everything.'

'Not quite, just set yourself back a little. *Nil desperandum*, my dear friend, *nil desperandum*.' With which he had to be content.

Lady Kempsey was in her early fifties, but illness made her look older. She had been a devoted wife who believed her spouse to be right in all things, unless it involved colours, for he had been colour-blind, and had laughingly said that he considered his calling to the Church a great blessing in itself, since he did not have to worry about what he wore each day. In her widowhood she was stoic, bearing both her loss and her infirmity with a quiet acceptance which her children found very moving. It had been her decision to live with her widowed sister rather than be a burden upon her children. Her excuse had been Augusta's proximity to excellent medical practitioners, but deep down all her children knew that their mother had made the decision so as not to trammel them with her ill health, which, when severe, almost confined her to her chair. They were grateful, but guilt-ridden for feeling relieved.

Sir Rowland was a loving son, though he was aware whenever he spent time with his mother his guilt was increased. His mama was also inclined to worry over her 'boys' and was apt to say 'Oh dear, what would your father advise' upon hearing of any decision they had taken. Telling her that he was contemplating matrimony was not, thought Sir Rowland, going to be easy, and he did not broach the topic with her for several days.

When he did so, he enumerated Miss Lound's excellent qualities, commending her good sense and competence, and carefully avoiding any mention that she did not share his mama's belief in male superiority in the least. Lady Kempsey was surprised, though as she said repeatedly, he was 'the right age to marry', which made him think of the Hesiod in the library at Tapley End. However, with such an important decision in life, she was acutely aware that her elder son was making his choice without his father's invaluable guidance, and was therefore agitated. Sir Rowland consoled himself with the fact that his sire would, he was sure, have liked Mary Lound, for all her independence, for she was genuine and honest.

After five days with his mama, Sir Rowland parted

from her affectionately, and went on to London, which he enjoyed more than usual because so much of what he did there was connected with Mary. He even had a list of purchases, which he ticked off as he made them. Sweetmeats from Gunter's was the simplest, and he came away not only with a prettily wrapped box of sugared almonds, but also some Turkish delight, which he thought the ladies in the dower house might not have encountered very often, if at all, and some sugar plums, which he knew his brother would enjoy if they were in the house.

When it came to perfumes, there were plenty of vendors in Bond Street, but he went to the one with which he was familiar, Mr Floris in Jermyn Street, whose emporium was the longest established. It was only once he had entered the portals of the shop that he felt the embarrassment of his situation. A husband might purchase a perfume that his wife or even, if he strayed, his mistress adored, but he was doing so for two ladies with whom he was bound by neither blood nor yet intimacy, and unless he simply asked for lavender water and attar of roses, would be making a wild guess. He cleared his throat rather self-consciously, and began hesitantly.

'I, er, wish to purchase some lavender water and a perfume that would please a lady who favours the scent of roses.'

The assistant gave a small smile.

'Can you give me some further description of the lady,

perhaps, sir?' he enquired. 'It sometimes helps to form an image of what she would suit, though of course her own natural fragrance will subtly alter a perfume.'

'She is young, but not straight from the schoolroom, and likes the fresh smells of outdoors, grass, flowers, that sort of thing.' Sir Rowland did not think adding that she liked to fish would help much.

'Well, sir, if she already shows a preference for the rose, then might I suggest our White Rose? It is a perfume that Mr Floris created with rose at its very heart, but with subtle additions that enhance it, making it more complex than a simple attar of roses. You may detect jasmine and violet, and it has a hint of grassy freshness. Let me show you.' The assistant selected a bottle from the shelf and dipped the end of a narrow strip of good, thick paper into it. He then handed the paper to Sir Rowland. 'There, sir, let your senses take up the fragrance.'

Sir Rowland sniffed, a little gingerly. It reminded him of the scent of Miss Lound up close, but it was not just a bunch of roses under his nose. He imagined her with this perfume clinging to her hair, on her skin, being close enough to him for him to take it in, and his eyes half closed. The assistant, well used to gentlemen 'imagining', did not say a word.

'Yes', said Sir Rowland, slowly. 'Yes, this would please her, I am sure. I will take a bottle of that, and the lavender water.'

Five minutes later, with his purchases carefully

wrapped in tissue paper, and tied prettily with ribbon, Sir Rowland left the shop feeling pleased with himself. He walked up to Piccadilly, and thence into Bond Street, and in New Bond Street saw an advertisement in the window of Mr Phillips' auction offices for a sale the following day. Sir Rowland did not come up to London very often, and this seemed a good opportunity to see if there were any items that he might think suited to Tapley End. He entered, and Mr Phillips, who recognised him by sight even though he was not so frequent a purchaser as to be known by name, greeted him as if the encounter had just enhanced his day.

'We have the contents of an estate coming up for sale tomorrow, sir, and the late Lord Stinsford had a good eye. There are some nice Dutch paintings, and some good bronzes.'

Sir Rowland decided that he might spend a very pleasant hour or so viewing the sale on a cold November day, and surveyed the lots with a critical eye. He was very taken with a van der Neer landscape by moonlight, and could imagine it upon the wall in the yellow saloon. It was only when he had finished inspecting the paintings that he noticed a cabinet containing miniatures, and when he looked down at the images his heart skipped a beat. Among them was one of a man with coppery hair and a neatly trimmed beard, staring boldly from the little oval frame. He was quite young, and dressed in a slashed doublet of green and gold, and was fingering a golden chain which lay upon his breast. In a flowing script it was annotated 'Anno Dom. 1586 and *Aetatis suae* 28'. Beneath the miniature was written 'Unknown gentleman by Nicholas Hilliard'. Could it be Valentyne Lound, wondered Sir Rowland? Date and age fitted, as did the garb. He asked to inspect it more closely, and asked for a magnifying lens. One was brought and he looked at the tiny picture intently, not so much for clues as proof, for he felt instinctively that this was the right man. Seeing a resemblance to Sir Robert Lound was too easily done if one wished to find it, and could not be trusted, but the hand that held the chain wore a gold signet ring. Was it fanciful to think that the marks upon it, tiny as it was, were 'VL'? Sir Rowland tried to clear the excitement from his thought processes. If one added all the evidence together, what chance was there that another copper-haired man, aged eight and twenty, wearing green and gold and fingering a golden chain, had been painted by Hilliard in 1586?

'Is there the provenance to this piece?' Sir Rowland asked, and the porter fetched Mr Phillips.

'A very nice miniature,' announced Mr Phillips, 'acquired by Lord Stinsford from a sale in Cirencester in 1778. He made notes of his purchases, which makes matters so very much easier, though the sitter is, alas, unknown.'

That, thought Sir Rowland, clinched the matter. Whilst an item might have travelled a great distance in over a century and a half, if it was only as far away from Tapley End as Cirencester in 1778, this must be

Valentyne. Perhaps a previous Lord Cradley, or the descendants of his steward, if it was he who had stolen it originally, had chosen to sell and realise its value in money. He thanked Mr Phillips, checked the time of the sale for the morrow, and went away with a feeling of eagerness tempered by the realisation that he could not simply buy the piece at whatever the cost. The estimate he had been given was quite reasonable, but he had seen items he liked reach double the estimate or more in the past. There was also the issue of returning it to Miss Lound. She might jib at him giving it to her as a gift. A bottle of perfume was one thing, but this was another. Could it be an engagement gift? Handing back a lady's ancestor sounded rather outlandish, and a jewel would be more normal. This made him contemplate the jewellers' shop windows in a manner he had not done previously, though nothing particular caught his eye.

He was not a regular attendee of his club, and November was hardly a month in which it was busy, but as he sat by a cheering fireside after dinner, he was hailed by a man he knew, which made for a pleasant evening. Knowing the gentleman spent far more time in the Metropolis, Sir Rowland asked his opinion for the best place to find 'something a bit special' for a lady.

'Rundell and Bridge, my dear fellow. Not cheap, of course, but always the best quality and my mama would not go anywhere else even to have her jewels cleaned.

You will find them in Ludgate Hill. Mr Bridge could sell a blind man a pair of spectacles, and I am sure he flatters the ladies into purchases, but he knows his jewels.'

The next morning, Sir Rowland, who by nature kept country hours and rose early, took a cab to Ludgate Hill and entered the premises of Rundell, Bridge and Rundell, to give them their full name. Having discounted purchasing a ring upon the grounds that he did not know the size of her fingers, Sir Rowland was taken with the idea of a bracelet, and it was these that he asked to see. He knew she wore aquamarines, and there was a very pretty aquamarine and diamond chip bracelet that caught his eye. He was not to be swayed, even by the silver tongue of Mr Bridge, into a bracelet of emeralds, for if she had no other pieces they were too gaudy, and they were also considerably more expensive. Since he wanted to conserve his guineas for the salesroom in the afternoon, he left with a velvet-lined box containing a gift which would not look parsimonious but would not break the bank. Sir Rowland was not a man who spent money without thought and made a point of settling his bills very promptly. A tiny part of him was quite shocked at his own behaviour, dashing about Town expending considerable sums, and upon a lady who was not, as yet, promised to him. The greater part, however, was filled with delight and anticipation of how she would react.

The auction room in New Bond Street was well

attended, but not as crowded as Sir Rowland had encountered on other occasions. He was fortunate in that quite a few present were interested in a Vermeer interior, and after that had been sold they drifted away. It meant that Sir Rowland was able to purchase the van der Neer at the lowest end of the estimate. However, when it came to the miniatures the prices were higher. Sir Rowland hoped that this was because the first three that were sold were of known individuals. It was with a racing pulse that he raised a hand to commence the bidding upon Lot 82. It was apparent from the start that there was one other interested bidder, but of course it only took one to send the price beyond reach. However, at mid-estimate the gentleman shook his head with a small smile, leaving Sir Rowland the poorer in guineas, but the joyous owner of Valentyne Lound's missing portrait. He could imagine the moment he presented it to her already, and there was not a shred of doubt in his mind that she would be speechless with delight.

The post road to Oxford was very good, and by setting out early Sir Rowland was able to arrive in time for a slightly late luncheon. He sauntered to Merton, exchanged pleasantries with the head porter, who remembered him, and then sought out his brother, whom he found looking rather less pleased to see him than he had expected. In fact, Tom looked rather sickly and very sheepish.

'Roly, I . . . I have been an almighty fool.'

Sir Rowland's heart sank, imagining an entanglement

with some young woman of dubious morals.

'You have?'

'Yes. It was Arthur Stirchley's birthday yesterday, and the end of term and . . . We were on the go a bit. Not sure quite how it happened, but we ended up in a gaming house.' He saw his brother wince. 'Yes, I know. Goodness knows I am no gamester by choice, but my wits were not with me, and of course neither was luck, if such a thing exists in such a place. I am afraid I left vowels to the tune of fifty pounds, Roly, and I do not possess that much, not at the end of term.'

Sir Rowland shook his head.

'So you need me to bail you out.'

'Rather. I will pay y—'

'Do not be an even bigger fool, Tom. I am glad you had at least the sense to make a clean breast of it, however much I resent losing the money. It is far easier learning by other people's mistakes than one's own, but we all make them. Your "error" was in getting so foxed you were not able to think, and I doubt you will let yourself go as easily in the future.'

'You can say not. Especially if I want a career in the Foreign Office. One can scarcely lose one's faculties in diplomatic situations. It could cause immeasurable harm.'

'Well, give me the direction and I will go and settle for you. Then hopefully you will be recovered enough to dine with me tonight and we can set off for Gloucestershire in the morning.'

'You do not want me to come with you?'

'No, Tom, I will handle this myself.'

Tom looked both guilty and relieved, and wrote down the address, which he said he had obtained from Mr Stirchley that morning. He also added, rather cryptically, that he had some very important information for his brother, but that it could wait.

Sir Rowland found the gaming den to be an unassuming-looking house, the door of which was answered by a man who had clearly been employed for his bulk rather than his politeness, and who was at first unwilling to let the unknown gentleman over the threshold. When it was explained that he was come to redeem vowels from the previous evening his manner thawed, and Sir Rowland was let in, and shown up to the first floor, where he waited in a chamber that smelt of stale spirits. After some minutes he heard a low-voiced conversation outside in the passage, and then the door was opened by a man perhaps younger than himself, but with marks of dissipation upon his face, and a hastily tied cravat.

'Good afternoon. I do hope I have not disturbed you,' said Sir Rowland, his voice heavy with sarcasm. 'My name is Kempsey, and I have come to redeem the vowels of my brother, who was so unfortunate as to enter this house last night in a state of inebriation.'

'I hold his vowels, but I doubt you have a roll of soft large enough.'

'Indeed? What sum are you claiming?'

'Claiming? Why, what it says upon the paper, five hundred pounds.'

'Show me.'

'Why should I do that?' The man scowled.

'Because my brother does not lie, and he told me the sum was fifty pounds.'

'He was foxed. He did not know what he was doing.'

'Ah yes, and you, despite being "a man of honour", thought him just the lamb to fleece?' Sir Rowland's voice was very even.

'I cannot prevent a young fool from being a fool.'

'Oh, you do yourself an injustice. I am sure you could, really.'

'The sum is five hundred pounds.'

The man withdrew a slightly ragged piece of paper from an inner pocket, being sure to hold it so that Sir Rowland might not be able to snatch it. Sir Rowland laughed.

'No, really, you cannot expect anyone to treat that as genuine. The amount is in numerals and an extra nought has been clearly added in a different hand.'

'He made a mistake and was too drunk to alter it.'

'No, you, my friend, are the one who made the mistake. Even if the cards were not fuzzed, which is debatable, setting up tables where the young men are green as grass and many of them minors is hardly the done thing. I will pay you the fifty pounds, and not a penny more, and if you object, well the university owns the majority of the leases hereabouts. Need I say more?'

The man's scowl became more pronounced.

'No.' He thrust out his hand. Without haste, Sir Rowland drew precisely fifty pounds in notes from his pocket, and gave them to him, at the same time taking the piece of paper on which Tom had scrawled his signature.

'I will not say it is a pleasure doing business with you, sir, for it is not. Good day.' With which Sir Rowland turned and walked out, closing the door behind him, so that should the gentleman seek to rush out and try to push him down the stairs, he would be forewarned. However, he reached the street unscathed, and returned to Merton, where he went to have a quiet word with the Warden.

CHAPTER EIGHTEEN

The brothers returned to Tapley End to discover a number of invitations had arrived for Christmastide parties, since everyone wanted to have some gathering over the twelve days, and Tom, who rather fancied a break from Greek tragedy for a week or so, happily declared they would scarcely have an evening at home, which was an exaggeration, but only a slight one. Sir Rowland was pleased, but mostly because he correctly assumed that those who sent invitations to Tapley End were also sending cards to the dower house, and this would mean he could spend more evenings if not with, then in sight of, Miss Lound. The first part of the month was also showing signs of being socially busy. The Roxtons were holding a ball, one which was designed for Madeleine to make her come out among those she knew, prior to her 'official' come out in the spring. It was only two days hence, being on the feast of St Nicholas, and thus at the beginning of all the December socialising. Lady Roxton had decided it was far better to lead the way than be lost in the middle of a round of engagements, and it meant everyone else's party would have a lot to live up to if it wished to be remembered. Sir Rowland dashed off his acceptance, with the explanation of its tardiness being due to absence, although he was sure that it was well enough known in the district.

He visited the dower house the following day, but found that the ladies had gone to Cheltenham to buy whatever necessities were required for the festive season. It was therefore on the morning of the ball at Hazelwood that he was able to see how the woman he loved had coped with his absence. He was pleased that she did not look wan, and her welcoming smile was all he could have wished. He brought the sweetmeats and perfume, sure that the first would be genuinely appreciated and hopeful for the second. Lady Damerham was cast into transports, for whilst both the confectionery and lavender water could be purchased in Cheltenham or in Gloucester, neither had the cachet of a London name. When it came to the perfume for Miss Lound, he tried to make it clear that the assistant had guided him, but if it was not to her liking he would—

What he would do was never revealed, for she

shook her head as she unwrapped the tissue paper from around the bottle, removing the stopper with care.

'I have never smelt anything like it, Sir Rowland.'

'Is that good or bad?'

'Oh, my dear sir, it is good. This is not simply a scent of roses, for there is more to it, which actually raises the rose within it. Thank you so very, very much.'

'I said you ought to make Sir Rowland some gift, dearest,' Lady Damerham reminded her.

'Yes, Mama, but you were thinking of knitting or embroidery, and I fear anything I presented in that line would be an awful disappointment.'

'You need not fear, Miss Lound. I did not buy you a gift in expectation of reciprocation,' Sir Rowland assured her.

She did not reveal that she had made him a gift, but that it was nothing connected to the contents of a workbox, and she had not revealed it to her mama.

'You are too generous, Sir Rowland,' sighed Lady Damerham.

'But I like you being "too generous",' added Miss Lound, her eyes lit with what he could tell was more than gratitude. If she looked like that at him, he thought, his generosity could be boundless. He smiled at her, but then his face grew more serious.

'There is something that I think you ought to know before the Roxtons' ball, though it is not for public knowledge, as yet. I was hoping you might let Miss

Banham know of it, though I will be advising Lord Roxton.'

'That sounds very serious indeed, sir.' Miss Lound frowned.

'It is. Lord Cradley is a married man.'

'What?'

'He is married, and his wife is with his mother in Bedfordshire, and apparently carrying his child.'

'Good grief!' cried Lady Damerham and put her hands to her cheeks.

'The . . . cur.' Miss Lound's surprise emerged as outrage. 'And there he has been, going about the shire as if he were a single man, no doubt entertaining himself by making up to Madeleine Banham with obviously no honourable intentions, and throwing a rub in the way of decent men like Harry Penwood. I never liked him, but even I would not have thought he would be that bad. How came you by this information, Sir Rowland?'

'Tom overheard a student, who is Cradley's cousin, sneering at the fact that he had married in haste to cover his debts last year, a cit's daughter, straight out of an expensive seminary for young ladies. The poor girl's family were only too pleased to "sell" her to the heir to a title, thinking it would give her position and security. I gather Cradley sent her to his mother as soon as it was clear she was increasing.'

'That is disgraceful. One cannot but feel for the poor soul. No doubt he played his charms upon her and her family whilst he needed to do so, and then, once he had her money, he found her an inconvenience. Well, if he does eventually bring her here, we must try and be welcoming.' Miss Lound looked grim. 'Men have much to answer for.' She saw Sir Rowland wince and amended her words. 'Some men, Sir Rowland. You cannot think I would place you in the same category as Lord Cradley, even if you do catch trees not fishes.' She softened her tone, and a ghost of a smile returned to her. 'I will do my best to speak with Madeleine tonight as early as possible, though I am sure it will diminish her enjoyment of the evening. I would not have her deceived. At least we can be sure that Lord Cradley will be shown in his true colours and the neighbourhood will be in no doubt as to his black-heartedness.'

'He might try to excuse himself on the grounds that his wife is not fit to travel long distances in her condition,' suggested Lady Damerham.

'No doubt he will do so, but that is not an excuse for omitting any mention of her, and going out of his way to appear a bachelor, ma'am. I doubt many doors will open to him hereafter.' Sir Rowland thought the man despicable.

'Thus, the latest Risley has proved true to type.' Miss Lound tossed her head, and her lip curled.

'I am sorry that I had to be the bearer of the information, for it has soured my visit.' Sir Rowland sighed.

'No, sir, "your" visit has been very welcome, and if the message is unpleasant, it is not the fault of the messenger.' Miss Lound held out her hand, and he took it, and clasped it firmly.

'Tonight you will dance with me?' He made it half command, half entreaty.

'Yes, Sir Rowland, if you are that brave, I shall.'

'Then I will leave you ladies to your preparations. Until tonight.'

He left, wondering if she waltzed.

Whilst Mary hoped she would not disappoint Sir Rowland, what occupied her mind most was finding the opportunity to take Madeleine Banham to one side, before she might put Lord Cradley's name on her dance card. As the daughter of the house, she would be in the receiving line. When Madeleine had made her curtsey to Lady Damerham she beamed at Mary, her eyes alight with delight.

'I am so very glad you have come. Everyone is here, all our friends, and Lord Cradley and Sir Rowland and his brother, and although we know everyone it is my first ball and so exciting.' There was nothing false about the degree of her anticipation.

'I am sure everyone will have a lovely evening,' replied Miss Lound, though what she must tell the innocent Miss Banham would tarnish that pleasure. She passed on into the large room created by folding back the panels that divided the morning room from the drawing room. It was already quite full, and she judged that there must be about forty persons present.

It was the sort of evening she could enjoy, since it was small enough for everyone to know everyone else and thus to be at ease, not playing roles, which was how it always felt in large gatherings.

She saw Sir Rowland Kempsey at the far end and with his back towards her. She did not ask herself how it was that she espied him so quickly, but made a conscious effort not to approach him and cause gossip.

'I wonder, ma'am, if your "pupil" will seek entertainment rather than education this evening,' Lord Cradley murmured from just behind her left shoulder. 'Will you dare reprimand him? I am not sure it would be wise.' His drawl was more noticeable than usual, but there was nothing soft about his voice. It was, Miss Lound felt, as though it was shot through with shards of ice, hard, cold, unfeeling. She refused to turn and look at him.

'You are determined to persist in your misconception, sir. Perhaps you think it amusing, but I am sure what amuses you would not amuse most other people.'

'How little you know the world, Miss Lound.' He smiled.

She so wanted to turn and confront him with his perfidy and denounce him in front of everyone, see how 'the world' would recoil from him, but it was not her house, her ball, and making a scene would be unthinkable. She clenched her gloved hands, and Lord Cradley, believing he had scored another hit, smiled the more.

Sir Rowland turned at that moment, but though he saw Miss Lound and her expression, he could not go to her, for he had just seen Lord Roxton enter the room, and he needed to speak privately with him as soon as possible. He made his excuses to the young lady with whom he and his brother were conversing, and worked his way, avoiding any appearance of undue haste, towards his host. Lord Roxton was naturally rather taken aback to receive a request for a private interview at a ball, but seeing Sir Rowland's expression, agreed at once. Ten minutes later it was a host whose outward manner remained congenial, but whose eyes were implacable, who emerged from his library.

It was thus Harry Penwood who 'rescued' Mary from Lord Cradley, who noted the angry look in the young man's eyes.

'Here comes the dependable Sir Harry, in the guise of, yes, a faithful dog. Do you think he will bite me, Miss Lound?' Lord Cradley did not await an answer, but acknowledged the very curt nod he was given with a bow.

'Penwood. What a pleasant evening, and with such a delightful "Belle of the Ball".' He could almost hear Sir Harry's teeth grind, and his eyes narrowed with amusement. 'Now, I really do think I will withdraw and avoid bite marks. Miss Lound, I do hope you find someone to dance with you this evening.' He stressed the 'someone' as though they would be the only one.

'I would rather not dance at all than dance with you, sir.'

'Indeed, ma'am.' He turned away, apparently very amused.

'How dare he—'

'No, really, Harry, I am not hurt by it.' Mary did not want to draw attention, and it was almost true.

'He is quite the centre of attention,' grumbled Harry, glaring after him.

'Well, he has novelty value, and of course some people like to think the "town bronze" will mean he is fascinating. It is just a veneer, though. Never fear, for his true colours, which are those of an adder, will soon be shown. I cannot say more just now.'

'That sounds cryptic.'

'Mmm.' She was glaring at Lord Cradley's back at that moment. 'Poisonous man.' she declared, and reverted her gaze to the honest face of Harry Penwood. 'Did you think I needed rescuing?' An eyebrow was raised.

'Not exactly. I have been practising the boulanger since you reminded me of the steps, so, dear Mary, would you favour me by putting me down as your partner for the first one?'

'So it is perfect before you ask Miss Banham?' She smiled at him, and he blushed.

'No, no. Stop roasting me.' Harry paused. 'You look lovely, by the way.'

'Thank you.'

* * *

Sir Rowland was unable to seek out Miss Lound as soon as he himself returned to the party, for Lady Roxton, in blissful ignorance of what he had said to her spouse, introduced him to a shy young lady as a dancing partner.

Miss Lound watched him dance, and without any pang of jealousy, for which she commended herself, since Madeleine Banham was 'safe', dancing with Mr Potterne, but as the music ended she seemed to disappear into thin air. When Sir Rowland came to her after the dance, Mary Lound looked worried.

'I saw her dancing, Sir Rowland, but now she has disappeared, and I cannot keep asking after her. It would be too obvious.'

'I understand. Instead of you seeking her alone, place your hand upon my arm, and we will look as if we are not looking for anyone, merely moving from room to room, enjoying each other's company.'

'Sir Rowland, I am not just "looking" as if I enjoy your company.'

'I am glad of that, Miss Lound.' As she laid her hand on this arm his other hand was, very fleetingly, placed over hers. She looked up at him, not affronted, just questioning if it was real and not a dream.

Sir Rowland and Miss Lound worked their way around the room, giving every sign of nonchalance, and then into the salon set aside for refreshments.

'She is not here, sir,' murmured Miss Lound.

'No, and what is worse, I have not seen Cradley.'

'She is not so foolish as to slip away alone with him,

surely? She is naïve, yes, but I do not think she is empty-headed.' Miss Lound sounded worried.

'Sadly, ma'am, the art of being a "good" seducer is being able to get decent young women to cast sense and decorum to the winds.'

'You do not think . . . at her own ball . . . ?'

'No, no, but a stolen kiss, a further assignation . . . Miss Lound I have a confession to make.'

'Do not tell me you are a reformed seducer, Sir Rowland, because I will not believe it.'

'Now, is it that you do not believe I could reform, or be a seducer in the first place?' He gave a low laugh.

'The latter sir, as you well know, and because of your character, not a lack of abil—Oh dear, that sounds wrong.'

'I comprehend you, Miss Lound, and thank you.' He was serious once more and revealed his own knowledge of Jasper Risley's 'seductive' past. 'My sister was then fortunate enough to find a very decent man who adores her, and she him, and no harm was done, but when I met Cradley I recognised him. His name I had forgotten, for it was five years ago and we had never spoken.'

'Then all the more reason for us to find Madeleine. There is the orangery, of course. It is small, but I hardly think it would be crowded with lovers in such company as this, where most courtship is done openly and with approval.'

'Then let us try the orangery.'

* * *

Madeleine Banham was confused. She had agreed to Lord Cradley leading her from the main reception rooms because he had pleaded with her so earnestly, and after her second glass of champagne, and buoyed by excitement, her guard was a little down. He was a very charming gentleman, and when he was with one it was hard to see him as duplicitous. He said things which made one feel very grown up and now he was telling her how she would shine out among the ladies being brought out next Season.

He thought he had said enough to make her amenable to a little foray over the bounds of propriety, although he would not go so far as to scare her. One needed patience. He was standing very close to her, and with one hand he took hers and raised it to his lips.

'You are the most captivating young lady,' he purred, letting go of the hand and running the back of his finger down Madeleine's cheek. Her eyes widened in surprise, but she did not back away. That gave him encouragement. His smile lengthened a fraction and he bent his head.

'I hear congratulations are in order, Cradley. Will Lady Cradley be coming into Gloucestershire for her confinement?' Sir Rowland's voice rang clear and, however 'congratulatory', had a distinct edge to it. His words had immediate effect. Miss Banham pulled back, shaking Lord Cradley's arm from her own with a horrified 'How could you?', and burst into tears. Cradley whipped round to see Sir Rowland with Miss Lound upon his arm.

Miss Lound held out her hand to Madeleine. 'Go to your mama and keep your poise as best you can. Nothing happened here.' She spoke softly, and Madeleine, bosom heaving, nodded and half ran from the orangery. Sir Rowland wondered why Miss Lound had not accompanied her.

Cradley's first thought was that it had been Miss Lound who had proved his nemesis, discovering his 'secret', for the enmity with her was thinly disguised, and he had no doubt she, like all women, pried.

'You think yourself so very clever, Miss Lound,' he snarled.

Sir Rowland stiffened, but Miss Lound gave him stare for stare, and then, to the surprise of both gentlemen, stepped forward and delivered a ringing slap to his cheek.

'You, sir, are a cur, and that is from Miss Banham and all decent women. I pity your poor wife.'

For one moment Cradley's face was murderous, and his right arm moved as if he would strike her back, but as Sir Rowland took the first pace to prevent him, he relaxed.

'Miss Lound the hound, was it? All that sniffing about for something detrimental?' sneered Cradley.

'You are under a misapprehension, Cradley. It was I who discovered that you are married, or rather information came to me, and by chance. Miss Lound has not been "sniffing".' Sir Rowland spoke curtly. 'If you wish to pick a fight, make it with me. I am perfectly willing to oblige.' He took another step forward, belligerently.

Miss Lound could sense how close both men were to grappling with each other. She did not think she could part them without also drawing attention to the fracas, so resorted to sarcasm.

'That's right, create even more of an embarrassment. Why not announce it to the entire party and we can watch fisticuffs on the dance floor. I am sure Lady Roxton would be delighted for so unusual an entertainment. It would be talked of for months.' Miss Lound's tongue was equally scathing to both gentlemen. She then turned to Sir Rowland. 'And if you do not solicit me for the next dance I . . . I will not let you fish with a Lound's Lucky when the season begins.' As a threat it sounded, even to her own ears, rather weak.

Lord Cradley looked at her in bemusement. Sir Rowland merely bowed.

'In the face of such a threat, ma'am, what can I do but entreat you to return to the ballroom with me and partner me in the next dance, whatever it may be.'

'Er,' Miss Lound swiftly consulted her dance card, and then blushed. 'It is a waltz, sir. I can waltz but have rarely done so in public.'

He smiled; she was so deliciously honest.

'Then I am especially honoured.' He held out his arm, and she took it, looking up at him, fleetingly, her confidence draining. They ignored Lord Cradley and went back to the sound of the fiddles. A cotillion had ended, and, having waited a few moments so as not to be the first upon the dance floor, Sir Rowland led Miss Lound onto it and placed his hand, lightly, at her waist. He looked down at her, but did not speak until the music began, and they had commenced twirling about the room. Miss Lound was a competent dancer, though he felt her a little stiff. She did not look him in the face but stared somewhere in the middle of his cravat.

'I apologise, Sir Rowland,' she said, just loud enough to be heard. 'It was the only way I thought I could prevent you from knocking him down.'

'Well, I am pleased you were confident that I would do so, and you were probably right. You can be very dictatorial, you know.' He sounded quite casual about it, as though commenting upon the weather. It could even have been described as caressing, but Mary Lound had never had a man speak to her in such a way, and did not hear the caress, only the truth of the words.

'Yes,' she admitted, and if there was a trace of regret it disappeared as she continued, looking up and into his face, 'but in fairness, someone has to manage things, and too often there is nobody else.' Her eyes held a spark of challenge.

'As ever, O pragmatic Miss Lound, you are very right.' He smiled, casting all thoughts of Cradley aside and giving in to how breathtakingly beautiful he found her, especially in a ball gown with very much more Mary Lound visible than when fishing or riding, and this time she did feel the caress.

She had told herself over and over that the sort of falling in love that she saw even Harry Penwood tumble into was not for her, but her heart was betraying her; her body was betraying her. She had ceased to be sensible and pragmatic when it came to Rowland Kempsey. She had not sought love, but love had sneaked in and conquered her. The last few weeks had felt magical, a dream, because his barriers too had been lowered, and she felt love had reached out to love and entwined, and tonight they had been achingly close.

Her thoughts twirled more than the steps of the waltz and suddenly she felt a little sick and very dizzy. A look of panic crossed her face and she went very pale.

'Sir Rowland . . . I am sorry . . . I feel . . . dizzy . . .'

He felt her sag slightly and drew her instantly from the floor and to a chair by a window embrasure, where she sank more than sat. Her head drooped, and for a moment he wondered if she might pass out completely and collapse. He cast a swift glance about the room, hoping to see Lady Damerham, but she was not in view. He wondered if it was indeed the unfamiliarity of revolving, and in a warm room, that had caused Miss Lound's indisposition. She was hardly the weak and feeble sort of female. He leant down and took her hand.

'Can I fetch you a glass of water? I cannot see Lady Damerham . . .'

'In a moment, perhaps . . . please . . . do not leave me just yet.' It was a gasping whisper.

'I will not leave you.' It was a promise, and he did not let go of her hand.

Mary tried to take deep breaths, for that was what

one was meant to do if feeling faint, she remembered. Remembering anything in an ordered way seemed impossible, and the only solid thing in her dizzy world was his hand holding hers. She felt it as though it alone was preventing her from slipping into oblivion.

'Is Miss Lound taken unwell?'

Sir Rowland straightened slightly and found Lord Roxton before them.

'Yes. I believe the twirling of the dance after . . .' Sir Rowland wondered if his host was as yet aware of what had gone on in the orangery, but the look he received gave him the answer. 'It is also very warm with the number of persons. If we could perhaps assist her somewhere cooler and more private?'

'Of course. Miss Lound, let me help you to stand, and Kempsey will be upon your other side. We will have you right as a trivet once you are somewhere quiet.' Lord Roxton actually hauled Mary to her feet, and with the gentlemen supporting her, she went with faltering steps. As she left the room she heard a girlish voice say, 'Poor Miss Lound. She is too old to take up the waltz.'

Once in the passage Sir Rowland, seeing how white she remained, cast propriety to the winds, and lifted her into his arms.

'A chamber with a chaise, my lord, and if we could send for water?'

'Yes, yes of course. Last woman I would expect to faint, you know. Most unexpected.' Lord Roxton led the way to a door which he opened into darkness. 'I will bring a branch of candles. Here, Thomas, fetch a glass of water, and do not dawdle.' He addressed a servant, who was walking past with a tray of glasses, then took a candelabrum from a side table and led Sir Rowland, with his fair burden, into a small room with a sofa and such furnishings as marked it as a chamber where ladies sat cosily to do needlework or read.

'Here, set her down gently, Kempsey. I shall go and find Lady Damerham.' Lord Roxton left them, as Sir Rowland gently settled Miss Lound upon the sofa. Her eyes were shut, but she bit her lip, so was not insensible. She swallowed and took a deep breath.

'I am so sorry . . . never done anything as foolish in my life . . .'

'If this is the most "foolish" thing you have ever done, Miss Lound, I can only commend your inestimable good sense. Lie quietly, and water will be brought directly.' He tried to sound unconcerned and positive, though he was worried about her. There came a knock, and Thomas entered, bearing not only a glass upon a tray, but a full jug of water. Just for a second Sir Rowland wondered if the man was expecting him to throw it over her.

'Thank you. Please leave the door not quite closed, and direct Lady Damerham within as soon as she comes.'

'Yes, sir.' Thomas bowed and withdrew.

'Let me assist you to sit up a little, Miss Lound, and then you can take a little water. It will make you feel very much more the thing.' Sir Rowland poured a glass of water and helped her into a sitting position, setting the glass to her lips. Her hand, shaking slightly, moved to take it, and their fingers touched. He wondered if she could possibly have felt it as he did. She sipped, and then spoke in a less disjointed voice, though a whisper.

'I am sorry,' she repeated. 'What a poor creature you must think me.'

Before he could answer, Lady Damerham bustled into the room, all words and her own tears of concern. Privately, Sir Rowland thought she did more harm than good, but it was right that she should be there.

'It would be best, no doubt, if you took Miss Lound home, ma'am. Let me arrange for your carriage to be brought round, and your cloaks fetched.'

'Yes, yes. Thank you, Sir Rowland. Oh, dear me! My poor girl! She has never fainted in her life before. I do hope it does not presage something serious. Oh dear!'

Sir Rowland left, with Lady Damerham fussing and Miss Lound feebly trying to reassure her, and found that Lord Roxton had already ordered the carriage.

'Seemed best, Kempsey. Poor girl. And as for what happened . . . damnable, despicable. He will be shunned by every decent family in the district.' The insult to his daughter was now uppermost in his lordship's mind. However, he saw Lady Damerham and Miss Lound to their carriage with solicitude, and Sir Rowland withdrew and left him to it. He took a couple of minutes to organise his own thoughts, and went back into the ballroom.

Sir Harry Penwood, ostensibly his normal self, but with glittering eyes, approached.

'Is Mary all right? I was with Lady Roxton and . . .' His voice dropped to an angered whisper. 'I will call him out, damn him.'

'No you will not. Think, man.' Sir Rowland guided him to a corner where there was far less risk of being overheard. 'Nothing happened, do you hear me? Miss Banham has been upset by realising how close she came to something less than discreet, that is all.'

'Yes, but—'

'Undoubtedly, Cradley is as Miss Lound described him to his face, a cur, and she hit him too, by the by, but if Miss Banham has suffered more than a jolt, I would be very surprised. Look at it from her point of view, Penwood. Cradley is a fashionable man of the world who paid her court, lavished attention on her, whether to keep himself from boredom or because he is a rake I neither know nor care, but beyond being flattered, and loving the sensation of the other young ladies all envying her, do you think she really fell in love with him? A man like that? She is too good, and not as feather-headed as many of her age. If you were to call Cradley out, it would make a mountain out of a molehill and the chatter would run that he took more advantage than a few seductive words. Moreover, you are not her brother, and nor are you, as yet, her intended. You will not deny that it is your aim, and so I say listen to my advice. How much better will she feel after this when a man she trusts, and her parents trust, shows her care and attention?'

'She is going to London for the Season in the spring.

Lady Roxton will be seeking a good match for her.' Harry Penwood's rage was melting into despondency.

'From what I have seen, the Roxtons love their daughter very much. You are no pauper, and if she marries you, she will not be disappearing from their lives as she would if she married some fellow hunting for a bride in London. I know which choice I would prefer. Treat her gently, let her see you care, for her and about her, and when she goes to the Metropolis it will be to pick bride clothes.'

'I thought you had little experience of women?' Harry Penwood regarded him with cautious optimism.

'Barely any at all, my dear fellow. If I did, then I doubt I would still be . . .' Sir Rowland halted, and a little colour crept into his cheek.

'Well, it sounds to me as if you have a dashed good idea, and your advice is sound. Thank you. I am not one normally to charge pell-mell like a hothead.' Sir Harry held out his hand and Sir Rowland shook it. 'If it is of any use to you, since I have known Mary Lound since before I was breeched, I have never seen her this way. Not fainting, I mean, but for a reason I never thought to see. Good luck, not that you need it.'

CHAPTER NINETEEN

Sir Rowland came to the dower house the following afternoon, despite a strong and biting cold wind, and appeared very much the friendly neighbour, eager to make sure that the ladies had everything set in store should the weather deteriorate further. He engaged Lady Damerham in conversation for a full ten minutes, before he turned to Mary, and their gaze met and held. The little creases at the outer aspect of his hazel eyes, and the warmth within them, the gentleness in his voice, gave her a colour the warmth of the fire could not.

'I am glad you are recovered from last night, Miss Lound. Being overcome by the heat is not, as you seem to believe, some sign of an inherent weakness in character. There is no shame in it.'

'Perhaps you could not imagine a woman who could

be "dictatorial" being so feeble, though, Sir Rowland?' She just had to know.

'I apologise if that remark was taken seriously.' He frowned. 'What you did, both in chastising Cradley, and taking us both to task for letting our male instincts override good behaviour, was completely correct, and I admire you for it, as I do your other qualities.' It was not flattery, nor was it praise, but his deep feeling.

'At least that would be a short list, sir,' she managed, with an attempt at making light of his words, and blushed the more.

'We must have differing definitions of short.' He watched her and noted that her breathing was a little fast. She could not be under any illusions from now on, however much she put herself down. He would let her recover her equilibrium. 'Are you ladies attending the Lissetts' musical evening on Friday? I believe Tom is hoping to sing a duet with Miss Banham, but I get the feeling that Penwood will beat him to it. Alas, poor youth, he will have to wait a few years before a young lady casts him soft looks.'

'Will Miss Banham attend, do you think?' asked Lady Damerham.

'I doubt her parents would permit her to cry off unless genuinely unwell. She did reappear at the ball, after supper, upon the excuse that the flounce of her gown had been trodden upon and it had taken some time to repair. Penwood was at her elbow much of the time, and later she danced with him, Tom, and a couple of other young sprigs she has known since they were in short coats. I have hopes that only we, the Roxtons and Penwood know what happened, or more accurately, what did not happen. She was indiscreet enough to be persuaded, we do not know by what words, to be alone with the man, and no doubt he would have kissed her, given the chance, but that chance was denied. She was obviously upset at the revelation of his perfidious character, and at her own behaviour, but it amounts to nothing.'

'What do you think Lord Cradley will do now, Sir Rowland?' asked Miss Lound.

'If he has any sense, he will absent himself and return to his wife and parent for Christmas, and bring the latter back here, her condition permitting, either in the New Year, or after her confinement. As you said, the wife will be treated with compassion, and that in itself might mean Cradley is accepted back into local society, though not made warmly welcome. Most people will forget he seemed to be courting Miss Banham and be aggrieved only that he duped them by omission by failing to announce his marital state.'

'I would not have him cross my threshold,' declared Miss Lound.

'You will not be required t—I doubt he would accept, for fear of you.' Sir Rowland it was who coloured this time, having begun to reply instinctively, imagining her as Lady Kempsey. His invitation to dinner on Christmas Eve was thus slightly rushed, but accepted with every sign of pleasure. 'Now, I wish to leave before the dusk, lest I trip over some fallen branch upon my walk back to the house.' He stood and would have bowed over the hands of both ladies, but even as Lady Damerham pulled the bell for Atlow, Miss Lound moved towards the door also, offering to show him out herself. He opened it, and she passed out of the room before him. The hall was empty, and more dimly lit than the parlour. They could hear Atlow's faint groans as he ascended from below stairs with arthritic knees. Sir Rowland took her hands, swiftly, and squeezed them, leaning so that she felt his breath upon her cheek.

'I have no doubts,' he whispered, near her ear. 'None.' As he straightened, his lips brushed her cheek, so delicately she might have imagined it. 'It is a shame the weather is so inclement,' he said, his voice raised to normal as Atlow approached. 'If by chance it does improve, I do hope you will ride with me, Miss Lound. I fear the winter will keep our mounts stable-bound for much of it.'

'Indeed, Sir Rowland. We must take advantage of whatever chances are given to us.'

Was she implying something more than the obvious? He thought she was. Christmas Eve could not come quickly enough.

There were but two opportunities to ride, and both required that the horses keep up a reasonable pace to keep warm. On each occasion, Mary returned to the house with pink cheeks, but since her nose was also rather pink, Lady Damerham did not assume Sir Rowland had been paying her excessive attentions. The realisation that Mary was very likely to receive a proposal of marriage had grown slowly in her mind, since she had so long been convinced otherwise, but these last few weeks it had become evident to her that it was only a matter of time. She did wonder why that period of time was being drawn out, but no doubt Sir Rowland had his reasons. She said nothing to Mary, who had not developed the habit of dropping his name into every possible conversation, or shown other 'maiden in love' traits, but who was noticeably happier, except when thrown into unexpected dejection. These swings of mood were, Lady Damerham felt, symptomatic of her emotional state.

The musical evening was one where Mary Lound was very content to listen, and to sit just in front of Sir Rowland, aware of his presence as if it gave off an aura that encompassed her. She thought that not sitting beside him would avoid wagging tongues, and was quite relieved that the gossip was about Lord Cradley's 'invisible' wife.

Madeleine Banham was present, and if she looked a little reserved and shy, most thought it was from nervousness at performing before quite so large an audience. As Sir Rowland had surmised, Harry Penwood was in close enough attendance for it to be noted, not least by other admirers, and when she took to the pianoforte to play, it was he who was instantly available to turn the pages for her. However, when it came to her singing, she asked if Mr Kempsey would sing with her, which made Tom blush with pleasure. Sir Rowland did notice however, the look that Miss Banham cast Sir Harry before she did so, a look which he thought asked permission. He was, he felt, learning at last to 'read' unspoken female messages, even if he sometimes mistranslated. Lady Roxton, also noting the look, smiled to herself.

Lord Roxton had been convinced that his wife would be as every match-making mama, and eager for her daughter to marry, if not a duke, since they were in short supply, at the very least a viscount. He himself simply wanted her happy and content, and decently established.

'My dear, if young Penwood is as serious as he appears . . .'

'I would not say the word against it.'

'You would not?' Lord Roxton had sounded amazed.

'*Naturellement*, I wish for the best for Madeleine, but the best need not be the highest rank. 'E would be always the caring 'usband, would be steady, and we would not "lose" *la Petite*, for she would be so close.'

'So if – and I say if – he should request permission to pay his addresses, you would not mind?'

'That is what I 'ave been saying.'

His lordship smiled.

'You are always right, my dear.'

'This I know.' She smiled back at him.

Christmas Eve was a busy day in most residences, with the greenery being brought into decorate stairs, beams and mantelshelves in garlands and swags, and at Tapley End there was plenty to decorate. Mrs Peplow was in charge, having seen to the preparations for many years, and all ran smoothly. Sir Rowland wandered about the house like a restless ghost, which made that dame mutter under her breath that gentlemen had a nasty habit of getting under one's feet. He had invited the ladies from the dower house over early, so that the fire in the huge fireplace in the great hall could be lit as the darkness fell. It was his intention to show Miss Lound the portrait of Valentyne and then lead into his declaration, and hopefully the excitement would not diminish appetites for the dinner over which Cook was slaving below stairs.

He greeted his guests in the great hall and showed off the large portion of a tree trunk that had been set over carefully positioned kindling wood in the hearth, but he only had eyes for Miss Lound. When she divested herself of her thick and serviceable fur-trimmed cloak it revealed her in the dress of pomona green that he admired the first time she had come to dine, but on this occasion, though it was not a ball, she was wearing the emeralds from her grandmother, which sparkled in the soft golden glow of the candles, already lit to ameliorate the afternoon gloom.

'You look beautiful,' he said, simply.

'Thank you, sir. I admit the emeralds are a little excessive for a dinner, but it is a special one.'

He hoped it really would be so, and not for the reason she imagined. He also realised he might have bought the emerald bracelet after all, despite the cost, since she possessed both necklace and earrings.

'You do think them too grand?' she asked, for he was staring a little.

'No, oh no. I am sorry, I was thinking of something else.' He realised that was not very complimentary, and added hastily, 'That is, seeing you with such stones, which look glorious on you, I was reminded of a jewel I saw in London, in a shop window. It was very eye-catching, upon a bed of velvet, but not nearly as much as seeing emeralds upon your sk—person.' He was digging himself a hole and knew it. 'Forgive me.'

'Of course. You were distracted . . . by green gemstones. They are rather fine and belonged to Grandmama.'

'You enhance them.'

'You are in a complimentary mood, Sir Rowland.'

'I am.'

At this moment Tom Kempsey, entered the hall, apologising for his tardiness and blaming a recalcitrant cravat.

'Not recalcitrant fingers and thumbs, Mr Kempsey?' Mary smiled at him.

'Well, those generally do as I command them, ma'am, so the blame has to lie with the muslin. Has my brother shown you his new picture? He is very pleased with it, at least I am pretty sure he is, for he asks me to admire it every time I walk past it.'

'I am not sure you deserve mulled wine, Tom,' remarked Sir Rowland, 'though at least you arrived before the fire is lit. You will take a glass, Lady Damerham?'

'Yes, I will. Thank you.'

'But what painting, Sir Rowland? I am intrigued.' Mary, ignoring refreshment, looked at him.

'I will show you. It is on the wall in the yellow saloon. Would you care to see it also, Lady Damerham?'

To his great relief, her ladyship, denying all knowledge of art, said she would be very comfortable with her wine, and Mr Kempsey to entertain her, thereby giving the couple carte blanche to be alone for a few minutes. She had a feeling it might be 'useful'. Sir Rowland therefore led Mary to the yellow saloon, where he studied her while she studied the picture.

'I like it very much,' she said, after careful inspection.

'Mmmm.'

'I have never seen a painting using moonlight before. You would think it would make things indistinct in places, but he has used the play of it to such good effect. What is the name of the artist?'

'Artist?' He had been thinking how well she carried herself, the way she kept her chin raised.

'Yes, sir, the person who painted the picture.' She

turned and saw him looking at her in such a way that she felt warm all over. 'You were not paying attention to me.'

'I was, I promise. Just . . . not to what you actually said. How could I look at mere art when you are so close to me?'

'Have you been thinking up nice things to say all afternoon, Sir Rowland?'

'No. It is just that at this moment I feel free to say them. It has not previously been the right time, or the right place. It is now, in this house that still feels yours, on Christmas Eve.' He reached for her hand, and his fingers entwined with hers. 'We have a few precious moments alone. Mary I . . .'

She stepped so close their bodies touched, and placed a finger to his lips for an instant, then removed it and lifted her face to his.

'Then no time for words,' she whispered, and, with great daring, she offered herself for his kiss. There was no rush, no indecent haste of passion. His lips met hers and his free hand went to her cheek. It was as if all five senses colluded in that kiss, for he could taste her, touch her, smell her, see her through half-closed eyes, hear the soft sound she made that was part sigh, part sob. It was everything he wanted, and yet but the tip of the iceberg. They lingered, savouring, committing every sensation to memory, for since the season meant that they must perforce meet indoors, being completely alone together would be rare and had to be treasured. They parted, slowly, and stared at each other. There was silence, silence in which he thought he could hear as well as feel his own heartbeat as they descended from a private alt.

'Moments well spent,' he murmured, and she nodded. 'You asked me a question.'

'The artist? It would be embarrassing to be asked and not know.'

'Van der Neer. I like the picture even more now, by its association.'

'We ought to return to the hall.'

'Yes,' his hand slid from hers, 'we ought.'

When they entered the hall, Lady Damerham was disappointed, for she expected an announcement and tears and smiles. It was a remarkably composed couple who came in, discussing landscape painting. What was the point, she thought, of giving them time together if they did not use it profitably?

Tom Kempsey, who was rather more astute at reading people, and especially his brother, did not think for one moment that it had not been 'profitable'.

Sir Rowland went to the fireplace and took a piece of wood from the mantelshelf. He had got the head gardener to find a branchlet and turn the end into a feather stick that would catch easily and could be applied to several points beneath the great log. Mary thought there was an almost schoolboy excitement to him. He handed Mary the feather stick and struck flint and steel and lit it for her.

'There, Miss Lound, you embody the history of this

house, so you lighting the yule log is the continuity we need.'

'I am here to bring good luck, Sir Rowland?'

'I think you are good luck,' he answered, quietly, and smiled at her.

Blushing, she pushed the burning feather-stick into the kindling, and Sir Rowland set the footman to watch the fire and ensure it was kept alight long enough for the log to begin to burn.

'And now, Miss Lound, I have something to show you that I think will surprise you.' He drew from his pocket a box, but it was not the velvet case for a jewel. He removed the lid. 'Show me your palm.' She obeyed, and he withdrew something small and oval from tissue paper and laid it on her extended hand. 'He is home, Miss Lound.'

Sir Rowland did not say who 'he' was, but Mary stared at the tiny portrait and then gave a strange squeak.

'It is Valentyne! It is, surely it is. Oh, Sir Rowland, where . . . ? How . . . ?' Her eyes pricked with sudden tears, and she held the portrait to her bosom for a moment.

'Serendipity, I have to admit. I went to an auction in New Bond Street, where I picked up the van der Neer, and there was a small collection of miniatures. They all came from a collector near Cirencester. I cannot believe that Hilliard would have painted another young man that year, of that age, with that hair and in those clothes. From the description in Sir Robert's letter, I am certain this is Valentyne. Seeing a resemblance might be going a bit far but . . .'

'It is him. I see it, and feel it. This is so wonderful, having him back in the house. Valentyne, returned at last.'

'I was hoping,' his hand took her free one, 'that he might be mine too, by marriage. Will you do me the great honour, Miss Lound, of—'

There was a sudden interruption, a heavy knocking upon the door and insistent tugging of the bell. It was the worst possible time for it to happen, but it disrupted Sir Rowland's flow and all eyes went to the door. 'Answer it, man,' admonished Sir Rowland, looking to the fire-watching footman. The footman bowed and went to the door, opening it to admit a heavily caped figure in a low-crowned beaver hat.

'What sort of welcome is it when a man returns for Christmas and finds his nearest and dearest have gone to . . . Good God!' The man stared at Sir Rowland.

'Edmund, my dear son!' cried Lady Damerham, spilling wine from her glass as she leapt to her feet and rushing to throw herself upon his chest.

'Oh no,' moaned Mary, 'not him.'

'So you are Damerham. How extraordinary,' said Sir Rowland, calmly.

'You have met?' Mary looked from her brother to Sir Rowland.

'In Oxford. In a gaming den. You told me your brother had gone abroad. He does not appear to have got very far upon that journey. Perhaps he decided it was more profitable fleecing minors at cards.' Sir Rowland's voice was very level.

'He . . .' She closed her eyes, and then turned slowly to stare at her brother. 'Was it indolence, or was it shame?' she asked, scathingly.

'It is none of your concern,' responded Lord Damerham, crisply.

'But Edmund, you were so set upon going away from England.' His mother looked a little confused, however pleased she was to see him.

'I only got as far as Ireland. I was vilely sick, if you must know, and disembarked in Cork when the ship stopped there to pick up more passengers.'

'So it seems you did inherit at least one thing from your Lound ancestors,' noted Mary, unimpressed.

'I do not like your attitude, miss.'

'And I do not like to have a card sharp as a brother,' she came back at him.

'There is nothing wrong with gambling for money. It is perfectly gentlemanly,' he said, a little defensively.

'Well, you used to lose, consistently, so either you improved very suddenly, or you prey upon those even less skilled than yourself, and if it is youths fresh from school then shame upon you. There is no honour in that.'

'Stop talking to me as if you were my father.'

'Well, even he would have drawn the line at fuzzing the cards.' She had lost her temper. At the very moment when her life was about to change, when a new dawn beckoned, here was the past, disreputable, and making her feel besmirched by association.

With no answer to this, Lord Damerham changed tack.

'What I want to know is why you and Mama are here, of all places.'

'Because they were invited.' Sir Rowland did not sound best pleased either. He was aware that his carefully planned proposal had been ruined. He did not doubt that whenever he did ask her, Mary Lound would say yes, but this had been a perfect setting in time and occasion, and it was lost.

'I am head of the family, and I demand that you both come home.'

'Until you sold it over our heads this was our home,' Mary reminded him.

'I mean the dower house. I do not want you . . . consorting with these men, men who offer nothing but insult, and do so from what ought to be ours, were it not for mischance.'

'I can see you are doomed to disappointm—' began Sir Rowland but stopped suddenly as Lady Damerham burst into tears.

'Mama?' Mary, however unwilling to be close to her brother, stepped away from Sir Rowland, and put her hand out to her mother, as that lady lifted her head from her son's chest.

'I cannot bear it,' she cried. 'I cannot bear you to be at odds like this.' She sounded on the verge of hysterics. 'He is safe, not eaten by bears.' That this was a possibility had not occurred to Mary, or indeed her brother, who looked suitably surprised.

Mary looked over her shoulder at Sir Rowland, beseeching him to understand.

'I . . . I should get her home,' she said, very quietly. 'It is with the utmost regret that I . . . we . . . cannot remain to dine, Sir Rowland. Forgive me.'

'I will call for your carriage.' His eyes did not leave her face. 'It is unfortunate that the evening has been curtailed, but it changes nothing.' He needed her to know that.

'Thank you. Keep Valentyne here for me, will you?'

'Yes.'

Their cloaks were brought, and Sir Rowland himself set hers about her shoulders. It gave him the chance to whisper in her ear.

'I am here for you also. Neither of us will wait long.' She was not quite sure whether he meant himself and Valentyne, or them as lovers, for since they loved each other, that was what they were.

When the door closed upon them, Sir Rowland, grim-faced, turned to face the now merrily burning fire.

'Damn.'

'What do we do now, Roly?' asked Tom.

'We eat dinner.'

Christmas morning was not filled with goodwill. The atmosphere was tense, and Lady Damerham talked incessantly, hoping that whilst her progeny could not get a word in edgewise they would not be able to fight. The return of the prodigal son was traditionally greeted with joy, feasting and the killing of the fatted calf, noted Mary, sarcastically, but in the dower house there was a modest roasted goose, which they were intending to make last for several days, and they could not afford a feast. Her brother looked daggers at her.

When the family went to church, her smouldering anger turned to acute embarrassment. Lord Damerham, with his mother leaning upon his arm, and his sister several paces behind, stalked into the church as though he owned it, and processed up the aisle, to the gasps and whispers of the rest of the congregation, without looking to right or left. He went straight to the box pew, despite Lady Damerham whispering that they could not use it. Mary was left either having to follow within or to turn away and take her usual place in the open pews of the nave.

'This is not ours,' she hissed, as he closed the door of the pew behind them.

'Of course it is. It is the Damerham pew.'

'It is the pew for the lord of the manor, for Tapley End, and you gave up the right, and the advowson, remember, when you sold it.'

'Mere semantics.'

'Truth, Edmund. What will happen when Sir Rowland and his brother arrive?'

'They can sit out there.' Damerham was dismissive.

'No, they will not.' Mary was outraged, and then caught the sound of a voice she recognised and loved. In contrast to Lord Damerham, Sir Rowland entered the church, acknowledging the parishioners as they nodded or dipped in respect, wishing 'Happy Christmas' to them and, when he saw that Mrs Shaw was cradling a swathed bundle which indicated she had been safely delivered of her seventh child, he halted, shook Nathaniel Shaw warmly by the hand in congratulation, and gave a half-crown to the new mother. The contrast to Damerham was stark. Eyes watched as he went to take the lord's pew, wondering what would happen. As he drew close, he could see it was occupied, but his expression did not change. He entered, with Tom Kempsey right behind him, and smiled at Mary.

'Happy Christmas,' he said, and sat down, facing her. 'How nice of you to join us.' He looked delighted. In truth he was thinking how wonderful it would be having Mary in the pew every week, by right, and accepted that it would seem churlish to leave Lady Damerham isolated in the main part of the church.

'What are you doing?' spluttered Lord Damerham, in an angry whisper.

'Attending Matins.'

Mary found it hard to concentrate upon the service, being prey to such tangled emotions. She was outraged by her brother, shamed by him, and at the same time thrilled by Sir Rowland's proximity, and the fact that, when their eyes met, so much was communicated. At the conclusion of the service, Damerham rose swiftly, wishing to take precedence and lead, with his mother beside him. Sir Rowland did not prevent him, but smiled at Mary and offered her his arm. She hesitated a moment, and then walked down the aisle at his side, with Mr Kempsey in their wake. She wondered if the next time she did this it might be as a bride.

They parted at the lychgate, and her day diminished. When she arrived back at the dower house she went to her room, and remained there until luncheon, writing a letter which she gave to Atlow with instructions that it be sent up to the house before dark.

When Sir Rowland received it, he opened it with care, and read it several times.

My dear Sir Rowland,

Never have I begun a letter and meant the appellation so truly.

Yesterday was almost perfect, ruined at the last by the untimely arrival of Damerham. I know what you were about to say, and you know what my response would have been, for my behaviour in the yellow saloon was proof of my feelings.

I am confident that Damerham has returned only for the Christmas period, since it means no expense for him, and he has revealed that he will not be returning to Oxford but hoping to try 'his luck' in Cambridge. It appears that the college that owns the lease of the house in which he conducted his business has revoked it, since they let it out as a dwelling, not a gaming house. He blames you for this, and I do hope he is right. During his sojourn it will be difficult to meet, and I beg you not to come here, for it would be most awkward for Mama. He has no power to forbid me seeing you, but I am thinking of her in this, not us.

You said that nothing has changed, but use this time to consider. I would not see your name tarnished by association. You are not bound, for no offer was made, and allying yourself with my name would link you to a man who seems capable of bringing nothing but shame and embarrassment to his family. He would almost certainly try to get money from you at some point.

If you remain firm in your wish you will find me, dearest sir,

Yours,
Mary Lound

He was torn between delight and frustration. They might meet only at the houses of neighbours for the next couple of weeks, and he felt she was trapped in a house where she was not happy, for it was clear that she and Damerham were at odds and she was concerned for her mother. At the same time the short letter exuded her love. There was nothing to consider, and all he must do was bide his time.

CHAPTER TWENTY

Sir Rowland's hopes of even meeting upon neutral ground were dashed two days later when he awoke to a sky thick with snow that was coming down in a blizzard, and with already six inches of it outside the house. All thought of travelling was set aside, and the yule log in the great hall that could have warmed a throng, could cheer but the two Kempsey brothers and the servants as they went about their tasks. There seemed no end to the heavy flakes, and for two days the snow deepened until over two feet, and then the wind began to move it into drifts reaching the height of a man's shoulders. It was bitterly cold. The farmers struggled out to rescue sheep, and Sir Rowland, faced with a siege of snow, gathered the male servants, donned the garb he had last worn for fishing, and led them out to at least clear a path the width of a horse to the gatehouse. He recalled the prognostication of Old Matthew and saw no reason to think the snow would melt away within days. He warned Tom that returning to Oxford for the beginning of term would be impossible, especially across the tops of the Cotswolds. A total cessation of all movement in the community could not last for long, however. Each household did what it could, and from the viewpoint of the crows scouring the landscape for animals that had succumbed to the weather, little tendrils of cleared pathways spread slowly but surely, linking house to house where neighbour checked upon neighbour, and, after a week, some villages could be reached by a cart pulled by a heavy horse.

Sir Harry Penwood, who had survived the retreat to Corunna under Sir John Moore, was not put off by a couple of feet of English snow, nor wedded to sartorial elegance. He was one of the first to re-establish communication with the dower house, and also with Hazelwood, where his reception was nearly as warm. Madeleine slipped easily from finding him a support to a feeling of reliance. She liked the feeling, and when the weather had kept them apart for nearly a week, missed him. If she was not in love with him, she was aware of increasing affection, and a willingness to love.

Twelfth Night came and went with far less festivity than had been planned, and Mary's hope that her brother would leave came to nothing. Even she admitted that this was unavoidable. Travelling long distance was impossible, and there were new heavy snowfalls, but gradually the community began to function a little more normally, despite the white world. Sleds were constructed, wood was brought to old neighbours who could not get about, church services resumed, for the vicar had been unable to even reach the church door from his own the first Sunday, and if the congregation was the thinner, they prayed fervently enough for all. An old man died, and the sexton was unable to dig a grave, the ground being frozen solid, and the vicar was in great perturbation as to what should be done. When Mary heard, she sent a note to him, suggesting that as a temporary measure, the service take place and the coffin be placed in the Lound family vault, if church protocol permitted that it might be moved and interred in the earth when that became possible. The vicar was most relieved, but when Damerham was told what she had done there was an almighty row, for he said she had no right to give permission, and he would not have illiterate yokels in the resting place of the Lounds. Mary replied that something had to be done, since the coffin could not remain in the house, or on view in the church, and nobody knew when the churchyard would be usable again.

'Besides, illiterate he may have been, but Jethro Fleet was at least honest. I cannot think our ancestors would begrudge him a few weeks in their company. His ancestors were their tenants, and they understood responsibility as you do not, for all you think of is your rights.' She stalked off in high dudgeon, and there was a stony silence between the siblings for two whole days.

When Harry called upon them a second time he found Mary at the end of her tether, sharp-tempered even with him.

'I am sorry, Harry,' she apologised. 'It is being cooped up, and with Edmund. I have not been outside this house for over two weeks, nor parted from him by more than a few walls. Mama panics if I as much as suggest riding out. Added to which . . .' She bit her lip. 'Have you been to Tapley End?'

'No, but I saw Kempsey and his brother two days ago, going to as many of the tenant farmers as they could, seeing the situation for themselves. Has he not come to—'

'He will not come while my brother is here.' She coloured, and then told him about Oxford. Harry was horrified.

'Poor Mary.' As his own romantic life was showing signs of flowering, he saw that hers had become, like the ground, frozen. 'Let me see what I can think up to help.'

'There is nothing that can be done while the weather is bad,' sighed Mary, resignedly.

'Do not be too sure.'

Harry was not idle. He went to Tapley End, and then on to Hazelwood, and the next day, as if to confirm he was doing the right thing, a pale sun pierced the clouds, and as the morning advanced there was even the occasional drip from the end of an icicle. Harry arrived at the dower house in company with Miss Banham, who was otherwise unescorted, which surprised Mary.

'We need you, Mary, to come skating with us. I know you used to have skates, and, as I recall, you fell over less often than James or I did.'

'Skating?'

'Yes. It will do you good to get out. Wrap up warm, find your skates, and be adventurous. Besides, if you do not do so, I will have to escort Madeleine straight back to Hazelwood, for there is nobody else who could, er, act as chaperone.'

'Harry, really.' Mary laughed for the first time in days, and noted he was on first name terms with his companion. 'I just hope my ice skates can be located.' She left the pair to converse with Lady Damerham, since her brother had slunk off in a huff upon hearing the familiar voice in the hall. He did not much like Penwood, and the feeling was mutual.

Mary dressed in a hurry, with a fur tippet about her throat and a thick cloak over her riding habit, and a fur hat that was not as new as Madeleine's but just as warm. She felt excited, and was the more so when Harry led them not, as she had vaguely supposed, to the river, but up the drive to Tapley End.

'We are going to skate on the lake,' he announced. 'It is all arranged.'

They were met at the house by Sir Rowland and Tom, who looked very pleased to see them. Harry Penwood had brought two extra pairs of ice skates, since Sir Rowland admitted to being so thoughtless as to not have ever purchased any.

'Which means I am very likely to embarrass myself and give you the opportunity to laugh at my tumbles.'

'You must let Mary guide you, then, Kempsey. She was always very good.' Harry laughed.

'I might at that. Will you save me, Miss Lound?' Sir Rowland looked at her, and her smile was all the answer needed.

Reaching the frozen lake meant traversing virgin snow, but Harry and Tom gallantly offered to lead the way and trample a path as best they could so that the ladies did not have snow reaching up under their skirts. At the edge they attached their skates, and Harry led the slightly nervous Madeleine Banham onto the ice. She had not skated for several years.

'The art, Sir Rowland, is to keep moving, and glide. Observe.' Mary set off slowly, feeling a little odd skating in her riding dress, but moving smoothly.

'My fear is that if you assist me, and I slip, I will bring you down also.'

'I am not afraid. Come along.'

If his first few steps were wobbly, and he flailed once or twice, he soon grew in confidence, and Tom, who had skated on the frozen Cherwell in his first year at Oxford, was not in need of coaching. They performed several circuits about the edge of the lake, the activity giving them pink cheeks. Madeleine forgot her fears and became quite giggly, daring Harry to go faster. She could certainly glide very elegantly, and weave about prettily. In a moment of gay abandon, she commanded him to try and catch her, and set off on a meandering course closer to the centre of the lake. She was teasing him and then suddenly her voice became a scream, and the ice gave way beneath her.

'Madeleine,' yelled Harry, and would have immediately dashed to her, but Mary halted him.

'No, no! You will go in also and break a larger hole. You are heavier.' She turned to Tom Kempsey. 'Get to the boathouse, for there should be rope in there, a painter at the very least.' She cast her cloak aside. 'I will go forward and try to grab her hands to at least keep her head above water.'

'But she will freeze.'

'Not as soon as she will drown.' Mary skated a little closer, then went down on her knees and thence lay upon the ice, edging forward. Madeleine had disappeared twice already, and Mary was very frightened. A hand reached up, a hand clawing at air, and Mary made a grab for it, even as she felt the ice beneath her tremble. She pulled the arm, and Madeleine's white face appeared above the dark water, but Mary felt very insecure.

'Grab my ankles, in case the ice gives way,' she cried, and a minute later strong hands grabbed her boots. 'Hold on, Madeleine. You will be safe.' Mary willed her to hold on to consciousness as much as her hand. The icy water was already chilling her bosom as it came over the sagging ice beneath her own person. She prayed Tom Kempsey was swift. She heard his voice.

'He is coming,' came Sir Rowland's voice from behind her.

'Wait,' cried Harry. 'Make a loop in the rope. She will be too cold to grip it with her hands.'

There was muttering, but Mary could not look over her shoulder. She was watching Madeleine too intently, and when one hand let go of her and a length of rope appeared at her shoulder, she was almost surprised by it. Manoeuvring the loop one-handed was not easy, and she realised that looping it as she had imagined, about Madeleine's body, was impossible to achieve. She therefore worked it about her wrists and pulled it tight. Her gloves might protect the skin a little, and if there were rope burns, well, that was the least harm there could be.

'Pull,' she shouted. 'Pull now.'

The rope tensed.

'You must edge back or the combined weight will have you both in.' It was Sir Rowland, his voice urgent. He pulled upon her ankles, and she felt herself move back as the ice cracked and complained and Madeleine was dragged onto the icy surface. After a few feet Mary tried to kneel up, though she was shaking, and turned to see Harry and Tom, skates discarded, trying to keep a purchase on the ice as they pulled. At least once

Madeleine was flat upon the ice she slid more easily, and as soon as she was far enough from the hole, Harry let go of the rope and scrambled to her.

'It will be safer and quicker to pull her than carry her,' warned Sir Rowland, himself coatless, and added his hands to his brother's. It looked heartless, but he was right. Mary, on all fours, slid and crawled to her cloak. Getting up on her feet felt impossible. As she saw Madeleine near the bank, she called to Sir Rowland to wrap Madeleine in her cloak. He came to her, and took it, as Harry Penwood, now distraught, begged Madeleine to speak, and lifted her up.

'Tom. Get to the house, and have Mrs Peplow have a fire lit in a guest chamber and the sheets warmed. Swiftly now.' Sir Rowland assisted Harry to drape the cloak about the pallid figure, and went back to Mary, who was shivering as much with reaction as cold. He helped her up, and then even as she protested, placed his own coat about her shoulders. 'You too must get warm,' he said, firmly, and his arm went about her. Her knees buckled a little, and he would have picked her up, but she objected, for they would make better speed if both were on foot.

'And I do not wish to be dropped in the snow, sir,' she managed, then paused. 'Is she breathing?' The question was whispered.

'Yes,' he answered.

* * *

It seemed to take a long time to reach the house, and Mary was focused upon placing one foot before the other, and on the secure arm about her waist. The warmth of the house was sudden and made her feel dizzy. She swayed a little.

'I will have a bed prepared for you also,' decided Sir Rowland.

'No, no, I will be better directly.'

'You cannot remain in wet clothes, however, and it will take time to send a servant to the dower house for dry garments.' He sent Hanford for his valet to go to his chamber and led Mary up the stairs.

'I realise that inviting you into my bedchamber sounds sinister in the extreme, but I assure you as you enter it, I shall leave. My valet will find a nightshirt from my press, and I have a very thick winter dressing gown. Irregular clothing it may be, but not indecorous, and it will be dry. He opened the door for her, but did not step within.

'You were very brave, and very sensible, and I love you,' he said, simply.

Alone in the room, Mary almost staggered to a chair, and sat, damply. A maid entered and lit the fire, and a minute later a dapper individual, with remarkably rosy cheeks, knocked and entered. He announced himself to be Lyng, Sir Rowland's man, and went straight to a figured mahogany press from which he drew forth a neatly folded nightshirt.

'If you would permit, madam, I would assist you

from your wet coat, for it will be exceedingly difficult for you to extricate yourself unaided.'

'Thank you.' Mary let him help her, and then he brought forth a very warm-looking dressing gown and laid it upon the bed, bowed, and left her. She undressed as swiftly as she might, for the room was still chill. Parts of her body felt numb, but her mind was overflowing with jumbled thoughts. She was worried about Madeleine, aware of her own physical discomforts, and also, as she pulled the nightshirt over her head, preternaturally aware that what lay now against her skin normally lay against Sir Rowland's. Logic said it was laundered cambric and nothing more, but to be wearing what he did, in his bed, felt not, she realised, shameful, but exciting. It was far too long in the arms, and very loose about the body, but would be covered by the dressing robe. This, she discovered, she could wrap so as to be double-breasted and still not tight. She knotted the cord firmly about her waist, and seeing a pair of slippers placed beside the bed, slipped her feet into them, although she could do no more than shuffle in them for they were so large. Being barefoot, however, felt indecent.

She left the bedchamber and closed the door softly behind her. Sir Rowland was a few paces away, speaking earnestly with his brother. He nodded, tapped Tom on the shoulder and turned as his brother went to do as he had been requested.

'Miss Banham is conscious. I have sent a groom to

Lord Roxton and also one for the doctor, if he can be reached. Mrs Peplow and now Penwood are with her. Word has also been sent to the dower house.'

'She will be all right?'

'I have every reason to hope so.' Sir Rowland looked more serious than usual. 'Are you warm enough, now?'

'Yes, indeed. But you, sir, have not attended to yourself. Your shirt is still damp.'

'The sight of you warms me.' The words sprang to his lips without thinking, and he stepped forward, took the hand she had instinctively held out to him and kissed it. 'I like you in my dressing gown. You look beautiful.'

She looked up into his eyes, a small frown between her own.

'But I am not at all like Madeleine Banham.'

'A different beauty, though it is not the primary reason that I fell in love with you.'

'You have fallen in love with me?' She did not doubt it, and yet it was amazing. 'Me.'

'Yes, you.' His eyes held warmth. 'On Christmas Eve, events prevented me from making my declaration in full.' An arm went about her waist, and he lifted her chin and placed a soft kiss upon her lips. 'But you knew what I was asking.' He smiled lovingly at her. 'Will you do me the immense honour of becoming my wife?'

'Oh! Oh, Rowland!'

'Yes will do,' he suggested, mildly.

'But I should not,' her face paled suddenly, as a thought struck her.

'Now, do not tell me that you have secretly contracted a marriage with old Wilmslow. I simply will not credit it.'

'No, but—'

'Then there is no reason which means you cannot say yes.'

'But I have deceived you,' she murmured, and her eyes filled with tears.

'I think you will find that you have not, my love,' he replied, holding her a little tighter.

'I have, I have. I set out to entrap you. I threw out lures.'

'You know, you are rather better with an artificial fly than live bait. I will acknowledge you to be an outstanding angler, but you do not throw lures with such craft, though you are immeasurably "al-luring". Nevertheless, behold me, a happy fish, truly hooked and eager to be landed. Just do not assault me with anything heavy and lethal, I beg you.' He sounded remarkably unperturbed by her admission, in fact rather amused.

'But you do not understand. I set out to get you to marry me so that I might live in Tapley End again as my home.'

'Congratulations. You have succeeded. You should be triumphant.'

'But . . .' She looked at him through a film of tears.

'Listen to yourself. If you were the heartless deceiver out only for the securing of your home, you would not have told me this now, before we are married. You have given the lie to the claim by revealing it. You never deceived me, Mary, though I was briefly put off when you commenced your attempts, and they ended long ago. If it is the time for confession, then there is mine, and what is more, I soon found your flirting terribly sweet, which I am sure will annoy you. You see, my love, what entranced me was not just that you are beautiful, and to me you are very beautiful, but the honesty of you, the practical good sense, the humour. You do not, as some women tend to do, wrap everything in pretence. They say no when they mean yes, they learn the "steps" of dalliance and perform the dance, and you are no dancer. You are a creature not of ballrooms and flirting fans, but of outdoors. That is your element, and you are as straight as the arrows you send into the target with such precision.' The amusement had left his voice now and been replaced by tender passion that made it slightly husky.

'How can you love me when I was not honest and true? I set out to get you to marry me, coldheartedly.'

'And a very sensible plan it was too. But if it had been as you first, erroneously, thought, and Cradley had been me, could you have done it?'

'No.' She shook her head.

'No. And your heart did not stay cold, not for long. I felt that. There was, from the moment I saw you, something that drew me to you, even when you were fierce and angered. My darling, you needed no lures, you did not have to "try" to make me love you.'

'I even tried not to love you for a little while, tried to keep it calculated, but I could not, Rowland.' Her fingers touched his cheek and trembled slightly.

'I have one more confession to make to you.' The words came slowly, for he was lost in the touch of her fingertips. 'I learnt to fish when I was ten.'

Her hand, which had been making small stroking motions, stopped.

'But you said . . .'

'I told you a lie, Mary. I hope it is the only one I ever do. You see, I saw it as a way to be close to you when you were happy and—'

'You were so clumsy.'

'It was really difficult, but I had to need those lessons, and you know, I was so focused on you, making a mess of it became easier the closer I was to you. Forgi—'

'I love you. I love you oh so much. I . . .' The words tumbled from her lips, but were curtailed by his pressing his own to them. He kissed her with a thoroughness and enthusiasm that more than made up for his paucity of osculatory experience, and Miss Lound found it entirely satisfactory.

'I have been wanting to do that again since Christmas Eve,' he murmured, a little breathlessly, 'and for weeks before that, too.'

'You have?'

'Yes. That night at the Roxtons' ball, just before you became dizzy, it was so very nearly overpowering I almost kissed you in the middle of the dance floor, you were so beautiful.'

'I . . . I thought you were disappointed in me, being so "dictatorial" and . . .'

'No, I simply could not trust myself with you in my arms, even in just a dance hold.'

'It does show I got something right, then. I always thought I showed to advantage in that gown.'

'You show to advantage even in your fishing garb.' He grinned, and there was an appreciative sparkle in his eyes.

'You are besotted, sir.' She put both arms about his neck. 'Would you k—'

'Mary!' Lady Damerham exclaimed, more in surprise than shock, for although she was fully in the expectation of her daughter marrying Sir Rowland, the actual sight of her in a man's arms was unimaginable. The couple pulled a little apart, not without some reluctance, and turned to see Lady Damerham and her son upon the stair, her ladyship bearing a small valise. Damerham looked the more appalled.

'Damn it, I should call you out for this, seducing my sister. Unhand her this instant.'

If he expected Sir Rowland to be outraged at the suggestion, he was in for a shock, for Sir Rowland kept his arm firmly about Mary's waist and let out a crack of laughter.

'If you think anyone could seduce your sister you cannot know her very well at all.'

'Stop being melodramatic, Edmund. I have not been seduced. Indeed, if anything, I appear to have "seduced" Sir Rowland,' declared Mary, tartly.

'And highly enjoyable it has been,' murmured Sir Rowland, quite prepared to cast fuel upon the flames of Damerham's wrath.

'I am so glad you think so, sir,' replied Mary, glancing up at him, her expression softening again for a moment.

'That I should hear my sister, a Lound of Tapley End, admitting to behaviour such as only a—'

'Be careful what you say, Damerham,' interjected Sir Rowland, swiftly. 'I will not have—'

'You dare, Edmund, stand there and spout "a Lound of Tapley End" at me when it has been you who has disgraced the name and brought us to ruin so that we are no longer of "Tapley End" at all?' Mary ignored her love and was focused upon her brother. 'That is rich. You did not think so much of this house or our name when you sold it to Lord Cradley, did you?' Her voice rose with her ire.

'I have brought you some dry clothes,' announced Lady Damerham, rather desperately, as though this might halt the spat between her children. She was ignored by both.

'Who is being melodramatic now?' Damerham threw back at Mary, and pointed his finger at Sir Rowland. 'You have set your cap at him for this house, and he has fallen for it.' Damerham curled his lip in a theatrical sneer at Sir Rowland. 'She's a hard piece and will rule the roost if you let her. All she wants is the house and the blasted lake, and . . .'

Mary felt Sir Rowland tense, and turned a little in his hold to place her hand over his heart in a gesture of restraint, but he took it and carried it to his lips.

'What I want, what I need, so much more even than this house, is you,' she whispered. 'You must know . . .'

'I know, my love, I know.'

'And as head of the family I forbid the union!' shouted Damerham, in a final, and futile, attempt to gain the upper hand.

'Oh, go away, Damerham. Get out before I have the servants throw you out.' Sir Rowland sounded bored and had apparently lost interest in him, which was not surprising given the way Mary was leaning into his shoulder, snuggling as close as a very well-padded dressing gown would permit.

Lady Damerham, not sure whether she should leave with her son or remain to chaperone her daughter, made odd dithering noises, and looked from one to the other. Damerham was also indecisive, not certain as to whether the threat would actually be put into effect. It was then that Tom appeared in the hall below.

'What the devil is he doing here again?' he exclaimed, flushing.

'Nothing to any purpose, Tom. Please see him out. By the by, he is going to be my brother-in-law, so curb your natural desire to punch him on the nose.'

'You mean he is—Lady Damerham, your servant, ma'am. Apologies for the language, did not at first see you . . .' Tom was struggling to assimilate all the information. 'I will be glad to take that valise from you in just a minute.' He set his foot upon the first stair, and then glared at Damerham.

It could not be said that Tom Kempsey was a heavily built young man, but he did look unusually pugnacious at this moment, and even if he could not forcibly eject Lord Damerham from the house, there would be a very undignified scuffle, which Damerham did not want.

'I wash my hands of you,' Damerham shouted at his sister, sounding petulant, and turned to descend muttering 'Yes, yes, I am leaving' as he brushed past Tom. Hanford opened the front door again, his face impassive, and bowed him out.

'If you will put the valise in the blue bedchamber, Tom.' Sir Rowland then kissed the top of Mary's head. 'I am sure you would feel better for wearing your own clothes, my love, and your mother will no doubt be eager to hear all that has happened.'

'Yes. Mama, do await me there and I will be with

you in a moment.' Mary turned her head and smiled at her mother, upon whom the full import of the situation seemed only just to have dawned. Lady Damerham smiled back and nodded. She of course needed no directions to the blue bedchamber.

Left alone again, Sir Rowland drew Mary to face him.

'Your brother is wrong. I know I do not need Tapley End to be "an inducement" to get you to marry me, but I do want to make you happy, and you will be happiest here, where your heart lies.'

'It lies with you, even more.'

'Bless you, my darling.' He kissed her tenderly. 'When shall we be married? I fear the weather does not look as if travelling will be easy . . .'

'But, Rowland, we must be married before Tom goes back to Oxford and then honeymoon here, at Tapley End of course, since you have just said that this is where I am happiest, and returning to live in it was my "reason" for deciding we must be married.' She grinned at him. 'I made you some "Lound's Lucky" flies as a Christmas gift, but never had the chance to give them to you. I think I ought to design a new fly as a wedding present and call it "Kempsey's Catcher".' She giggled. 'There is perfect light for making them in The Ladye's Chamber on bright mornings. Also, if there should be further heavy snowfalls, we shall be blissfully undisturbed by bride visits and other mundane things.'

'Eminently sensible, my love. Just us.'

'And the servants, Rowland.'

'I will ensure they wait an extra long time after knocking before entering a room.'

'Why?' Her gaze was wide-eyed and innocent, but her lips twitched.

'Because I would hate us to be disturbed whilst . . . discussing angling,' his hold tightened once more, 'from all angles.'

'I am looking forward to being married already.'

'So am I, my darling, so am I.'

AUTHOR'S NOTE

Angling was an outdoor pursuit in which ladies might engage during the Regency period, and an 1814 angling guide by Thomas Salter was actually dedicated to HRH The Duchess of York, whom he described as occasionally enjoying 'the amusement of angling', though the methods of casting were not those of modern anglers. For this novel I have used *The Art of Angling*, by Thomas Best, seventh edition (1807) for the methods described, and the genuine fishing-fly names of the period.

Sophia Holloway read Modern History at Oxford and also writes the Bradecote and Catchpoll medieval mysteries as Sarah Hawkswood.

@RegencySophia
sophiaholloway.co.uk

Sophy Hadlow does not want to return for another London Season. Her own debut into Society was marred by self-consciousness and her cringing embarrassment every time she was announced as 'The Lady Sophronia Hadlow'. Yet, much to her dismay, Sophy is back in London to oversee the debut of her younger sister and their wild cousin, Susan Tyneham, who risks ruining both her own and her innocent cousin's chances of marriage.

Sophy, a most reluctant chaperone, is left to guide her sister and attempt to keep Susan from complete disaster, all whilst dealing with her own unexpected feelings for the disarming Lord Rothley.

Celia Mardham's first London Season should have been a great success, but a near fatal riding accident has left her with a pronounced limp which means she cannot even curtsy, let alone dance.

Her mother, Lady Mardham, makes one last effort to save her daughter from a life of spinsterhood. She draws up a list of guests for a country house party, selecting an array of potential suitors as well as young ladies who will not be rivals, or so she thinks. Among the gentlemen is Lord Levedale and when he meets Celia he sees her, not the limp. However, accidents, misunderstandings and spiteful interventions litter the path ahead, and may succeed in driving them apart for good.